Read
I & D

1.50

"Glenn?"

"Yes?"

Her throat felt swollen and constricted, her chest, suddenly tight as if tears were brewing just beneath the surface. "Did I understand you right? Did you— just now—suggest that you and me—the two of us— get married?"

"That's exactly what I'm suggesting." Glenn didn't hesitate. He'd never been more sure of anything in his life. He'd lost one woman; he wasn't going to lose Maggie.

"When?"

"Tonight."

Glenn was crazy. They both were. Talking about marriage, running away tonight. Reno. None of it made sense, but nothing in all her life had sounded more exciting, more wonderful, more right. And Maggie felt like an adventurer, daring and audacious, dauntless and intrepid, reckless and carefree. There'd be problems. She realized that. But tonight, with Glenn at her side, there wasn't anything she couldn't conquer.

D1010102

Dear Reader:

Romance offers us all so much. It makes us "walk on sunshine." It gives us hope. It takes us out of our own lives, encouraging us to reach out to others. Janet Dailey is fond of saying that romance is a state of mind, that it could happen anywhere. Yet nowhere does romance seem to be as good as when it happens *here*.

Starting in February 1986, Silhouette Special Edition is featuring the AMERICAN TRIBUTE—a tribute to America, where romance has never been so wonderful. For six consecutive months, one out of every six Special Editions will be an episode in the AMERICAN TRIBUTE, a portrait of the lives of six women, all from Oklahoma. Look for the first book, *Love's Haunting Refrain* by Ada Steward, as well as stories by other favorites—Jeanne Stephens, Gena Dalton, Elaine Camp and Renee Roszel. You'll know the AMERICAN TRIBUTE by its patriotic stripe under the Silhouette Special Edition border.

AMERICAN TRIBUTE—six women, six stories, starting in February.

AMERICAN TRIBUTE—one of the reasons Silhouette Special Edition is just that—Special.

The Editors at Silhouette Books

DEBBIE MACOMBER
White Lace and Promises

Silhouette Special Edition

Published by Silhouette Books New York

America's Publisher of Contemporary Romance

To Maggie Osborne
with deep respect and affection

SILHOUETTE BOOKS
300 East 42nd St., New York, N.Y. 10017

Copyright © 1986 by Debbie Macomber

All rights reserved, including the right to reproduce
this book or portions thereof in any form whatsoever.
For information address Silhouette Books,
300 East 42nd St., New York, N.Y. 10017

ISBN: 0-373-09322-5

First Silhouette Books printing July 1986

All the characters in this book are fictitious. Any
resemblance to actual persons, living or dead, is
purely coincidental.

SILHOUETTE, SILHOUETTE SPECIAL EDITION and colophon
are registered trademarks of the publisher.

America's Publisher of Contemporary Romance

Printed in the U.S.A.

Books by Debbie Macomber

Silhouette Special Edition

Starlight #128
Borrowed Dreams #241
Reflections of Yesterday #284
White Lace and Promises #322

Silhouette Romance

That Wintery Feeling #316
Promise Me Forever #341
Adam's Image #349
The Trouble with Caasi #379
A Friend or Two #392
Christmas Masquerade #405
Shadow Chasing #415
Yesterday's Hero #426
Laughter in the Rain #437

DEBBIE MACOMBER

has quickly become one of Silhouette's most prolific authors. A wife and mother of four, she not only manages to keep her family happy, but she also keeps her publisher and readers happy with each book she writes.

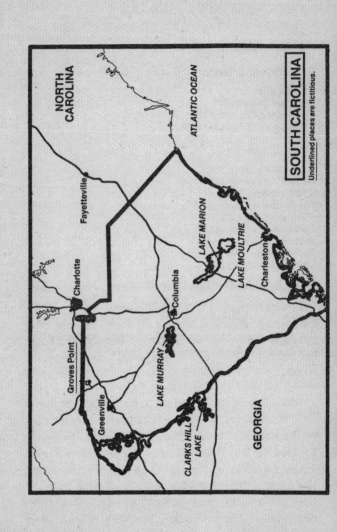

SOUTH CAROLINA

Underlined places are fictitious.

Chapter One

Maggie Kingsbury ground the gears of her royal-blue Mercedes and pulled to a screeching halt at the red light. Impatient, she glanced at her wristwatch and muttered silently under her breath. Once again she was late. Only this time her tardiness hadn't been intentional. The afternoon had innocently slipped away while she painted, oblivious to the world.

When Janelle had asked her to be the maid of honor for the wedding, Maggie had hesitated. As a member of the wedding party, unwelcome attention would be focused on her. It wasn't until she had learned that Glenn Lambert was going to be the best man that she'd consented. Glenn had been her friend from the time she was in grade school: her buddy, her co-conspirator, her white knight. With Glenn there everything would be perfect.

But already things were going badly. Here she was due to pick him up at San Francisco International and she was ten minutes late. In the back of her mind, Maggie realized that her tardiness was only another symptom of her discontent.

The light changed and she roared across the intersection, her back tires spinning. One of these days she was going to get a well-deserved speeding ticket. But not today, she prayed, please not today.

Her painting smock was smudged with a full spectrum of rainbow colors. The thick dark strands of her chestnut hair were pinned to the back of her head, disobedient curls tumbling defiantly at her temples and across her wide brow. And she had wanted to look so good for Glenn. It had been years since she'd seen him—not since high school graduation. In the beginning they had corresponded back and forth, but soon they'd each become involved with college and had formed a new set of friends. Their letters had dwindled to a chatty note on a Christmas card. Steve and Janelle had kept her updated with what had been going on in Glenn's life, and from what she understood, he was a successful stockbroker in Charleston. It sounded like a job he would manage well.

It surprised Maggie that in all those years, Glenn hadn't married. At twenty-nine and thirty they were the only two of their graduation class who hadn't. Especially now that Janelle was marrying Steve. Briefly she wondered what had kept Glenn away from the altar. As she recalled, he had always been easy on the eyes. But twelve years was a lot of time and things could have changed.

Her mind conjured up a mental picture of a young Glenn Lambert. Tall, dark, athletic, broad shouldered, thin—she smiled—he'd probably filled out over the years. He was the boy who lived next door and they had been great friends and at times worst enemies. Once, in the sixth grade, Glenn had stolen her diary and as a joke made copies and sold them to the boys in their class. After he found her crying, he had spent weeks trying to make it up to her. Years later his patience had gotten her a passing grade in chemistry and she had fixed him up with a date for the Junior-Senior prom.

Arriving at the airport, Maggie followed the freeway signs that directed her to the passenger-pickup area. Almost immediately she sighted Glenn standing beside his luggage, watching the traffic for a familiar face. A slow smile blossomed across her lips until it hovered at a grin. Glenn had hardly changed, and yet he was completely different. He was taller than she remembered, with those familiar broad shoulders now covered by a heather-blue blazer instead of a faded football jersey. At thirty he was a prime specimen of manhood. But behind his easy smile, Maggie recognized a maturity—one he'd fought hard for and painfully attained. Maggie studied him with fascination, amazed at his air of deliberate casualness. He knew about her inheritance. Of course he knew; Steve would have told him. Involuntarily, her fingers tightened around the steering wheel as a sense of regret settled over her. As much as she would have liked to, Maggie couldn't go back to being a carefree schoolgirl.

She eased to a stop at the curb in front of him and leaned across the seat to open the passenger door. "Hey, handsome, are you looking for a ride?"

Bending over, Glenn stuck his head inside the car. "Muffie, I should have known you'd be late."

Maggie grimaced at the use of her nickname. Glenn had dubbed her Muffie in high school, but it had always sounded to Maggie like the name of a poodle. The more she'd objected the more the name had stuck until her friends had picked it up. The sweet, innocent Muffie no longer existed.

After checking the side-view mirror for traffic to clear, she opened her door and stepped out. "I'm sorry I'm late, I don't know where the time went. As usual I got carried away."

Glenn chuckled and shook his head knowingly. "When haven't you gotten carried away?" He picked up his suitcase and tucked it inside the trunk Maggie had just opened. Placing his hands on her shoulders, he examined her carefully and gave her a brief hug. "You look fantastic." His dark eyes were somber and sincere.

"Me?" she choked out, feeling the warmth of many years of friendship chase away her earlier concerns. "You always could lie diplomatically." Maggie had recognized early in life that she was no raving beauty. Her eyes were probably her best feature—dark brown with small gold flecks, almond shaped and slanting upward at the corners. She was relatively tall, nearly five foot eight, with long shapely legs. Actually, the years hadn't altered her outwardly. Like Glenn's, the changes were more inward. Life's lessons had left their mark on her as well.

Looking at Glenn, Maggie couldn't hide the feeling of amused nostalgia she was experiencing. "The last time I looked this bad I was dressed as a zucchini for a fifth-grade play."

He crossed his arms and regarded her in the spirit of relaxed friendship. "I'd say you were wearing typical Muffie attire."

"Jeans and sneakers?"

"Seeing you again is like stepping into the past."

Not exactly. She didn't stuff tissue paper in her bra these days. Momentarily, she wondered if Glenn had ever guessed that she had. "I've got strict instructions to drop you off at Steve's. The rehearsal's scheduled at the church tonight at seven." This evening he'd have the opportunity to see just how much she had changed. Of all the people Maggie knew, Glenn would be the one to recognize the emotional differences in her. She might have been able to disguise them from others, but not from Glenn.

"With you chauffeuring me around there's little guarantee I'll make the wedding," Glenn teased affectionately.

"You'll make it," she assured him and climbed into the car with supple ease.

Glenn joined her and snapped the seat belt into place. Thoughtfully he ran his hand along the top of the dashboard. "I heard about your inheritance and wondered if it'd made a difference in your life."

"Well, I now live in a fancy beach house, and don't plan to do anything with the rest of my life except paint." She checked his profile for a negative response and finding none, she continued. "A secretary handles the mail, an estate planner deals with the finances, and there's a housekeeper and gardener as well. I do exactly as I want."

"Must be nice."

"I heard you haven't done so shabbily yourself."

"Not bad, but I don't lounge around in a beach house." He said it without censure. "I've had dealings with a lot of wealthy people the past few years. As far as I can see, having money can be a big disappointment."

The statement was open-ended, but Maggie refused to comment. Glenn's insight surprised her. He was right. All Great-aunt Margaret's money hadn't brought Maggie or her brother happiness. Oh, at first she had been filled with wonderful illusions about her inheritance. But these days she struggled to shroud her restlessness. To anyone else her life-style was a dream come true. Only Maggie knew differently.

"Money is supposed to make everything right. Only it creates more problems than it solves," she mumbled and pulled into the flow of traffic leaving the airport. Glenn didn't respond and Maggie wasn't sure he heard her, which was just as well, because the subject was one she preferred to avoid.

"It's hard to imagine Steve and Janelle getting married after all these years." A lazy grin swept across his tanned face.

Maggie smiled, longing to keep things light. "I'd say it was about time, wouldn't you?"

"I've never known two people more right for each other. The surprising part is that everyone saw it but them." .

"I'm really happy for those two."

"Me, too," he added, but Maggie noted that Glenn's tone held a hint of melancholy, as if the wedding was going to be as difficult for him as it was for her. Maggie couldn't imagine why.

"Steve's divorce devastated him," Maggie continued, "and he started dating Janelle again. The next thing I knew they decided to march up the aisle.'' Maggie paused and gestured expressively with her right hand.

Glenn's eyes fell on Maggie's artistically long fingers. It surprised him that she had such beautiful hands. They looked capable of kneading the stiffest clay and at the same time gentle enough to soothe a crying child. She wore no rings, nor were her well-shaped nails painted, yet her hands were striking. He couldn't take his eyes from them. He had known Maggie most of her life and had never appreciated her artistic hands.

"Are you going to invite me out to your beach house?" he asked finally.

"I thought I might. There's a basketball hoop in the gym and I figured I'd challenge you to a game."

"I'm not worried. As I recall the only slam dunk you ever made was with a doughnut."

Hiding her laugh, Maggie answered threateningly, "I'll make you pay for that remark."

Their families had shared a wide common driveway, and Maggie had passed many an hour after school playing ball with Glenn. Janelle and Steve and the rest of the gang from the neighborhood had hung around together. Most of the friendships she had formed in her youth were as strong today as when they had graduated from high school. Admittedly, Maggie wasn't as trusting of people these days. Not since she had inherited the money. The creeps had come crawling out of the woodwork the minute the news of her good fortune was out. Some were obvious gold diggers and others weren't so transparent. Maggie had gleaned valuable lessons from Dirk Wagner and had nearly made the mistake of marrying a man who loved her money far more than he cared for her.

"I don't suppose you've got a pool in that mansion of yours?"

"Yup."

"Is there anything you haven't got?" Glenn asked with suddenly serious eyes.

Maggie didn't know where to start, the list was so long. She had lost her purpose, her ambition, her drive to succeed professionally with her art. Her roster of friends was meager and consisted mainly of people she had known most of her life. "Some things," she muttered, wanting to change the subject.

"Money can't buy everything, can it?" Glenn asked so gently that Maggie felt her throat tighten.

She'd thought it would at first, but had learned the hard way that it couldn't buy the things that mattered most: love, loyalty, respect or friendship.

"No." Her voice was barely above a whisper.

"I suppose out of respect for your millions, I should call you Margaret," Glenn suggested next. "But try as I might, you'll always be Muffie to me."

"Try Maggie. I'm not Muffie anymore." She smiled to take any sharpness from her voice. With his returning nod, her hand relaxed against the steering wheel.

She exited from the freeway and drove into the basement parking lot of Steve's apartment building. "Here we are," she announced, turning off the engine. "With a good three hours to spare."

While Glenn removed his suitcase from the car trunk, Maggie dug in the bottom of her purse for the apartment key Steve had given her. "I have strict instructions to personally escort you upstairs and give you a stiff drink. You're going to need it when you hear what's scheduled."

With his suitcase in tow, Glenn followed her to the elevator. "Where's Steve?"

"Working."

"The day before his wedding?" Glenn looked astonished.

"He's been through this wedding business before," she reminded him offhandedly.

The heavy doors swished closed and Maggie leaned against the back wall and pulled the pins from her hair. It was futile to keep putting it up when it came tumbling down every time she moved her head. Stuffing the pins in her pocket, she felt Glenn's gaze studying her. Their eyes met.

"I can't believe you," he said softly.

"What?"

"You haven't changed. Time hasn't marked you in the least. You're exactly as I remember."

"You have." They both had.

"Good Lord, don't I know it." Glenn sighed, leaned against the side of the moving elevator and pinched the bridge of his nose. "Some days I feel a hundred years old."

Maggie was mesmerized by him. He was different. The carefree, easygoing teen had been replaced by an introspective man with intense, dark eyes that revealed a weary pain. The urge to ask him what had happened burned on her lips, but she knew that if she inquired into his life, he could ask about her own. Instead she led the way out of the elevator to the apartment.

The key turned and Maggie swung open the door to the high-rise apartment that gave a spectacular view of San Francisco Bay.

"Go ahead and plant your suitcase in the spare bedroom and I'll fix us a drink. What's your pleasure?"

"Juice if there's any."

Maggie placed both hands on the top of the bar. "I'll see what I can do." Turning, she investigated the contents of the refrigerator and brought out a small can of tomato juice. "Will this do?"

"Give it to me straight," he tossed over his shoulder as he left the living room.

By the time he returned, Maggie was standing at the window holding a martini. She watched him take the glass of juice from the bar and join her.

"Are you on the wagon?" she asked impulsively.

"Not really. It's a little too early in the afternoon for me."

Maggie nodded as a tiny smile quirked at the corners of her mouth. The first time she had ever tasted vodka had been with Glenn.

"What's so amusing?"

"Do you remember New Year's Eve the year I was sixteen?"

Glenn's brow furrowed. "No."

"Glenn!" She laughed with disbelief. "After all the trouble we got into over that, I'd think you'd never forget it."

"Oh, Lord, was that the year we threw our own private party?"

"Remember Cindy and Earl, Janelle and Steve, you and me and . . . who else?"

"Brenda and Bob?"

"No...Betty and Bob."

"Right." He chuckled. "I never could keep the twins straight."

"Who could? It surprises me he didn't marry both of them."

Whatever happened to Bob?"

Maggie took a sip of her martini before answering. "He's living in Oregon, going bald, and has four kids."

"Bob? I don't believe it."

"You weren't here for the ten-year reunion." Maggie hadn't bothered to attend either, but Janelle had kept her informed.

"I'm sorry I missed it," Glenn said and moved to the bar. He lifted his drink and finished it off in two enormous swallows.

Mildly surprised at the abrupt action, Maggie took another sip of hers, moved to a deep-seated leather chair, sat and tucked her long legs under her.

Glenn took a seat across from her. "So what's been going on in your life, Maggie? Are you happy?"

She shrugged indolently. "I suppose." From anyone else she would have resented the question, but she'd always been able to talk to Glenn. A half hour after being separated for years and it was as if they'd never been apart. "I'm a wealthy woman, Glenn, and I've learned the hard way about human nature."

"What happened?"

"It's a long story."

"Didn't you just get done telling me that we had three hours before the rehearsal?"

For a moment Maggie was tempted to spill her frustrations out. To tell Glenn about the desperate pleas for money she got from people who sensed her soft heart. The ones who were looking for someone to invest in a sure thing. And the users, who pretended friendship or love in the hopes of a lucrative relationship. "You must be exhausted. I'll cry on your shoulder another time."

"I'll hold you to that." He leaned forward and reached for her hand. "We had some good times, didn't we?"

"Great times."

"Ah, the good old days." Glenn relaxed with a bittersweet sigh. "Who was it that said youth was wasted on the young?"

"Mark Twain," Maggie offered.

"No, I think it was Joan Collins."

They both laughed and Maggie stood, reaching for her purse. "Well, I suppose I should think about heading home and changing my clothes. Steve will be here in an hour. That'll give you time to relax." She fanned her fingers through her hair in a careless gesture. "I'll see you tonight at the rehearsal."

"Thanks for meeting me," Glenn said, coming to his feet.

"I was glad to do it." Her hand was on the doorknob.

"It's great to see you again."

The door made a clicking sound as it closed and Glenn turned to wipe a hand over his tired eyes. Damn, it was good to be with Maggie again, but frankly, he was glad she had decided to leave. He needed a few minutes to compose his thoughts before facing Steve. The first thing his friend was bound to ask him about was Angie.

Glenn stiffened as her name sent an instant flash of pain through him. She had married Simon two months earlier, and Glenn had thought that acceptance would become easier with time. It had, but it was far more difficult than he had ever expected. He had loved Angie with a reverence; eventually he had loved her enough to step aside when she wanted to marry Simon. He'd been a fool, Glenn realized. If he had acted on his instincts, he'd have had a new bride on his arm for this trip. Now he was alone, more alone than he could ever remember. The last place he wanted to be was a wedding. Every part of it would only be a reminder of what could have been his, and what he'd allowed to slip through his fingers. He didn't begrudge Steve any happiness; he just didn't want to have to stand by and smile serenely when part of him was dying.

Maggie shifted into third gear as she rounded the curve in the highway at twenty miles above the speed limit. Deliberately she slowed down, hating the urgency that forced her to rush home. The beach house had become her gilded cage. The world outside its door had taken on a steel edge that she avoided.

Although she had joked with Glenn about not being married, the tense muscles of her stomach reminded her of how much she envied Janelle. She would smile for the wedding pictures and be awed at all the right moments, but she was going to hate every minute of it. The worst part was she was genuinely happy for Janelle and Steve. Oh, Janelle had promised that they'd continue to get together as they always had. They had been best friends since childhood, and for a time they probably would see each other regularly. But Janelle wanted to start a family right away, and once she had a baby, Maggie thought, everything would change. It had to.

Automatically Maggie took the road that veered from the highway and a few minutes later turned onto the long circular driveway that led to the beach house. The huge house loomed before her, impressive, elegant and imposing. Maggie had bought it for none of those reasons. She wasn't even sure she liked it. The two-story single-family dwelling on Eastwood Drive where she had grown up was far more appealing. Even now she couldn't bring herself to sell that house and had rented it for far less than market value to a retired couple who kept the yard and flower beds meticulously. Sometimes during the darkest hour of a sleepless night, Maggie would mull over the idea of donating her money to charity. If possible, she would gladly return to the years when she had sat blissfully at her bedroom window, her chin resting on her crossed arms as she gazed into the stars and dreamed of the future. Childhood dreams that were never meant to come true.

Shaking herself from her reverie, Maggie parked the Mercedes in front of the house. This night she would put on her brightest smile. No one would ever know what she was feeling on the inside.

Janelle's mother looked as if she were preparing more for a funeral than a wedding. Flustered and worried, she waved her hands in five different directions, orchestrating the entourage gathered in the church vestibule.

"Girls, please, please pay attention. Darcy go right, June left and so on. Understand?"

The last time anyone had called Maggie a girl was in high school. Janelle, Maggie, the bridesmaids, the flower girl, and the ring bearer were all positioned, awaiting instructions. Maggie glanced enviously to the front of the church where Steve and Glenn were standing. It didn't seem fair that they should get off so lightly.

"Remember to count to five slowly before following the person in front of you," Janelle's mother continued.

The strains of organ music burst through the church and the first attendant, shoulders squared, stepped onto the white paper runner that flowed down the long aisle.

"I can't believe this is really happening," Janelle whispered. "Tomorrow Steve and I will be married. After all the years of loving him it's like a dream."

"I know," Maggie whispered and squeezed her friend's forearm.

"Go left, go left." Mrs. Longmier's voice drifted to them and Maggie dissolved into giggles.

"I can't believe your mother."

"The pastor assured her he'd handle everything, but she insisted on doing it herself. That's what I get for being the only girl in a family of four boys."

"In another twenty years or so you may well be doing it yourself," Maggie reminded her.

"Oops." Janelle nudged her. "Your turn. And for heaven's sake don't goof up. I'm starved and want to get out of here."

Holding a paper plate decorated with bows and ribbons from one of Janelle's five wedding showers, Maggie carefully placed one foot in front of the other in a deliberate, step-by-step march that seemed to take an eternity. The smile on her face was as brittle as old parchment.

Standing in her place at the altar, Maggie kept her head turned so she could see Janelle's approach. The happiness radiating from her friend's face produced a curious ache in Maggie's heart. If these feelings were so strong at the rehearsal, how would she react during the actual wedding? Maggie felt someone's eyes on her and glanced up to see Glenn's steady gaze. He smiled briefly and looked away.

The pastor moved to the front of the young couple and cracked a few old jokes. Everyone laughed politely. As the organ music filled the church, the bride and groom, hands linked, began their exit.

When it came time for Maggie to meet Glenn at the head of the aisle, he stiffly tucked her hand in the crook of his elbow.

"I never thought I'd be marching down the aisle with you," she whispered under her breath.

"It has all the makings of a nightmare," Glenn countered. "However, I'll admit you're kinda cute."

"Thanks."

"But so are lion cubs."

Maggie's fingers playfully bit into the muscles of his upper arm as she struggled not to laugh.

His hand patted hers as he whispered, "You're lovely."

"Is that so?" Maggie was shocked that she would flirt so blatantly. She turned her upper body just enough to offer him a glimpse of her cleavage.

They were nearing the back of the church. Glenn's dark eyes bored holes into her. "Are you looking for a lover?"

The question caught Maggie by surprise. The old Glenn would have swatted her across the rump and told her to behave. The new Glenn, the man she didn't know, was dead serious. "Not this week," she returned, deliberately flippant. "But if you're interested, I'll keep you in mind."

His gaze narrowed slightly as he tilted his head to one side. "How much have you had to drink?"

Maggie wanted to laugh outright and would have if not for a discouraging glare from Mrs. Longmier. "One martini."

The sound of a soft snort followed. "You've changed, Maggie." Just the way he said it indicated that he wasn't pleased with the difference.

Her spirits crashed to the floor with breakneck speed. Good grief, she thought angrily, it didn't matter what Glenn thought of her. He had made her feel like a teenager again and she'd behaved like a fool. She wasn't even sure why she was flirting with him. Probably to cover up how miserable the whole event was making her.

Casually, Glenn dropped her arm as they entered the vestibule and stepped aside to make room for the others who followed. Maggie used the time to gather her coat and purse. Glenn moved in the opposite direction and her troubled gaze followed him.

A flurry of instructions followed as Steve's father gave directions to the Grants' home, where dinner was being served to the members of the wedding party.

Maggie moved outside the church. There wasn't any need for her to stay and listen. She knew how to get to the Grants' house as well as her own. Standing at the base of the church steps, Maggie was fumbling inside her purse for a cigarette when Glenn joined her.

"I'm supposed to ride with you."

"Don't make it sound like a fate worse than death," she bit out, furious that she couldn't find a smoke when she needed one.

"Listen, Maggie, I'm sorry. Okay?"

"You?" Amazed, Maggie lowered the purse flap and slowly raised her dark eyes to his. "It's me who should apologize. I was behaving like an idiot in there, flirting with you like I was a kid again."

He lifted a silken strand of hair from her shoulder. "It's rather nice to be flirted with now and then," he said with a lazy smile that caressed her upturned face.

Maggie tore her gaze from his and withdrew her car keys. "Here," she said, handing the key chain to him. "I know you'll feel a whole lot safer driving yourself."

"You're right," he retorted, his mood teasing and jovial. "I still remember the day you wiped out two garbage cans and an oak tree backing out of the driveway."

"I'd just gotten my learner's permit and the gears slipped," she returned righteously.

"Unfortunately your skills haven't improved much."

"On second thought, I'll drive and you can do the praying."

Laughing, Glenn tossed an arm across her shoulders.

They chatted easily on the way to the Grants' home and parked behind Steve and Janelle in the driveway. The four car doors slammed simultaneously.

"Glad to see you still remember the way around town," Steve teased Glenn. The two men were nearly the same height, both with dark hair and brown eyes.

Steve smiled lovingly at Janelle and brought her close to his side. "I hope everyone's hungry," he said, waiting for Glenn and Maggie to join them. "Mom hasn't stopped cooking in two days."

"Famished," Glenn admitted. "The last time I ate was on the plane."

"Poor starving baby," Maggie cooed.

Glenn was chuckling when the four entered the house. Immediately Janelle and Maggie offered to help Steve's mother and carried the assorted salads and platters of deli meats to the long table for the buffet. Soon the guests were mingling and helping themselves.

Maggie loaded her plate and found an empty space beside Glenn, who was kneeling in front of the coffee table with several others. He glanced up from the conversation he was having with a bridesmaid when Maggie joined them.

"Muffie, you know Darcy, don't you?" Glenn asked.

"Muffie?" Darcy repeated incredulously. "I thought your name was Maggie."

"Muffie was the name Glenn gave me in high school. We were next-door neighbors. In fact, we lived only a few blocks from here."

"I suppose you're one of those preppy, organized types," Darcy suggested.

Glenn nearly choked on his potato salad. "Hardly."

Maggie gave him the sharp point of her elbow in his ribs. "Glenn thought he was being cute one day and dubbed me something offensive. Muffie, however, was better than Magpie—"

"She never stopped talking," Glenn inserted.

"—or Maggie the Menace."

"For obvious reasons."

"For a while it was Molasses." Maggie closed her eyes at the memory.

"Because she was forever late."

"As you may have guessed, we fought like cats and dogs," Maggie explained needlessly.

"The way a lot of brothers and sisters do," Glenn inserted.

"So where did the Muffie come in?"

"In high school things became a bit more sophisticated. We couldn't very well call her Magpie."

Darcy nodded and sliced off a bite of ham.

"So after a while," Glenn continued, "Steve, Janelle, the whole gang of us decided to call her Muffie, simply because she talked so much we wanted to muffle her. The name stuck."

"Creative people are often subjected to this form of persecution," Maggie informed her with a look of pure innocence.

"Didn't you two...?" Darcy hesitated. "I mean Steve and Janelle obviously had something going even then."

"Us?" Maggie and Glenn shared a look of shock. "I did ask you to the Sadie Hawkins dance once."

Glenn nodded, a mischievous look in his eyes. "She'd already asked five other guys and been turned down."

"So I drastically lowered my standards and asked Glenn. It was a complete disaster. Remember?"

Their eyes met and they burst into fits of laughter, causing the conversational hum of the room to come to an abrupt halt.

"Hey you two, let me in on the joke," Darcy said. "What's so funny?"

Maggie composed herself enough to begin the story. "On the way home, Glenn's car stalled. We learned later it was out of gas. Believe me, I wasn't pleased, especially since I'd sprung for new patent-leather shoes and my feet were killing me."

"I don't know why you're complaining; I took you to the dance, didn't I?"

Maggie ignored him. "Since I didn't have a driver's license, Mr. Wonderful here insisted on steering while I pushed his car—uphill."

"You?" Darcy was aghast.

"Now, Maggie, to be fair, you should explain that I helped push, too."

"Some help," she grumbled. "That wasn't the worst part. It started to rain and I was in my party dress, shoving his car down the street in the dead of night."

"Maggie was complaining so loud that she woke half the neighborhood," Glenn inserted, "and someone looked out the window and thought we were stealing a car. They phoned the police and within minutes we were surrounded by three patrol cars."

"They took us downtown and phoned Glenn's dad. It was the most embarrassing moment of my life. The Girls' Club had sponsored the dance and I was expecting roses and kisses in the moonlight. Instead I got stuck pushing Glenn's car in the rain and was darn near arrested."

"Believe me, Maggie made me pay for that one." Glenn's smiling eyes met hers and Maggie felt young and carefree again. It'd been so long since she had talked and laughed like this; she could almost forget. Almost. The present, however, was abruptly brought to her attention a few minutes later when Steve's cousin approached her.

"Maggie," he asked, crowding in next to her on the floor, "I was wondering if we could have a few minutes alone? There's something I'd like to ask you."

A heavy sensation of dread moved over her. It had happened so often in the past that she knew almost before he spoke what he would say. "Sure, Sam." As of yet, she hadn't found a graceful way of excusing herself from these situations.

Rolling to her feet, she followed Sam across the room to an empty corner.

"I suppose Steve's told you about my business venture?" he began brightly with false enthusiasm.

Maggie gritted her teeth, praying for patience. "No, I can't say that he has."

"Well, my partner and I are looking for someone with a good eye for investment potential who would be willing to lend us twenty-five thousand. Would you happen to know anyone who might be interested?"

Maggie noticed Glenn making his way toward them. As she struggled to come up with a polite rejection to Sam, Glenn stopped next to her.

"Sam," he interrupted, taking Maggie by the arm, "excuse us for a minute, will you?" He didn't wait for a response and led her through the cluttered living room and into the kitchen.

"Where are you taking me?" Maggie asked when he opened the sliding glass door that led to the patio.

"Outside."

"That much is obvious. But why are you taking me out here?"

Glenn paused to stand under the huge maple tree and looked toward the sky. "There's only a half-moon tonight, but it'll have to do."

"Are you going to turn into a werewolf or something?" Maggie joked, pleased to be rescued from the clutches of an awkward conversation.

"Nope." He turned her in his arms, looping his hands around her narrow waist and bringing her against the hard wall of his chest. "This is something I should have done the night of the Girls' Club dance," he murmured as he looked down at her.

"What is?"

"Kiss you in the moonlight," he whispered just before his mouth claimed hers.

Chapter Two

Maggie was too amazed to respond. Glenn Lambert, the boy who had lived next door most of her life, was kissing her. And he was kissing her as if he meant to be doing exactly that. His lips moved slowly over hers, shaping and fitting his mouth to hers with a gentleness that rocked her until the core of her being was a churning mass of conflicting emotions. This was Glenn, the same Glenn who had teased her unmercifully about "going straight" while she wore braces. The Glenn who had heartlessly beaten her playing one-on-one basketball. The same Glenn who had always been her white knight. Yet it felt so right, so good to be in his arms. Hesitantly, Maggie lifted her hands, sliding them over his chest and linking her fingers at the base of his neck, clinging to him for support. Gently parting her lips, she responded pliantly to his kiss. She luxuriated in the warm taste of him, the feel of his hands against the small of her back and the tangy scent of his after-shave. It seemed right for Glenn to be holding her. More right than anything had felt in a long time.

When he lifted his head there was a moment of stunned silence while the fact registered in Glenn's bemused mind that he had just kissed Maggie. Maggie. But the vibrant woman in his arms wasn't the same girl who'd lived next door. The woman was warm and soft and incredibly feminine, and he was dying for a woman's gentleness. Losing Angie had left him feeling cold and utterly alone. His only desire had been to love and protect her, but she hadn't wanted him. A stinging chill ran through his blood, forcing him into the present. His hold relaxed and he dropped his arms.

"Why'd you do that?" Maggie whispered, having difficulty finding her voice. From the moment he had taken her outside, Maggie had known his intention had been to free her from the clutches of Steve's cousin—not to kiss her. At least not like that. What had started out in fun had become serious.

"I'm not sure," he answered honestly. A vague hesitancy showed in his eyes.

"Am I supposed to grade you?"

Glenn took another step backward, broadening the space between them. "Good grief, no; you're merciless."

Mentally, Maggie congratulated him for recovering faster than she. "Not always," she murmured. At his blank look, she added, "I'm not always merciless."

"That's not the way I remember it. The last time I wanted to kiss you, I damn near got a fist in the stomach."

Maggie's brow furrowed. She couldn't remember Glenn even trying to kiss her and regarded him with surprise and doubt as she sifted through her memories. "I don't remember that."

"I'm not likely to forget it," he stated and arched one brow arrogantly. "As I recall, I was twelve and you were eleven. A couple of the guys at school had already kissed a girl and said it wasn't half-bad. There wasn't anyone I wanted to kiss, but for a girl you weren't too bad, so I offered you five of my best baseball cards if you'd let me kiss you."

Maggie gave him a wicked grin as her memory returned. "That was the greatest insult of my life. I was saving my lips for the man I planned to marry. At the time I think it was Dustin Hoffman."

"As I recall you told me that," he replied with a low chuckle. He tucked an arm around her waist, bringing her to his side. "Talking about our one and only date tonight made me remember how much I took you for granted all those years. You were great."

"I know," she said with a complete lack of modesty.

A slow, roguish grin grew across his features. "But then there were times..."

"Don't go philosophical on me, Glenn Lambert." An unaccustomed, delicious heat was seeping into her bones. It was as if she'd been standing in a fierce winter storm and someone had invited her inside to sit by the cozy warmth of the fire.

"We've both done enough of that for one night," Glenn quipped, looking toward the bright lights of the house.

Maggie didn't want to go back inside. She felt warm and comfortable with herself for the first time in what seemed like ages. If they returned to the house full of people, she'd be forced to paint on another plastic smile and listen to the likes of Steve's cousin.

"Do you ever wonder about the old neighborhood?"

Grinning, Glenn looked down on her. "Occasionally."

"Want to take a look?"

He glanced toward the house again, sensing her reluctance to return. The old Maggie would have faced the world head-on. The change surprised him. "Won't we be missed?"

"I doubt it."

Glenn tucked Maggie's hand in the crook of his arm. "For old times' sake."

"The rope swing in your backyard is still there."

"You're kidding!" He gave a laugh of disbelief.

"A whole new generation of kids are playing on that old swing."

"What about the tree house?"

"That, unfortunately, was the victim of a bad windstorm several years back."

His arm tightened around her waist and the fragile scent of her perfume filled his senses. She was a woman now, and something strange and inexplicable was happening between them. Glenn wasn't sure it was right to encourage it.

"How do you keep up with all this?" he asked, attempting to steer his thoughts from things he shouldn't be thinking, like how soft and sweet and wonderfully warm she felt.

"Simple," Maggie explained with a half smile. "I visit often." The happiest days of her life had been in that house in the old neighborhood. She couldn't turn back the clock, but the outward symbols of that time lived on for her to visit as often as needed. "Come on," she said brightly and took his hand. She was feeling both foolish and fanciful. "There probably won't be another chance if we don't go now."

"You'll freeze," Glenn warned, running his hands down the lengths of her bare arms and up again to cup her shoulders.

"No," she argued, not wanting anything to disturb the moment.

"I'll collect your coat and tell Steve what we're up to," Glenn countered.

"No," she pleaded, her voice low and husky. "Don't. I'll be fine. Really."

Glenn studied her for an instant before agreeing with a curt nod. Maggie was frightened. The realization stunned him. His bubbly, happy-go-lucky Maggie had been reduced to an unhappy, insecure waif. The urge to take her in his arms and protect her was nearly overwhelming.

"All right," he agreed, wrapping his arms around her shoulder to lend her his warmth. If she did get chilled he could give her his jacket.

With their arms around each other, they strolled down Ocean Avenue to the grade school, cut through the play yard and came out on Marimar near Eastwood Drive.

"Everything seems the same," Glenn commented. His smile was filled with contentment.

"It is."

"How are your parents doing?" he inquired.

"They retired in Florida. I told them they ought to be more original than that, but it was something they really wanted. They can afford it, so why not? What about your folks?''

"They're in South Carolina. Dad's working for the same company. Both Eric and Dale are married and supplying them with a houseful of grandchildren.''

A chill shot through Maggie and she shivered involuntarily. She was an aunt now, too, but the circumstances weren't nearly as pleasant. Her brother, Denny had also discovered that his inheritance wasn't a hedge against unhappiness. Slowly shaking her head, Maggie spoke. "Do you realize how old that makes me feel? Dale married—I'd never have believed it. He was only ten when you moved.''

"He met his wife the first year of college. They fell in love, and against everyone's advice decided not to wait to get married. They were both nineteen and had two kids by the time Dale graduated.''

"And they're fine now?''

"They're going stronger than ever. The boys are in school and Cheryl has gone back to college for her degree." There wasn't any disguising the pride in his voice.

"What about Eric?''

"He married an airline stewardess a couple of years ago. They have a baby girl." His hand rested at the nape of her neck in a protective action. "What about your brother?''

"Denny was already married by the time you moved, wasn't he? He and Linda have two little girls.''

"Is he living in San Francisco?''

"Yes," she supplied quickly and hurried to change the subject. "The night's lovely, isn't it?''

Glenn ignored the comment. "Is Denny still working for the phone company?''

"No," she returned starkly. "I can't remember when I've seen so many stars."

They were silent for a moment while Glenn digested the information. Something had happened between Denny and Maggie that she was obviously reluctant to discuss.

"Do you realize that there's never been a divorce in either of our families?" she said softly with sudden insight. She knew what a rarity that was in this day and age. Nearly thirty percent of their high school class were on their second marriages if not their third.

"I doubt that there ever will be a divorce. Mom and Dad believe strongly in working out problems instead of running from them and that was ingrained in all three of us boys."

"We're in the minority then. I don't know how Janelle is going to adjust to Steve's children. It must be difficult."

"She loves him," Glenn countered somewhat defensively.

"I realize that," Maggie whispered, thinking out loud. "It's just that I remember when Steve married Ginny. Janelle cried for days afterward and went about doing her best to forget him. Every one of us knew that Ginny and Steve were terribly mismatched and it would only be a matter of time before they split."

"I wasn't that sure they couldn't make a go of it."

Maggie bristled. "I was, and anyone with half a brain saw it. Ginny was pregnant before the wedding and no one except Steve was convinced the baby was his."

"Steve was in a position to know."

Maggie opened her mouth to argue, glanced up to see Glenn's amused gaze and gingerly pressed her lips tightly closed. "I don't recall you being this argumentative," she said after several moments.

"When it comes to the sanctity of marriage, I am."

"For your sake, I hope you marry the right woman then."

The humor drained from his eyes and was replaced with such pain that Maggie's breath caught in her throat. "Glenn, what did I say?" she asked, concern in her voice.

"Nothing," he assured her with a half smile that disguised none of his mental anguish. "I thought I had found her."

"Oh, Glenn, I'm so sorry. Is there anything I can do? I make a great wailing wall." From the pinched lines about his mouth and eyes, Maggie knew that the woman had been someone very special. Even when Maggie had known him best, Glenn had been a discriminating male. He had dated only a few times and, as far as she could remember, had never gone steady with one girl.

The muscles of his face tightened as he debated whether to tell Maggie about Angie. He hadn't discussed her with anyone over the past couple of months and the need to purge her from his life burned in his soul. Perhaps someday, he thought, but not now and not with Maggie, who had enough problems of her own. "She married someone else. There's nothing more to say."

"You loved her very much, didn't you?" Whoever she was, the woman was a fool. Glenn was the steady, solid type most women sought. When he loved, it would be forever and with an intensity few men were capable of revealing.

Glenn didn't answer. Instead he regarded her with his pain-filled eyes and asked, "What about you?"

"You mean why I never married?" She gave a shrug of indifference. "The right man never came along. I thought he might have once, but I was wrong. Dirk was more interested in spending my money than loving me."

"I'm sorry." His arm tightened around her as an unreasonable anger filled him over the faceless Dirk. He had hurt Maggie, and Glenn was intimately aware of how much one person could hurt another.

"Actually, I think I was lucky to discover it when I did. But thirty is looming around the corner and the biological clock is winding down if I want a family while I'm young enough to enjoy one. I'd like to get married, but I won't lower my standards."

"What kind of man are you looking for?"

He was so utterly blasé about it that Maggie's composure slipped and she nearly dissolved into laughter. "You mean in case you happen to know someone who fits the bill?"

"I might."

"Why not?" she asked with a soft giggle. "To start off, I'd like someone financially secure."

"That shouldn't be so difficult."

He was so serious that Maggie bit into her bottom lip to hide the trembling laughter. "In addition to being on firm financial ground, he should be magnanimous."

"With you he'd have to be," Glenn said in a laughter-tinged voice.

Maggie ignored the gibe. "He'd have to love me enough to overlook my faults—few as they are—be loyal, loving, and want children."

She paused, expecting him to comment, but he nodded in agreement. "Go on," he encouraged.

"But more than simply wanting children, he'd have to take responsibility for helping me raise them into worthwhile adults. I want a man who's honest, but one who won't shout the truth in my face if it's going to hurt me. A special man to double my joys and divide my sorrows. Someone who will love me when my hair is gray and my ankles are thick." Realizing how serious she'd become, Maggie hesitated. "Know anyone like him?" Her words hung empty in the silence that followed.

"No," Glenn eventually said, and shook his head for emphasis. Those were the very things he sought in a wife. "I can't say that I do."

"From my guess, Prince Charmings are few and far between these days."

They didn't speak again until they paused in front of the fifty-year-old house that had been Glenn's childhood home. Little had altered over the years, Glenn realized. The wide front porch and large dormers that jutted out from the roof looked exactly as they had in his mind. The house had been repainted, and decorative shutters were now added to the front windows, but the same warmth and love seemed to radiate from its doors.

Maggie followed Glenn's gaze to the much-used basketball hoop positioned above the garage door. It was slightly crooked from years of slam dunks. From the looks of things, the hoop was used as much now as it had been all those years ago.

"I suppose we should think of heading back. It's going to be a long day tomorrow." Maggie's gaze fell from the house to the cracked sidewalk. It hit her suddenly that in a couple of days Glenn would be flying back to Charleston. He was here for the wedding and nothing more.

"Yes," Glenn agreed in a low, gravelly voice. "Tomorrow will be a very long day."

The vestibule was empty when Maggie entered the church forty minutes before the wedding. Out of breath and five minutes late, she paused to study the huge baskets of flowers that adorned the altar, and released an unconscious sigh at the beauty of the sight. This wedding was going to be special. Hurrying into the dressing room that was located to her right, Maggie knocked once and opened the door. The woman from The Wedding Shop was helping Janelle into her flowing lace gown. Mrs. Longmier was sitting in a chair, dabbing the corner of her eye with a linen hankie.

"Oh, Maggie, thank goodness you're here. I had this horrible dream that you showed up late. The wedding was in progress and you ran down the aisle screaming how dare we start without you."

"I'm here, I'm here, don't worry." Stepping back, Maggie inspected her friend and could understand Mrs. Longmier's tears. Janelle was radiant. Her wedding gown was of a lavish Victorian style that was exquisitely fashioned with ruffled tiers of Chantilly lace and countless rows of tiny pearls. "Wow," she whispered in awe. "You're going to knock Steve's eyes out."

"That's the idea," Janelle said with a nervous smile.

Another woman from the store helped Maggie don her blushing-pink gown of shimmering taffeta. Following a common theme, the maid of honor's and the bridesmaids' dresses were also Victorian in style, with sheer yokes and lace stand-up collars. Lace bishop sleeves were trimmed with dainty satin bows. The bodice fit snugly to the waist and flared at the hip. While the woman fastened the tiny buttons at the back of the gown, Maggie studied her mirrored reflection. A small smile played on her mouth as she pictured Glenn's reaction when he saw her. For years he had seen her in nothing more elaborate than tight jeans and sweatshirts. She had worn a dress for the rehearsal, but this gown would amaze him. She was a woman now and it showed.

The way her thoughts automatically flew to Glenn surprised Maggie, but she supposed it was natural after their walk in the moonlight. He had filled her dreams and she'd slept wonderfully well. After talking to Glenn, Maggie's attitude toward the wedding had changed. She wouldn't be standing alone at the altar with her fears. Glenn, her friend from childhood, would be positioned beside her. Together they would lend each other the necessary fortitude to smile their way through the ordeal. Maggie realized her thoughts were more those of a martyr than an honored friend, but she'd dreaded the wedding for weeks. Not that she begrudged Janelle any happiness. But Maggie realized that at some time during the wedding dinner or the dance scheduled to follow, someone would comment on her single status. With Glenn at her side it wouldn't matter nearly as much.

From all the commotion going on outside the dressing room, Maggie realized the guests were beginning to arrive. Nerves attacked her stomach. This wasn't the first time she'd been in a wedding party, but it was the most elaborate. She pressed a calming hand to her abdomen and exhaled slowly.

"Nervous?" Janelle whispered.

Maggie nodded. "What about you?"

"I'm terrified," she admitted freely. "Right now I wish Steve and I had eloped instead of going through all this." She released her breath in a slow, drawn-out sigh. "I'm convinced that halfway through the ceremony my veil's going to slip or I'll faint, or something equally disastrous."

"You won't," Maggie returned confidently. "I promise. Right now everything's overwhelming, but you won't regret a minute of this in the years to come."

"I suppose not," Janelle agreed. "This marriage is forever and I want everything right."

"I'd want everything like this, too." Maggie spoke without thinking and realized that when and if she ever married she wanted it to be exactly this way. She wanted a flowing white dress with a long train and lifetime friends to stand with her.

Someone knocked on the door and, like an organized row of ducklings, the wedding party was led into the vestibule. Organ music vibrated through the church and the first bridesmaid, her gloved hands clasping a bouquet of pink hyacinths, stepped forward with a tall usher at her side.

Maggie watched her progress and knew again that someday she wanted to stand in the back of a church and look out over the seated guests who had come to share her moment of joy. And like Janelle, Maggie longed to feel all the love that was waiting for her as she slowly walked to the man with whom she would share her life. And when she repeated her vows before God and those most important in her life she would feel, as Janelle did, that her marriage was meant to last for all time.

When it was her turn to step onto the trail of white linen that ran the length of the wide aisle, Maggie held her chin high, the adrenaline pumping through her blood. Her smile was natural, not forced. Mentally she thanked Glenn for that and briefly allowed her gaze to seek him out in the front of the church. What she found nearly caused her to pause in midstep. Glenn was standing with Steve at the side of the altar and looking at her with such a wondrous gaze that her heart did a tiny flip-flop and lodged in her throat. This all-encompassing wonder was what Maggie had expected to see in Steve's eyes when he first viewed Janelle. A look so tender, so lambent it should be reserved for the bride and groom. The moment stretched out until Maggie was convinced everyone in the church had turned to see what was keeping her. By sheer force of will she continued with short steps toward the front of the church. Every resounding note of the organ brought her closer to Glenn. She felt a throb of excitement as the faces of people she'd known all her life turned to watch her progress. A heady sensation enveloped her as she imagined it was she who was the bride, she who would speak her vows, she who had found her life's love. Until that moment Maggie hadn't realized how much she yearned for the very things she had tried to escape in life, how much she was missing by hiding in her gilded cage, behind her money.

As practiced, she moved to the left and waited for Janelle and Steve to meet at center front. At that point she would join her friend and stand at Janelle's side. With the organ music pulsating in her ear, Maggie strained to catch Steve's look when he first glimpsed Janelle. She turned her head slightly, and paused. Her gaze refused to move beyond Glenn who was standing with Steve near the front of the altar. Even when Janelle placed her hand in Steve's, Maggie couldn't tear her eyes from Glenn. The pastor moved to the front of the church and the four gathered before him. Together they lifted their faces to the man of God who had come to unite Steve and Janelle.

The sensations that came at Glenn were equally disturbing. The minute Maggie had started down the aisle it had taken everything within him not to step away from Steve, meet her and take her in his arms. He had never experienced any sensation more strongly. He wanted to hold her, protect her, bring the shine back to her eyes and teach her to trust again. When she had met him at the airport he'd been struck by how lovely she'd become. Now he recognized her fragile vulnerability, and she was breathtaking. He had never seen a more beautiful woman. She was everything he'd ever wanted—warm, vibrant, alive and standing so close that all he had to do was reach out and touch her. He felt like a blind man who had miraculously and unexpectedly been gifted with sight. Maggie needed him. Charleston, with all its painful memories, lay on the other side of the world.

"Dearly beloved, we are called here today to witness the marriage vows between Janelle and Stephen."

The rush of emotion that assaulted Maggie was unlike anything she'd every known. She couldn't keep her eyes from Glenn, who seemed to magnetically compel her gaze to meet his. Their eyes locked and held as the pastor continued speaking. There was no exchange of smiles, no winks, nothing cute or frivolous, but a solemn mood that made that instant, that moment, the most monumental of their lives. Maggie felt a breathless urgency come over her, and an emotion so powerful, so real that it brought brimming tears that filled her vision. In order to keep her make-up from streaking, she held one gloved finger under each eye a hand at a time and took in several deep breaths to forestall the ready flow. The void, the emptiness in her life wasn't entirely due to her money. What she needed was someone to love and who would love her. Desperately, Maggie realized how much she wanted to be needed. Several seconds passed before she regained her composure. The tightening lessened in her breast and she breathed freely once again.

When the pastor asked Steve and Janelle to repeat their vows, Maggie's gaze was again drawn to Glenn's. He didn't speak, nor did Maggie, but together, in unison, each syllable, each word was repeated in their hearts as they issued the same vows as their friends. When the pastor pronounced them man and wife, Maggie raised stricken eyes to the man of God who had uttered the words, needing the reassurance about whom he had meant. It was as if he had been speaking to Glenn and her, as well, and as if the formal pronouncement included them.

The organ burst into the traditional wedding march and Steve and Janelle turned to face the congregation, their faces radiant with happiness. As the newly wedded couple moved down the aisle, Glenn's arm reached for Maggie's, prepared to escort her. At the touch of his hand at her elbow, Maggie felt a series of indescribable sensations race through her: wonder, surprise, joy. Their eyes met and for the first time that day, he smiled. An incredible, dazzling smile that all but blinded her. Their march down the aisle, her arm on his elbow, added to the growing feeling that that day, that moment was meant for them as well.

Family and friends gathered outside the church doors, spilling onto the steps, giving hearty applause as Steve turned Janelle into his arms and kissed her. A festive mood reigned as Janelle was joyously hugged and Steve's hand was pumped countless times. The photographer was busily snapping pictures, ordering the wedding party to pose one way and then another. For a brief second the fantasy faded enough to frighten Maggie. What game was Glenn playing with her? No. She'd seen the sincerity in his eyes. But pretending was dangerous, far too dangerous.

"Are you all right?" Glenn whispered in her ear.

Maggie didn't have the opportunity to answer. As it was, she wasn't sure how to respond. Under other circumstances, she would have asked him to drive her to the hospital emergency room. Her daydreams were overpowering reality. This wasn't her wedding, nor was the man at her side her husband. She had no right to feel sensations like these.

The next thing she knew, Glenn had disappeared. Maggie hardly had time to miss him when a shiny new Cadillac pulled to the curb. Just Married was painted on the back window. Glenn jumped out and opened both doors on the passenger side. Then, racing up the church stairs, he took Maggie by the hand and following on the heels of Steve and Janelle, pulled her through a spray of rice and laughter as he whisked her toward the car.

Amidst hoots and more laughter, Glenn helped her gather her full-length skirt inside the automobile before closing the door and running around the front to climb in beside her.

Maggie was still breathless with laughter when he flashed her another of his dazzling smiles and started the engine. A sea of happy faces was gazing in at them. Turning her head to look out the side window, Maggie was greeted with the well-wishes of several boys and girls—children of their friends—standing on the sidewalk and waving with all their might. Glenn checked the rearview mirror and pulled into the steady flow of street traffic.

"Maggie, it was just as wonderful as you claimed it would be," Janelle said softly from the back seat.

"Did you doubt?" Steve questioned, his voice thick with emotion.

"I'll have you know, Mr. Grant, that I nearly backed out of this wedding at the very last minute. The only thing that stopped me was Maggie. Somehow she convinced me everything was going to work out. And it did."

"Janelle, I hardly said anything," Maggie countered, shocked by her friend's admission.

"You said just enough."

"I'm eternally grateful," Steve murmured and from the sounds coming from the back seat he was showing Janelle just how grateful he was that she was his bride.

Glenn's hand reached for Maggie's and squeezed it gently. "You're lovely." He wanted to say so much more and discovered he couldn't. For weeks he had dreaded the wedding and having to stand at the altar with his friend when it should have been his own wedding. The day had been completely unlike anything he'd expected. Maggie alone had made the difference.

"You make a striking figure yourself," she said, needing to place their conversation on an even keel.

Glenn unfastened the top button of the ruffled shirt and released the tie. "I feel like a penguin."

Laughter bubbled up in Maggie's throat. She felt happy, really happy for the first time in a long while. When Glenn held out his arms, she scooted across the seat so that they were as close as possible within the confines of the vehicle.

The sounds of smothered giggles from the back seat assured Maggie that things were very fine indeed. They stopped at a light and Glenn's gaze wandered to her for a brief, glittering second, then back to the road. "Thank you for today," he said, just low enough for her to hear. "You made our friends' wedding the most special day of my life."

"I... felt the same way about you," she whispered, wanting him to kiss her so badly she could almost taste his mouth over hers.

"Maggie," Janelle called from the back seat. "Will you check this veil? I can't walk into the dinner with it all askew. People will know exactly what kind of man I married."

"Oh, they will, will they?" Steve said teasingly, and kissed her soundly.

Maggie turned and glanced over her shoulder. "Everything looks fine. The veil's not even crooked, although from the sound of things back there it should be inside out and backward."

"Maggie," Steve said in a low and somewhat surprised tone as he studied her, "I expected Janelle's mother to cry, even my own. But I was shocked to see you were the one with tears in your eyes."

"You were shocked?" she tossed back nonchalantly. "Believe me, they were just as much of a surprise to me. Tears were the last thing I expected."

"Count your blessings, you two," Glenn said, tossing a glance over his shoulder. "Knowing Muffie, you should be grateful she didn't burst into fits of hysterical laughter." He glanced over to her and leaned close to her her and whispered. "Actually, they should thank me. It took everything in me not to break rank and reach for you." Glenn hadn't meant to tell her that, but those tears had nearly been his undoing. He had known when he'd seen her eyes bright with unshed tears that what was happening to him was affecting Maggie as greatly. He had come so close to happiness once, and like a fool, he'd let it slip away. It wouldn't happen again; he wouldn't allow it.

Everything was happening so quickly that Maggie didn't have time to react. Glenn's breath fanned her temple and a shiver of apprehension raced up and down her spine. They were playing a dangerous game. All that talk in the moonlight about the sanctity of marriage had affected their brain cells and they were daydreaming. No...pretending that this moment, this happiness, this love, was theirs. Only it wasn't, and Maggie had to give herself a hard mental shake to dislodge the illusion.

A long string of cars followed closely behind as the other members of the wedding party caught up with the Cadillac. Watching Glenn weave in and out of traffic, Maggie was impressed with his driving skill. However, everything about Glenn had impressed her today. Fleetingly, she allowed her mind to wander to what would happen when he left on Monday. She didn't want this weekend to be the end, but a beginning. He lived in Charleston, she in San Francisco. The whole country separated them, but they were only hours apart by plane and seconds by phone.

When he turned and caught her studying him, Maggie guiltily shifted her attention out the side window. The way her heart was hammering, one would think she was the bride. She struggled for composure.

Janelle's family had rented a huge Victorian hall for the dinner and dance. Maggie had no idea that there was such a special place in San Francisco and was assessing the wraparound porch and second-floor veranda when the remainder of the wedding party disembarked from the long row of cars that paraded behind the Cadillac. Wordlessly, Glenn took her by the elbow and led her up the front stairs.

Everything inside the huge hall was lushly decorated in antiques. Round tables with starched white tablecloths were set up to serve groups of eight. In the center of each table was a bowl of white gardenias. A winding stairway with a polished mahogany banister led to the dance floor upstairs.

Being seated at the same table as Steve and Janelle added to the continuing illusion. Somehow Maggie made it through the main course of veal cordon bleu, wild rice and tender asparagus spears. Her appetite was nonexistent and every bite had the taste and the feel of cotton. Although Glenn was at her side, they didn't speak, but the communication between them was louder than mere words. Twice she stopped herself from asking him what was happening to them, convinced he had no answers and the question would only confuse him further.

When Janelle cut the wedding cake and hand-fed the first bite to Steve, the happy applause vibrated around the room. The sound of it helped shake Maggie from her musings and she forced down another bite of her rice. The caterers delivered the cake to the wedding guests with astonishing speed so that all the guests were served in a matter of minutes.

Glenn's eyes darkened thoughtfully as he dipped his fork into the white cake and paused to study Maggie. He prayed she wasn't as confused as he. He didn't know what was happening, but was powerless to change anything. He wasn't even convinced he wanted anything different. It was as if they were in a protective bubble, cut off from the outside world. And although they sat in a room full of people, they were alone. Not knowing what made him do anything so crazy, Glenn lifted his fork to her mouth and offered Maggie the first sample of wedding cake. His eyes held her immobile as she opened her mouth and accepted his offering. Ever so lightly he ran his thumb along her chin as his dark, penetrating eyes bored into hers. By the time she finished swallowing, Glenn's hand was trembling and he lowered it.

Promptly Maggie placed her clenched fingers in her lap. A few minutes later she took a sip of champagne, her first that day, although she knew that enough was happening to her equilibrium without adding expensive champagne to wreak more damage.

The first muted strains of a Vienna waltz drifted from the upstairs dance floor. Maggie took another sip of champagne before standing.

Together, Steve and Janelle led their family and friends up the polished stairway to the dance floor.

When he saw the bride and groom, the orchestra leader stepped forward and announced: "Ladies and gentlemen, I give you Mr. and Mrs. Stephen Grant."

Steve took Janelle in his arms and swung his young bride around the room in wide fanciful steps. Pausing briefly, he gestured to Glenn, who swung Maggie into his arms.

Again the announcer stepped to the microphone and introduced them as the maid of honor and best man. All the while, the soft, melodic music continued its soothing chorus and they were soon joined by each bridesmaid and usher couple until the entire wedding party was on the dance floor.

As Glenn held Maggie in his arms, their feet made little more than tiny, shuffling movements that gave the pretense of dancing. All the while Glenn's serious, dark eyes held Maggie's. It was as though they were the only two in the room and the orchestra was playing solely for them. Try as she might, Maggie couldn't pull her gaze away.

"I've been wanting to do something from the moment I first saw you walk down the aisle."

"What?" she asked, surprised at how weak her voice sounded. She thought that if he didn't kiss her soon she was going to die.

Glenn glanced around him to the wide double doors that led to the veranda. He took her by the hand and led her through the crowd and out the curtained glass doors.

Maggie walked to the edge of the veranda and curled her fingers over the railing. Dusk had already settled over the city and lights from the bay flickered in the distance. Glenn joined her and slipped his arms around her waist, burying his face in her hair. Turning her in his arms, he closed his eyes and touched his forehead to hers. He took in several breaths before speaking.

"Are you feeling the same things I am?" he asked.

"Yes." Her heart was hammering so loud, Maggie was convinced he'd hear it.

"Is it the champagne?"

"I had two sips."

"I didn't have any," he countered. "See?" He placed the palm of her hand over his heart so she could feel its quickened beat. "From the moment I saw you in the church it's been like this."

"Me too," she whispered. "What's happening to us?"

Slowly, he shook his head. "I wish to God I knew."

"It's happening to me, too." She took his hand and placed it over her heart. "Can you feel it?"

"Yes," he whispered.

"Maggie, listen, this is going to sound crazy." He dropped his hands as if he needed to put some distance between them and took several steps back.

"What is?"

Glenn jerked his hand through his hair and hesitated. "Do you want to make this real?"

Chapter Three

Make this real?" Maggie echoed. "What do you mean?"

Glenn couldn't believe the ideas that were racing at laser speed through his mind. Maggie would burst into peals of laughter and he wouldn't blame her. But even that wasn't enough to turn the course of his thoughts. He had this compulsion, this urgency to speak as if something were driving him to say the words. "Steve and Janelle are going to make this marriage a good one."

"Yes," Maggie agreed. "I believe they will."

The look she was giving him was filled with questions. Surely she realized he hadn't asked her onto the veranda to discuss Steve and Janelle. After Angie, Glenn hadn't expected to feel this deep an emotion again. And so soon was another shock. Yet when he'd seen Maggie that first moment in the church the impact had been so great it was as though someone had physically assaulted him. She was lovely, possessing a rare beauty that had escaped his notice when they were younger. No longer had he been standing witness to his best friends's wedding, but he'd participated in a ceremony with a woman who could stand at his side for a lifetime. Maggie had felt it, too; he had seen it in her eyes. The identical emotion had moved her to tears.

"Glenn, you wanted to say something?" She coaxed him gently, her mind pleading with him to explain. He couldn't mean what she thought.

Remembering the look Maggie had given him when Steve and Janelle exchanged vows gave Glenn the courage to continue. "Marriage between friends is the best kind, don't you think?"

"Yes," she answered, unable to bring her voice above a husky whisper. "Friends know everything about each other, whether good or bad, and then choose to remain friends."

They stood for a breathless moment, transfixed, studying each other. "I'd always believed," Glenn murmured, his voice low and seductive, "that it would be impossible for me to share my life with anyone I didn't know extremely well."

"Oh, I agree." Maggie's mind was formulating impossible thoughts. Glenn was leading this conversation down meandering paths she'd never dreamed of traveling with him.

"We're friends," he offered next.

"Good friends," she agreed, nodding.

"I know you as well as my own brothers."

"We lived next door to each other for fifteen years," she added, her heart increasing its tempo to a slow drumroll.

"I want a home and children."

"I've always loved children." There hadn't been a time in her life when the pull was stronger toward a husband and family.

"Maggie," he said, taking a step toward her, but still not touching her, "you've become an extremely beautiful woman."

Her lashes fluttered against the high arch of her cheek as she lowered her gaze. Maggie didn't think of herself as beautiful. "Thank you."

"Any man would be proud to have you for his wife."

The sensations that raced through her were all too welcome and exciting. "I . . . I was just thinking that a woman . . . any woman would be extremely fortunate to have you for a husband."

"Would you?"

Her heart fluttered wildly, rocketed to her throat and then promptly plummeted to her stomach. Yet she didn't hesitate. "I'd be honored and proud."

Neither said anything for a timeless second while their minds assimilated what had just transpired, or what they thought had.

"Glenn?"

"Yes."

Her throat felt swollen and constricted, her chest suddenly tight as if tears were brewing just beneath the surface. "Did I understand you right? Did you—just now—suggest that you and me—the two of us—get married?"

"That's exactly what I'm suggesting." Glenn didn't hesitate. He'd never been more sure of anything in his life. He had lost one woman; he wasn't going to lose Maggie. He would bind her to him and eliminate the possibility of someone else stepping in at the last moment. This woman was his and he was claiming her before something happened to drive her from his arms.

"When?"

"Tonight."

She blinked twice, convinced she hadn't heard him right. "But the license, and . . ."

"We can fly to Reno." Already his mind was working out the details. He didn't like the idea of a quickie wedding, but it would serve the purpose. After what they had shared earlier they didn't need anything more than a few words to make it legal.

Stillness surrounded them. Even the night had gone silent. No cars, no horns, no crickets, no sounds of the night—only silence.

"I want to think about it," she murmured thoughtfully. Glenn was crazy. They both were. Talking about marriage, running away tonight. Reno. None of it made sense, but nothing in all her life had sounded more exciting, more wonderful, more right.

"How long do you want to think this over?" A thread of doubt prompted the question. Perhaps rushing her wasn't the best way to proceed, but waiting was equally impossible.

A fleeting smile touched and lifted the curved fullness of Maggie's mouth. They didn't dare tell someone they would do anything so ludicrous. She didn't need time, not really. She knew what she wanted: she wanted Glenn. "An hour," she said, hoping that within that time frame nothing would change.

The strains of another waltz drifted onto the veranda and wordlessly he led her back to the dance floor. When he reached for her, Maggie went willingly into his arms. His hold felt as natural as breathing, and she was drawn into the warmth of his nearness. The past two days with Glenn had been the happiest, most exciting in years. Who would have thought that Glenn Lambert would make her pulse pound like a jackhammer and place her head in the clouds where the air was thin and clear thought was impossible? Twenty-four hours after his arrival, and they were planning the most incredible scheme. Their very best scheme.

"This feeling reminds me of the night we stole out of the house to smoke our first cigarette," Glenn whispered in her ear. "Are we as daring and defiant now as we were at fourteen?"

"Worse," she answered. "But I don't care as long as you're with me."

"Oh, Maggie." He sighed her name with a wealth of emotion.

Her hands tightened around his neck as she fit her body more intimately to the unyielding contour of his. Her breasts were flattened to his broad chest; her nipples, hard and erect, seemed to swell with each swaying movement. They were melded together, thigh to thigh, hip to hip, as close as humanly possible and still giving the guise of dancing.

Every breath produced an incredible range of new sensations. Maggie felt drugged and delirious, daring and darling, bold and extraordinarily shy. Every second in his arms brought her more strength of conviction. This night, in less than an hour she was going to walk out of this room with Glenn Lambert. Together they would fly to Reno and she would forever link her life with his. There was nothing to stop her. Not her money. Not her pride. Not her fears. Glenn Lambert was her friend. Tonight he would become her lover as well.

Unable to bear the terrible sweetness of his touch a second longer, Maggie rained a long series of kisses over the jutting line of his jaw. The need to experience the intimate touch of his hands flowered deep within her.

Glenn's hold at her waist tightened and he inhaled sharply. "Maggie, don't tease me."

"Who's teasing?" They'd known each other many years and in all that time he had only kissed her once. But it was enough, more than enough to know that the loving between them would be exquisite.

Without her even being aware, Glenn had maneuvered her into a darkened corner of the dance floor where the lighting was the dimmest. His eyes told her he was about to kiss her and hers told him she was eager for him to do exactly that. Unhurriedly, Glenn lowered his mouth to hers with an agonizing slowness. His kiss was warm and tender and lingering, as if this were a moment and place out of time meant for them alone. Her soft mouth parted with only the slightest urging from his tongue and her arms tightened around his neck as she drew his probing tongue into her mouth, then happily gave him hers. He teased her; she tormented him. He delved; she stroked. Together they became masters of exploration in their need to discover all they could about kissing each other. In minutes, they made up for years of lost time.

Trembling in his embrace, Maggie drew in a long unsteady breath. Glenn's kisses had been filled with such aching tenderness, such sweet torment that Maggie felt tears stinging for release. Tears for a happiness she had never hoped to find. At least not with Glenn. This was a wondrous surprise. A gift. A miracle so unexpected it would take a lifetime to fully appreciate.

"I want you," he whispered, his voice hoarse with desire. His breath warmed her lips.

"Yes" she returned, vaguely dazed. "I want you, too."

His arms tightened and Maggie felt the shudder that rocked him until her ribs ached with the tender violence. Gradually his hold relaxed as his gaze polarized hers. "Let's get out of here."

"Should . . . should we tell anyone?" *No*, her mind shouted. Someone might try to talk them out of this and she wanted it. Desperately she wanted everything that Glenn was suggesting.

"Do you want to tell Steve and Janelle?" Glenn asked.

"No."

Tenderly he brushed his lips across her forehead. "Neither do I. They'll find out soon enough."

"It'll be our surprise." She smiled at him, the warm happy smile of someone about to embark on the most exciting adventure of her life. And Maggie felt like an adventurer, daring and audacious, dauntless and intrepid, reckless and carefree. There'd be problems; she realized that. But tonight with Glenn at her side there wasn't anything she couldn't conquer.

Glenn raised her fingertips to his lips and kissed each one. "I'm not letting you out of my sight. We're going directly to the airport."

"Fine." She had no desire to be separated from him, either.

"I'll call a taxi."

"I'll get my purse."

The night air brought a chill to her arms, but it didn't sharpen any need to analyze what they were doing. If Glenn expected her to have second thoughts as they breezed through the streets of San Francisco, she found none. Even the busy airport, with its crowded concourses and people who stared at their unusual dress, wasn't enough to cause her to doubt.

Glenn bought their airline tickets, and she found a seat while he used the pay phone to make hotel reservations. When he returned, the broad smile reached his eyes and Maggie was struck anew with the wonder of what was happening.

"Well?"

"Everything's been taken care of."

"Everything?" It seemed paramount that they get married tonight. If they were forced to wait until morning there could be second thoughts.

"The Chapel of Love is one block from city hall and they're going to arrange for the marriage license." He glanced at his watch and hesitated. "The plane lands at ten-thirty and the ceremony is scheduled for eleven-fifteen." He sat in the seat beside her and reached for her hand. "You're cold."

"A little." Despite her nerves she managed to keep her voice even. She didn't doubt they were doing the right thing and wanted to reassure Glenn. "I'm fine. Don't worry about me."

Rising to his feet, Glenn stripped the tuxedo jacket from his arms and draped it over her shoulders. "Here. We'll be boarding in a few minutes and I'll get you a blanket from the stewardess." His dark eyes were full of warmth and he was smiling at her as if they'd been sitting in airports, waiting for planes to fly them to weddings every day.

His strong fingers closed over hers and for the first time she admired how large his hands were. The fingers were long and tapered and looked capable of carving an empire or soothing a crying child. "Are you—" Maggie swallowed convulsively, almost afraid to ask "—are you having any second thoughts?"

"No," he answered quickly. "What about you?"

"None." She was never so positive of anything in her life.

"I'll be a good husband to you."

"I know that." She placed her free hand over the back of his. "And I'll be a good wife."

His returning smile, filled with warmth and incredible wonder, could have melted a glacier.

"My parents are going to be ecstatic." Shocked too, her mind added, but that didn't matter.

"Mine will be pleased as well," Glenn assured her. "They've always liked you."

He bent his head toward her and Maggie shyly lifted her face and met him halfway. His kiss was filled with soft exploration, and they parted with the assurance that everything was perfect.

"After we're married, will you want me to move to Charleston?" Maggie ventured.

"No," he said on a somber note. "I'll move to San Francisco." The time had come to leave Charleston. Glenn wanted to bury the unhappiness that surrounded him there. The brief visit to San Francisco had been like coming home. With Maggie at his side he'd build a new life in San Francisco. Together they'd raise their family and live in blissful happiness. No longer would he allow the memory of another woman to haunt him.

Maggie felt simultaneously relieved and confused. Her career in art made it possible for her to work anywhere. For Glenn to move to San Francisco would mean giving up his Charleston clientele and building up a new one on the West Coast. It didn't make sense. "I don't mind moving, really. It would be easier for me to make the change. You've got your career."

He slid his hand from her arm to her elbow, tightening his hold. "I'll transfer out here." Turning his wrist he glanced at his watch, but Maggie had the feeling he wasn't looking at the time. "I'm ready for a change," he murmured after a while. "You don't mind, do you?"

Did she? No, Maggie decided, she loved California. "No, that'll be fine. You'll like the beach house."

"I don't doubt that I will."

Their flight number was announced and Maggie returned Glenn's tuxedo jacket before they boarded the plane. The flight attendant came by a few minutes later, after they were comfortably seated, to check their seat belts. She paused and commented that they both looked as if they were on their way to a wedding. Glenn and Maggie smiled politely, but neither of them opted to inform the young woman that it was exactly what they were doing. Maggie feared that if they let someone in on their plan it would somehow shatter the dream. Briefly she wondered if Glenn shared her fears.

The flight touched down on the Reno runway precisely on schedule. With no luggage to collect, Glenn and Maggie walked straight through the airport and outside, where a taxi was parked and waiting.

"You two on your way to a wedding?" the cab-driver asked with a loud belly laugh as he held the door open for Maggie.

"Yes," Maggie answered shyly, dismissing her earlier fears.

"Ours," Glenn added, sliding into the seat next to Maggie and reaching for her hand.

The heavyset cabbie closed the door and walked around to the driver's side. He checked the rearview mirror and merged with the traffic. "Lots of people come to Reno to get married, but then a lot of folks come here to get unmarried, too."

A thundering silence echoed through the close confines of the taxi. "There won't be any divorce for us," Glenn informed him.

The driver tipped back the rim of his cap with his index finger. "Lot of folks say that, too." He paused at the first red light, placed his arm along the back of the seat and turned to look at Glenn. "Where was it you said you wanted to go?"

"Chapel of Love," Glenn said firmly and glanced over to Maggie. "Do you want to change your mind?" he whispered low enough for only her to hear.

"You're not backing out of your proposal, are you?" The words nearly stuck in her throat.

"No."

"Then we're getting married," she murmured, more determined than ever. "I didn't come this far in a shimmering pink taffeta gown to play the slot machines."

"Good."

"Very good," she murmured, unwilling to let anyone or anything ruin her joyous anticipation of this night.

A half hour later, after arriving at the chapel, Maggie had freshened her makeup and done what she could with her hair. They stood now before the proprietor of the wedding chapel.

"Organ music is fifteen dollars extra," Glenn told her as he reached for his back pocket.

Her hand stopped him. "I don't need it," she assured him with perfect serenity. "I'm still hearing the music from the church."

The impatience drained from his eyes and the look he gave her was so profound that it seemed the most natural thing in the world to lean forward and press her lips to his.

The justice of the peace cleared his throat. "If you're ready we can start the ceremony."

"Are you ready?" Glenn asked with smiling eyes.

"I've been ready for this all night," she answered, linking her arm with his.

The service was shockingly short and sterile. They stood before the justice and repeated the words that had already been spoken in their hearts. The stark ceremony wasn't what Maggie would have preferred, but it didn't diminish any of the happiness of the moment. This wedding was necessary for legal reasons; their real vows had already been exchanged earlier that day as they stood witnesses for Steve and Janelle. Those few moments in the church had been so intense that from then on every moment of her life would be measured against them. Maggie yearned to explain that to Glenn, but mere words were inadequate. He, too, had experienced it, she realized, and without analyzing it, he had understood.

Their room at the hotel was ready when they arrived. With the key jingling in Glenn's pocket they rode the elevator to the tenth floor.

"Are you going to carry me over the threshold, Mr. Lambert?" Maggie whispered happily and nuzzled his ear. She felt a free-flowing joyousness unlike anything she'd ever experienced. That night and every night for the rest of her life would be spent in Glenn's arms.

"I'll see what I can manage," Glenn stated seriously as he backed her into the corner of the elevator and kissed the side of her neck.

Maggie shot him a dubious look. "I'm not that heavy, you know."

"What I suggest we do," he murmured as he nibbled on her earlobe, "is have me lift one of your legs and you can hop over the threshold."

"Glenn," she muttered, breaking free. "That's crazy."

Chuckling, he ignored the question. "On second thought I could probably manage to haul you piggyback."

Deftly her fingers opened his tie and she teased his throat with the moist tip of her tongue. If he was going to joke with her then she'd tease him as well. "Never mind," she whispered. "I'll carry you."

The elevator came to a grinding halt and the doors swished open. Glenn glanced around him, kissed Maggie soundly and with a mighty heave-ho, hauled her over his shoulder fireman fashion.

"Glenn..." she whispered fiercely, stunned into momentary speechlessness. "Put me down this instant."

Chuckling, he slowly rubbed his hand over her prominently extended derriere. "You said you wanted me to carry you over the threshold. Only I can't very well manage you, the key and the door all at once."

Using her arms against his shoulders for leverage, Maggie attempted to straighten. "Glenn, please," she begged, laughing until it was difficult to speak and probably just as impossible to be understood.

He shifted her weight when he fidgeted with the key. Maggie couldn't see what was happening, but the sound of the door opening assured her all was well. Her eyes studied the same door as it closed and the narrow entryway as he carried her halfway into the room. The next thing Maggie knew, she was falling through space. She gave a frightened cry until the soft cushion of the mattress broke her rapid descent.

Panting and breathless with laughter, Maggie lay sprawled across the bed. She smiled up at Glenn playfully and raised her arms to her husband of fifteen minutes. Glenn knelt beside her, his eyes glowing with the fire of passion as he lowered his mouth to hers in a deep kiss that sent her world into a crazy tailspin. She clung to him, her fingers ruffling the thick, dark hair that grew at his nape. Wildly, she returned his kiss, on fire for him, luxuriating in the feel of his body over hers, pressing against her breasts and stomach. With loving gentleness his hands stroked her breasts, his touch feather-light, lingering over each quivering nipple until they throbbed and stood erect, pleading for his touch.

Unexpectedly, he tore his mouth from hers and lifted his head. Without a word, he brushed the soft wisps of hair from her temple and dipped his head a second time to sample her mouth. When he broke away and moved to the long dresser that dominated one side of the hotel room, Maggie felt a sudden chill throughout her body and rose to a sitting position.

A bottle of champagne was resting in a bed of crushed ice. With his back to her, Glenn peeled off the foil covering that was wrapped around the top and removed the cork. He ached with the need to take her physically, but feared his building passion would frighten her. Silently, Glenn cursed himself for not having approached the subject sooner. He wanted her, but did he dare take her so soon?

The dresser mirror revealed Glenn's troubled frown and Maggie felt a brooding anxiety settle over her. For the first time she could see doubt in his eyes. The breath jammed in her lungs. No, not doubt, but apprehension, even foreboding. Maggie was feeling it, too. Maybe advancing from friends to lovers in the space of a few hours wasn't right for them. Maybe they should think it through very carefully before proceeding with what was paramount on both their minds. There wasn't any reason to wait. They were married. They knew each other better than most newlyweds. The certificate in Glenn's coat pocket granted them every right.

With her weight resting on the palm of one hand, she felt her heart throb painfully. "Glenn," she whispered brokenly, not knowing what exactly to say, or how to say it.

The sound of her voice was drowned by the cork, exploding from the bottle. Fizzing champagne squirted across the dresser. Glenn deftly filled the two glasses and returned the dark bottle to its icy bed.

Handing her a goblet, Glenn joined her on the side of the mattress. "To my wife," he whispered tenderly and touched the edge of her glass to his.

"To my husband," she murmured in return. The bubbly liquid tickled her nose and she smiled shyly at Glenn as she took another sip. "I suppose this is when I'm supposed to suggest that I slip into something more comfortable."

"I'm for that." He quickly stood and strode across the room for the bottle, setting it on the floor next to the bed as he sat down again, avoiding her eyes the whole time.

"However, we both seemed to have forgotten something important." She bit her bottom lip in a gesture of uncertainty and laughter.

He glanced up expectantly. "What's that?"

"Clothes," she said and giggled. They had been so afraid to leave one another for fear something would happen to change their minds that they hadn't even stopped to pack an overnight bag.

"We're not going to need them." In that instant Glenn realized that they weren't going to wait. He wanted her. She wanted him; it was in her eyes and the provocative way she batted her long lashes. "We have two days," he murmured, "and I can't see any need we'll be having for clothes."

He was so utterly serious that laughter rumbled in her throat. Where there had once been anxiety there was expectancy. "Maybe we could get away with that sort of thing on the Riviera, but believe me, they arrest people for walking around nude in Reno."

Smiling, he tipped back his head and emptied his glass. "You know what I mean."

Maggie set their champagne glasses aside. "No," she said breathlessly as she lightly stroked the neatly trimmed hair at his temple. "I think you'll have to show me."

Gently, Glenn laid her back on the bed and joined her so the upper portion of his body was positioned over the top of hers. His arms went around her, pressing her to his hard strength until her breasts strained against him. "I have every intention of doing exactly that."

He captured her mouth in a deep, consuming kiss, his exploring tongue parting her lips. Boldly her tongue met his in a loving duel in which they were both winners. Maggie could hear the slow, steady beat of his heart and the sound excited her all the more.

His lips left hers to investigate her ear before tracing their way back across her cheek and reclaiming her delectable mouth.

Maggie buried her face in the hollow of his throat, drawing in a deep shuddering breath as his busy hands fumbled with the effort to locate the tiny buttons at the back of her dress. Every place his fingers grazed her sensitized skin, a glowing warmth spread. Again Maggie opened her mouth to explore the strong cord of his neck, savoring his salty-tasting skin. She heard the harsh intake of his breath when she pulled his silk dress shirt free and sensuously began to stroke his muscular back.

"Oh, Glenn," she whispered urgently when she didn't think she could stand it anymore. Her shoulders were heaving when he lifted his weight from her.

He rolled onto his back and she heard him release a harsh breath. "Maggie." His voice was thick and husky. "Listen, are you sure about this? We can wait."

"I'm sure," she whispered and switched positions so that now it was she who was sprawled half atop him. "Glenn, I'm so sure it hurts."

"Maggie, oh Maggie." He repeated her name again and again in a broken whisper. "Oh, dear God, you're going to be good for me. I've needed you so long."

"And I need you." The surge of emotion that went through her caused her voice to crack. She had spent a lifetime searching for him when all along he'd been so close and she hadn't known.

His arms crushed her then, and his mouth passionately sought hers with a greedy ardor that seemed to want to devour her. He took; she surrendered. He gave; she received. They were starved for each other and the physical love their bodies could share. His mouth and tongue alternately caressed and plundered hers. With her arms wrapped securely around him, Maggie met his ravaging hunger with her own needs. When he half lifted her from the mattress she was trembling with desire.

"Glenn," she whispered brokenly. "Oh, Glenn, don't ever let me go."

"Never," he promised, sitting on the edge of the bed with her cradled in his lap. "This is forever." His words were a vow. Carefully, in order not to tear her dress, his fingers released each tiny button at the back of her gown. As each one was freed he pressed his lips to the newly exposed skin.

"Forever," she repeated, and twisted so she could work loose the tuxedo tie and the buttons to the ruffled shirt. She pulled the shirt free of his shoulders and slid her hand down his chest to his tightening abdomen.

"Maggie," he warned hoarsely.

"Love me," she whispered. "Oh, Glenn, make me your wife. Please."

His open mouth ran greedily over her, seeking her breast, teasing her taut nipple until she was weak with longing.

Maggie's fingers clutched frantically at his thick dark hair as he continued to stroke her heaving breast.

"Now, oh please, now." The words could barely escape her parched throat. She was on fire for him. Consumed with desire, lost in a primitive world, aware of nothing but the desperate need he awoke within her body.

Moving quickly he laid her upon the mattress and eased his body over hers. He kissed her until Maggie felt as if she would melt. Urgently, she opened her thighs, her hands eager as she guided him. With a throaty groan, Glenn thrust deeply into her. Maggie's startled eyes shot open and gasping with pleasure, she called out his name.

His mouth found hers and she clamped her arms around his neck as they began to move. Whimpering with joy and relief, Maggie arched her back as their bodies created their own intimate rhythm.

"Oh, Glenn," she cried out of happiness as a delicious trembling spread through her body.

Glenn tossed his head back, his eyes clenched tightly as his body heaved and shuddered once, then relaxed.

A long moment passed before he gathered her in his arms and rolled onto his side, taking her with him.

Lying cradled in his embrace, their legs entwined, Maggie closed her eyes and released a contented sigh.

"It was beautiful," she whispered, still overcome with emotion.

Glenn kissed the top of her head. "You're beautiful."

"So are you," she added quickly. "Oh, Glenn, we're going to have such a good life."

"Yes," he agreed and kissed her forehead.

Maggie snuggled closer against him and kissed the nape of his neck when he reached down to cover them with the sheet and blanket.

Glenn held her close, kissing the crown of her head until her eyes closed sleepily. Her last thought as she drifted into the welcoming comfort of slumber was of warmth and security.

Maggie woke a couple of times in the darkest part of the night, unaccustomed to sharing her bed. Each time she experienced the unexpected thrill of finding Glenn asleep at her side. No longer was she alone. Her joy was so great that she felt ten years old again, waking up on Christmas morning.

She cuddled him spoon fashion, pressing her softness to his backside. Her body fit perfectly to his. Edging her hand over his muscular ribs she felt his strength and knew that this man was as steady as the Rock of Gibraltar. She had chosen her life mate well. Content, she drifted back to sleep.

A low, grumbling sound woke her when morning light splashed into the room from the small crack between closed drapes. Sitting up, Maggie yawned and raised her arms high above her head. She was ravenous, and pressed a hand to her stomach to prevent her rumbling from waking Glenn. A menu for room service sat by the phone and Maggie reached for it, studying its contents with interest, wondering if it would wake him if she ordered anything.

Glenn stirred and rolled onto his back, still caught in the last dregs of sleep. Gloriously happy, Maggie watched as a lazy smile grew on his face. Pride swelled in her heart as she realized their lovemaking was responsible for his look of blessed contentment. Maybe she wasn't so hungry after all.

Her long, tangled hair fell forward as she leaned down to press her lips to his. As she drew near, he whispered something. At first Maggie couldn't understand his words, then she froze. Stunned, her hand flew to her breast at the unexpected pain that pierced her. The arctic chill extended all the way to her heart and she squeezed her eyes closed to fight back the burning tears. Choking on humiliation, she struggled to untangle herself from the sheet. Her frantic movements woke Glenn from the nether land of sleep to the world of consciousness.

He turned on his side and reached for her hand. "Good morning," he said cheerfully. At the sight of her stricken face, he paused and rose to a full sitting position. "What's wrong?"

"The name is Maggie," she whispered fiercely, shoving his hand away. "And in case you've forgotten, I'm your wife as well."

Chapter Four

Tugging the sheet loose from the mattress, Maggie climbed out of bed. Her hands were shaking so badly that she had trouble twisting the material around her. Holding it together with one hand above her breasts, she sorted through the tangled mess of clothes on the floor. The tightness in her chest was so painful she could barely breathe. The room swayed beneath her feet and she closed her eyes, struggling to maintain her balance and her aplomb. Everything had been so beautiful. So perfect. How readily she had fallen into the fantasy, believing in each minute with a childlike innocence and trust. She'd been living in a twenty-four-hour dreamworld. That fantasy had been shattered by the reality of morning and she was shamed to the very marrow of her bones.

Glenn wiped a hand over his face and struggled to a sitting position. He vaguely recalled the contented pleasure of sleeping with a warm body at his side. In his sleep he must have associated this fulfillment with Angie. Damn that woman for haunting him in his marriage.

"Maggie, what did I say?"

Straightening, Maggie turned to regard him coolly before speaking. "You said enough." *More than enough,* her mind shouted. Clenching the sheet in one hand, her clothes in the other, she defiantly marched across the floor, her head tilted at a stately angle. She never felt more like crying in her life. Her pride and dignity remained intact but little else was as it should be.

Once inside the bathroom she leaned against the heavy door, her shoulders sagging. Covering her face with both hands in abject frustration, she let the sheet slip to the floor. Equal doses of anger and misery descended on her until Maggie was convinced she'd slump under the force of their weight. She didn't know what do do, but taking a bath seemed utterly important.

"Maggie." Glenn stood on the other side of the door, his voice low and confused. "Tell me what I said. At least talk to me."

"No," she shouted unreasonably, still reeling from the shock. "I don't want to talk. I've heard enough to last me a lifetime." Forcing herself into action, she turned on the faucet and filled the tub with steaming hot water. She had been a fool to believe in yesterday's illusions, she thought angrily. The morning had shattered the dream—only she didn't want it to end. Glenn was someone she had thought she could trust. In her heart she knew that he wouldn't be like all the rest.

"Maggie, for God's sake give me a chance to explain."

Sliding into the steaming bath, Maggie bit into her bottom lip and forced herself to think. She could demand that they divorce, but she didn't want that and Glenn didn't, either. For twelve hours she had been a happily married woman. Somehow Maggie had to find a way to stretch twelve hours into a lifetime.

In the other room Glenn dressed slowly, his thoughts oppressive. Things couldn't be worse. From the moment Maggie had met him at the airport he had seen how reserved and untrusting her inheritance had made her. Now he had hurt her, and he silently cursed himself for doing the very thing he vowed he wouldn't. He could still envision those stricken eyes glaring down at him when he woke. He had wanted to take her in his arms and explain, but she'd jumped from the bed as if she couldn't get away fast enough. Good God, he couldn't blame her. The worst part was that he couldn't guarantee it wouldn't happen again. Angie had been an integral part of his life for nearly two years. He had cast her from his thoughts with an all-consuming effort, but he had no control over the ramblings of his mind when he slept. Dear Lord, he wished he knew what he'd said. He stroked his fingers through his hair and heaved a disgusted sigh. Whatever it was, he wouldn't allow it to ruin this marriage. Somehow he'd find a way to make it up to Maggie.

The bathroom door opened and Glenn turned anxiously. He studied Maggie's face for evidence of tears and found none. He had forgotten what a strong woman she was and admired her all the more. With vivid clarity he recalled the time she was fifteen and broke her arm skateboarding. She'd been in intense pain. Anyone else would have been screaming like a banshee, but not Maggie. She had gritted her teeth, but hadn't shed a tear. He also remembered how the only person she had trusted to help her had been him. The guilt washed over him in dousing waves.

"Can we talk now?" he asked her gently.

"I think we should," she said, pacing because standing in one spot was impossible. "We need to make some rules in this marriage, Glenn."

"Anything," he agreed.

"The first thing you have to do is stop loving that other woman right now. This minute." Her voice trembled and she battled for control.

Glenn felt physically ill. Maggie was unnaturally pale, her cheeks devoid of color. Her dark, soulful eyes contained a sorrow he longed to erase and yet he knew he couldn't. His thoughts were in turmoil. "You know I'd never lie to you."

"Yes." Glenn might be a lot of things, she knew, but a liar wasn't one of them.

"Maggie, I want this marriage to work, but what you're asking me to do is going to be hard."

A tingling sensation went through her that left her feeling numb and sick. She wouldn't share this man— not even with a memory.

"In that case," she murmured and swallowed, "I've got some thinking to do." She turned from him and started toward the door.

"Maggie." Glenn stopped her and she turned around. Their eyes met and held. "You don't want a divorce, do you?"

The word hit Maggie with all the impact of a freight train. "No," she said, shaking her head. "I may be mad, Glenn Lambert, but I'm not stupid."

The door made an echoing sound that bounced off the walls as Maggie left the hotel room. Glenn felt his tense shoulder muscles relax. It had taken everything in him to ask her about a divorce. That was the last thing he wanted, but he felt he had to know where Maggie stood after what had happened that morning.

The curious stares that met Maggie as she stepped off the elevator convinced her that the first thing she had to do was buy something to wear that was less ostentatious. A wrinkled pink maid-of-honor gown would cause more than a few heads to turn, and the last thing Maggie wanted was attention. In addition, she couldn't demand that her husband give up his affection for another woman and love and care for her instead, when she looked like something the cat left on the porch.

The hotel had a gift shop where she found a summer dress of pale-blue polished cotton, which she changed into after purchasing it. A walk through the lobby revealed that Glenn was nowhere to be seen. With time weighing heavily on her hands, Maggie turned a ten-dollar bill into a roll of quarters. Already the hotel casino was buzzing with patrons eager to spend their money. Maggie was no exception. Standing in front of the quarter slot machine, Maggie inserted the first coin. Pulling down the handle she watched the figures spin into a blur and slowly wind down to two oranges and a cherry. Two quarters slid out and Maggie stared at them in disbelief. She didn't expect to win. Actually, it was fitting that she was in Reno. She had just made the biggest gamble of her life. The scary part was that Maggie felt like a loser and had felt like one almost from the minute she inherited her Great-aunt Margaret's money. She felt the ridiculous urge to laugh, but recognized that if she gave in to the compulsion tears wouldn't be far behind.

Glenn found her ten minutes later, still playing the slot machines. For several moments he stood watching her, wondering how to approach this woman he had known most of his life. The woman who was now his wife. There were so many issues facing them that had to be settled before he left for Charleston. Maggie's inheritance was one thing he wouldn't allow to hang between them like a steel curtain. It was best to clear the air of that and everything else they could.

A discordant bell clanged loudly and a barrage of quarters slipped from the belly of Maggie's slot machine. She looked stunned and stepped back as the machine emptied. Without emotion, she dumped the coins into a paper bucket. As she turned, their eyes clashed. Her breath caught in her throat and she hesitated, waiting for him to speak first. Like her, he had purchased another set of clothes, and again Maggie wondered why she'd never noticed how extraordinarily good-looking Glenn was. He was a man any woman would be proud to call her husband. If he'd come to tell her he wanted a divorce, she didn't know what she would say. The time spent in front of the slot machine had given her the perspective to realize that Glenn was as shocked by what had happened as she was. Desperately she prayed that he hadn't come for the reason she suspected. Maggie wanted this marriage. She had been so lonely and miserable. The previous day with Glenn had been the most wonderful day of her life. Maybe she was still looking at the situation through rose-colored glasses, but the deed was done. They were married now. The other woman had no claim to him. He might murmur ''her'' name in his sleep, but he was married to Maggie.

''Our plane leaves in two hours,'' he said, stepping forward. ''Let's get something to eat.''

Nodding required a monumental effort. Her body went limp with relief.

The receptionist at the restaurant led them to a booth and handed them menus. She gave Glenn a soft, slightly seductive smile, but Maggie was pleased to notice that he didn't pay the woman the least bit of attention. Glenn had never been a flirt. Beyond anything else, Maggie realized, Glenn was an intensely loyal man. For him to whisper another woman's name in his sleep had been all the more devastating for just that reason.

Almost immediately a waitress arrived, poured them each a cup of coffee and took their order.

''I want you to know that I'll do everything in my power to do as you ask,'' Glenn announced, his eyes holding hers. His hands cupped the coffee mug and there was a faint pleading note shining from his eyes. ''About this morning; I suppose you want to know about her.''

''Yes,'' Maggie whispered, hating the way his eyes softened when he mentioned his lost love.

A sadness seemed to settle over him. ''Her name is Angie. We were...'' He hesitated. ''Engaged. She decided to marry her childhood sweetheart. It's as simple as that.''

''You obviously cared about her a great deal,'' Maggie said softly, hoping to take some of the sting from her earlier comments. Talking about Angie, even now, was obviously painful for him.

He held her gaze without hesitation. "I did care for her, but that's over now. I didn't marry you longing for anyone else. You aren't a substitute. This marriage wasn't made on the rebound. We're both vulnerable for different reasons right now. I want you for my wife. Not anyone else, only you. We've known each other most of our lives. I like you a great deal and respect you even more. We're comfortable together."

"Yes, we are," she agreed. So Glenn regarded her as an old pair of worn shoes. He could relax with her and put aside any need for pretense...as she could. But then she hadn't exactly come into their marriage seeking white lace and promises. Or maybe she had, she thought. Maggie didn't know anymore; she was completely confused.

"We're going to work this out," he said confidently, smiling for the first time that day as he reached for her hand.

"We're going to try," she suggested cautiously. "I'm not so sure we've done the right thing running off like this. We were both half-crazy to think we could make a marriage work on a twenty-four-hour reacquaintance."

"I knew what we were doing every second," Glenn countered gruffly. "I wanted this, Maggie."

"I didn't know if it was right or wrong. I guess only time will tell if we did the right thing or not.

The flight back to San Francisco seemed to take a lifetime. Maggie sat by the window, staring at the miniature world far below. The landscape rolled and curved from jutting peaks to plunging valleys that reminded her of the first few hours of her marriage. Even now a brooding sense of unreality remained with her.

The days were shorter now that winter was approaching, and dusk had settled by the time the taxi pulled up in front of the beach house. While Glenn was paying the cabdriver, Maggie looked over the house where she had voluntarily sequestered herself, wondering how Glenn would view the ostentatious showplace. Undoubtedly he would be impressed. Her friends had praised the beach house that seemed to lack for nothing. There was a small gym, a sauna, a Jacuzzi, a swimming pool and a tennis court in the side yard that Maggie never used. The house held enough attractions to keep even the most discriminating prisoner entertained.

On the way from the airport they had stopped off at Steve's empty apartment and picked up Glenn's luggage. Seeing it was a vivid reminder that he was scheduled to leave in the morning. "What time is your flight tomorrow?" she asked, wondering how long they'd be in Charleston. They had already decided to make their home in San Francisco, but arrangements would need to be made in Charleston.

His mouth hardened. "Are you so anxious to be rid of me?"

"No." She turned astonished eyes to him, stunned at his sharp tongue. He made it sound as though she wouldn't be going with him. She should. After all, she was his wife. She could make an issue of it now, or wait until she was certain she'd read him right. They had already experienced enough conflict for one day and Maggie opted to hold her tongue. Her fingers fumbled with the lock in an effort to get inside the house. "I have to phone my brother," she announced once the door was open.

"Denny?"

"Yes, Denny, or is that a problem, too?"

He ran his fingers through his hair and expelled an angry breath. "I didn't mean to snap at you."

Maggie lowered her gaze. "I know. We're both on edge. I didn't mean to bite your head off, either." They were nervous and unsure of each other for the first time in their lives. What had once been solid ground beneath their feet had become shifting sand. They didn't know where they stood...or if they'd continue to stand at all.

Glenn placed a hand at the base of her neck and gently squeezed it. "My flight's scheduled for three. We'll have some time together."

He didn't plan to have her travel with him! That was another shock. Fine, she thought angrily. If he didn't want her, then she wouldn't ask. "Good," she murmured sarcastically. Fine indeed!

The entryway was paved with expensive tiles imported from Italy, and led to a plush sunken living room decorated with several pieces of furniture upholstered in white leather. A baby grand piano dominated one corner of the room. As she hung up Glenn's coat he wandered into the large living room, his hands in his pockets.

"Do you like it?"

"It's very nice" was all he said. He stood, legs slightly apart while his gaze rested on an oil painting hung prominently on the wall opposite the Steinway. It was one of Maggie's earlier works and her favorite, a beachscape that displayed several scenes, depicting a summer day's outing to the ocean. Her brush had captured the images of eager children building a sand castle. Another group of bikini-clad young girls were playing a game of volleyball with muscle-bound he-men. A family was enjoying a picnic, their blanket spread out on the sand, shaded by a multicolored umbrella. Cotton-candy clouds were floating in a clear blue sky while the ocean waves crested and slashed against the shore. Maggie had spent hours agonizing over the minute details of the painting. Despite its candor and realism, Maggie's beachscape wasn't an imitation of a snapshot recording, but a mosaiclike design that gave a minute hint at the wonder of life.

"This is a marvelous painting. Where did you ever find it?" Glenn asked without turning around. "The detail is unbelievable."

"A poor imitation of a Brueghel." A smile danced at the corners of her mouth.

"Who?"

"Pieter Brueghel, a sixteenth-century Flemish painter."

"A sixteenth-century artist didn't paint this," Glenn challenged.

"No. I did."

He turned with a look of astonished disbelief on his face. "You're not teasing, are you?" The question was rhetorical. His eyes narrowed fractionally as if reassessing her.

"It's one of my earliest efforts after art school. I've done better since, but this one's my favorite."

"Better than this?" His voice dipped faintly as though he doubted her words. "I remember you scribbling figures as a kid, but I never suspected you had this much talent."

A shiver of pleasure raced up her arm at the pride that gleamed from his eyes as he glanced from the painting back to her. "I had no idea you were this talented, Maggie."

The sincerity of the compliment couldn't be doubted. Others had praised her work, but Maggie had felt a niggling doubt as to the candidness of the comments. So often people wanted to gain favor because of her money. "Thank you," she returned, feeling uncharacteristically humble.

"I'd like to see your other projects."

"Don't worry, you'll get the chance. Right now, I've got to phone Denny. He'll wonder what happened to me."

"Sure. Go ahead. I'll wait in here if you like."

Maggie's office was off the living room. She hesitated a moment before deciding, then walked to the telephone on a table next to the couch. Her back was to Glenn as she picked up the receiver and punched out the number.

"Denny, it's Maggie."

"Maggie," he cried with obvious relief. "How was the wedding? You must have been late. I tried to get hold of you all day."

It was on the tip of Maggie's tongue to tell him about her marriage, but she held back, preferring to waylay his questions and doubts. She would tell him soon enough.

Her brother's voice softened perceptibly. "I was worried."

"I'm sorry, I should have phoned." Maggie lifted a strand of hair around her ear.

"Did you get the money transferred?"

Maggie sighed inwardly, feeling guilty. Denny knew all the right buttons to push with her. "The money will be ready for you Monday morning."

"Thanks. You know Linda and I appreciate it." His voice took on a honey-coated appeal.

"I know."

"As soon as I talk to the attorney about my case I'll let you know where we stand."

"Yes, Denny, do that." A large portion of Denny's inheritance had been lost in a bad investment and Maggie was helping him meet expenses. She didn't begrudge him the money: how could she when she had so much? What she hated was what it was doing to him. Yet she couldn't refuse him. Denny was her brother, her only brother.

After saying her goodbye, she replaced the receiver and turned back to Glenn. "I gave the housekeeper the weekend off. But if you're hungry, I'm sure I'll be able to whip up something."

"How's Denny?" Glenn ignored her offer.

"Fine. Do you want something to eat or not?"

"Sure." His gaze rested on the phone and Maggie realized that he'd probably picked up the gist of her conversation with Denny. More than she had intended. As a stockbroker Glenn would know what a foolish mistake her brother had made and she wanted to save her brother the embarrassment if possible.

Determined to avoid the subject of her brother, Maggie strolled past Glenn, through the dining room and into the expansive kitchen that was equipped with every conceivable modern cooking device. The double-width refrigerator/freezer was well stocked with frozen meals so that all that was required of her was to insert one into the microwave, push a button and wait.

The swinging doors opened as Glenn followed her inside. He paused to look around the U-shaped room with its oak cabinets and bright red-tiled countertops. His hands returned to his pockets as he cocked his thick brows. "A bit large, wouldn't you say? One woman couldn't possibly require this much space."

Of course the kitchen was huge, she thought, irritated. She hadn't paid an exorbitant price for this place for three drawers and a double sink. "Yes," she returned somewhat defensively. "I like it this way."

"Do you mind if I take a look outside?" he asked and opened the sliding glass doors that led to a balcony overlooking the ocean.

"Sure. Go ahead."

A breeze ruffled the drape as he opened and closed the glass door. Maggie watched him move to the railing and look out over the beach below. If she paused and strained her ears, she could hear the sounds of the ocean as the wild waves crashed upon the sandy shore. A crescent moon was barely visible behind a thick layer of clouds.

Leaning a hip against the counter, Maggie studied his profile. It seemed incomprehensible that the man who was standing only a few feet from her was her husband. She felt awkward and shy, even afraid. If he did head back to Charleston without her the situation would become increasingly unreal. Before Glenn turned to find her studying him, Maggie took out a head of lettuce from the refrigerator and dumped it into a strainer, and then placed it under the faucet.

Rubbing the chill from his arms, Glenn returned a minute later.

"Go ahead and pour yourself a drink," Maggie offered, tearing the lettuce leaves into a bowl. When he hesitated, she pointed to the liquor cabinet.

"I'm more interested in coffee if you have it."

"I'll make it."

"I will."

Simultaneously they moved and somehow Maggie's face came sharply into contact with the solid mass of muscle and man. Amazingly, in the exaggerated kitchen, they'd somehow managed to collide. Glenn's hand sneaked out to steady Maggie at the shoulders. "Are you all right?"

"I think so." She moved her nose back and forth a couple of times before looking up at him. "I should have known this kitchen wasn't big enough for the two of us."

Something warm and ardent shone from his eyes as his gaze dropped to her mouth. The air in the room crackled with electricity. The hands that were gripping her shoulders moved down her upper arms and tightened. Every ticking second seemed to stretch out of proportion. Then, very slowly, he half lifted her from the floor, his mouth descending to hers a fraction of an inch at a time. Maggie's heart skipped a beat, then began to hammer wildly. He deliberately, slowly, left his mouth a hair's space above hers so that their breaths mingled and merged. Holding her close, he seemed to want her to take the initiative. But the memory of that morning remained vivid in her mind. And now it seemed he intended to leave her behind in San Francisco as well. No, there were too many questions left unanswered for her to give in to the physical attraction between them. Still his mouth hovered over hers, his eyes holding her. At the sound of the timer dinging, Glenn released her. Disoriented, Maggie stood completely still until she realized Glenn had moved away. Embarrassed, she turned, making busy-work at the microwave.

"That smells like lasagna," Glenn commented.

"It is." Maggie's gaze widened as she set out the dishes. What an idiot she'd been. The bell she heard hadn't been her heart's song from wanting Glenn's kisses. It had been the signal from her microwave that their dinner was ready. The time had come to remove the stars from her eyes regarding their marriage.

Maggie noted that Glenn's look was thoughtful when they ate, as if something was bothering him. For that matter, she was unusually quiet herself. After the meal, Glenn silently helped her stack the dinner plates into the dishwasher. "Would you like the grand tour?" Maggie inquired, more in an effort to ease the tension than from any desire to show off her home.

"You did promise to show me some more of your work."

"My art?" Maggie hedged, suddenly unsure. "I'm more into the abstract things now." She dried her hands on a terry-cloth towel and avoided looking at him. "A couple of years ago I discovered Helen Frankenthaler. Oh, I'd seen her work, but I hadn't appreciated her genius."

"Helen who?"

"Frankenthaler." Maggie enunciated the name slowly. "She's probably the most historically impor-tant artist of recent decades and people with a lot more talent than me have said so."

Glenn looped an arm around her shoulders and slowly shook his head. "Maggie, you're going to have to remember your husband knows absolutely nothing about art.''

"But you know what you like," she teased, leading him by the hand to the fully glassed-in upstairs studio.

"That I do," he admitted in a husky whisper.

No one else had ever seen the studio, where she spent the vast majority of her time. It hadn't been a conscious oversight. There just had never been anyone she'd wanted to show it to. Not even Denny, who, she realized, only gave lip service to her work. She led Glenn proudly into her domain. She had talent and knew it. So much of her self-esteem was centered in her work. In recent years it had become the outpouring of her frustrations and loneliness. Her ego, her identity, her vanity were all tied up in her art.

Glenn noted that her studio was a huge room twice the size of the kitchen. Row upon row of canvases were propped against the walls. From the shine in her eyes, Glenn realized that Maggie took her painting seriously. She loved it. As far as he could see it was the only thing in this world that she had for herself. He hadn't liked what he'd innocently overheard in her telephone conversation with Denny. He had wanted to ask Maggie about it over dinner, but hesitated. He felt that it was too soon to pry into her relationship with her brother. As he recalled, Denny was a decent guy, four or five years older than Maggie. From the sounds of it, though, Denny was sponging off his sister— which was unusual since he had heard that Denny was wealthy in his own right. It was none of his affair, he had decided, and it was best that he keep his nose out of it.

Proudly Maggie walked around the studio, which was used more than any other room in the house. Most of the canvases were fresh and white, waiting for the bold strokes of color that would bring them to life. Several of the others contained her early experiments in cubism and expressionism. She watched Glenn as he walked around the room, studying several of her pictures. Pride shone in his eyes and Maggie basked in his approval. She wanted to hug him and thank him for simply appreciating what she did.

He paused to study a large ten-foot canvas propped at an angle against the floor. Large slashes of blue paint were smeared across the center and had been left to dry, creating their own geometric pattern. Maggie was especially pleased with this piece. It was the painting she had been working on the afternoon she was late meeting Glenn at the airport.

"What's this?" Glenn asked, his voice tight. He cocked his head sideways, his brow pleated in concentration.

"Glenn," she chided, "that's my painting."

He was utterly stupefied that Maggie would waste her obvious talent on an abstract mess. The canvas looked as though paint had been carelessly splattered across the top. Glenn could see no rhyme or pattern to the design. "Your painting," he mused aloud. "It's quite a deviation from your other work, isn't it?"

Maggie shrugged off his lack of appreciation and enthusiasm. "This isn't a portrait," she explained somewhat defensively. This particular painting was a departure from the norm, a bold experiment with a new balance of unexpected harmony of different hues of blues with tension between shapes and shades. Glenn had admitted he knew nothing about art, she thought. He wouldn't understand what she was trying to say with this abstract piece, and she didn't try to explain.

Squatting, Glenn examined the large canvas, his fingertips testing the texture. "What is this material? It's not like a regular canvas, is it?"

"No, it's unprimed cotton duck—the same material that's used for making sails." This type of porous material allowed her to toss the paint across the canvas; then point by point, she poured, dripped and even used squeegees to spread the great veils of tone. She spent long, tedious hours contemplating each aspect of the work, striving for the effortless, spontaneous appeal she admired so much in Helen Frankenthaler's work.

"You're not into the abstract stuff, are you?" she asked with a faint smile. She tried to make it sound as if it didn't matter. The pride she'd seen in Glenn's eyes when he saw her beachscape and her other work had thrilled her. Now she could see him trying to disguise his puzzlement. "Don't feel bad, abstracts aren't for everyone."

A frown marred his smooth brow as he straightened and brushed the grit from his hands. "I'd like to see some more of the work like the painting downstairs."

"There are a couple of those over here." She pulled a painting out from behind a stack of her later efforts in cubism.

Glenn held out the painting and his frown disappeared. "Now this is good. The other looks like an accident."

An accident! Maggie nearly choked on her laughter. She'd like to see him try it. "I believe the time has come for me to propose another rule for this marriage."

Glenn's look was wary. "What?"

"From now on everything I paint is beautiful and wonderful and the work of an unrecognized genius. Understand?"

"Certainly," he murmured, "anything you say." He paused to examine the huge canvas a second time. "I don't know what you're saying with this, but this is obviously the work of an unrecognized and unappreciated genius."

Maggie smiled at him boldly. "You did that well."

Chapter Five

Glenn muttered under his breath as he followed Maggie out of her studio. Her dainty back was stiff as she walked down the stairs. She might have made light of his comments, but he wasn't fooled. Once again he had hurt her. Twice in one day. *Damn*. The problem was that he was trying too hard. They both were. "I apologize, Maggie. I didn't mean to offend you. You're right. I don't know a thing about art."

"I'm not offended," she lied. "I keep forgetting how opinionated you are." With deliberate calm she moved into the living room and sat at the baby grand piano, running her fingers over the ivory keys. She wanted to be angry with him, but couldn't, realizing that any irritation was a symptom of her own insecurity. She had exposed a deeply personal part of herself. It had been a measure of her trust and Glenn

hadn't known or understood. She couldn't blame him
for that.

"I don't remember that you played the piano." He
stood beside her, resting his hand on her shoulder.

His touch was oddly soothing. "I started taking
lessons a couple of years ago."

"You're good."

Maggie stopped playing; her fingers froze above the
keys. Slowly, she placed her hands in her lap. "Glenn,
listen, the new rule to our marriage only applies to my
painting. You can be honest with my piano playing.
I'm rotten. I have as much innate rhythm as lint."

Glenn recognized that in his effort to make up for
one faux pas he had only dug himself in deeper. He
didn't know anything about music. "I thought you
played the clarinet."

"I wasn't much better on that, if you recall."

"I don't."

"Obviously," she muttered under her breath, rising to her feet. She rubbed her hands together in a
nervous gesture. "It's been a long day."

Glenn's spirits sank. It had been quite a day and
nothing like he'd expected. Yet he couldn't blame
Maggie—he had brought everything on himself. His
hand reached for hers. "Let's go to bed."

Involuntarily, Maggie tensed. Everything had been
perfect for the wedding night, but now she felt unsure
and equally uneasy. Glenn was her husband and she
couldn't give him the guest bedroom. But things were
different from what they had been. Her eyes were
opened this time, and white lace and promises weren't
filling her mind with fanciful illusions.

"Is something wrong?" Glenn's voice was filled
with challenge.

"No," she murmured, abruptly shaking her head. "Nothing's wrong." But then not everything was right, either. She led the way down the long hallway to the master bedroom, feeling shaky.

The room was huge, dominated by a brick fireplace, with two pale-blue velvet chairs angled in front of it. The windows were adorned with shirred drapes of a delicate floral design that had been especially created to give a peaceful, easy-living appeal. The polished mahogany four-poster bed had a down comforter tossed over the top that was made from the same lavender floral material as the drapes. This room was Maggie's favorite. She could sit in it for hours and feel content.

If Glenn was impressed with the simple elegance or felt the warmth of her bedroom, he said nothing. Maggie would have been surprised if he had.

His suitcase rested on the thick carpet, and Glenn sighed, turning toward her. "We have a lot to do tomorrow." Frustrated anger filled Glenn at his own stupidity. Everything he had done that day had been wrong. From the moment he had opened his eyes to the time he'd mentioned going to bed. He couldn't have been more insensitive had he tried. He didn't want to argue with Maggie and yet, it seemed, he had gone out of his way to do exactly that. There would be a lot of adjustments to make with their marriage and he had gotten off on the wrong foot almost from the moment they'd started. Maggie was uncomfortable; Glenn could sense that. He could also feel her hesitancy. But he was her husband, and by God he'd sleep with her this and every night for the remainder of their lives.

The mention of the coming day served to remind Maggie that Glenn was planning on returning to Charleston alone. That rankled. Sometime during the evening, she had thought to casually bring up the return trip. But with what had happened in her studio and afterward, the timing hadn't been right. Crossing her arms over her breasts, she met his gaze.

"Oh. What are we doing tomorrow?" She couldn't think of anything they needed to do that couldn't be handled later.

"First we'll see a lawyer, then—"

"Why?" she asked her voice unnaturally throaty. Alarm filled her. Glenn had changed his mind. He didn't want to stay married. And little wonder. She kept making up these rules and—

"I want to make sure none of your inheritance money is ever put in my name." With all the other problems they were facing, Glenn needed to assure Maggie that he hadn't married her for her wealth. If anything, he regretted the fact she had it. Her Great-aunt Margaret's money had been a curse as far as he was concerned. And judging by the insecure, frightened woman Maggie had become, she might even have realized that herself.

"I...I know you wouldn't cheat me." The odd huskiness of her voice was made more pronounced by a slight quiver. Of all the men she had known in her life, she trusted Glenn implicitly. He was a man of honor. He might have married her when he was in love with another woman, but he would never deliberately do anything to swindle her.

Their gazes melted into each other's. Maggie trusted him, Glenn realized. The heavy weight that had pressed against him from the moment she had turned her hurt, angry eyes on him that morning lessened. Damn, but there'd been a better way to handle that business with her paintings, he thought. She had talent, incredible talent, and it was a shame that she was wasting it by hiding it away.

"After the lawyer we'll go to a jeweler," he added.

"A jeweler?"

"I'd like you to wear a wedding ring, Maggie."

The pulse in her neck throbbed as she beat down a rush of pure pleasure. "Okay, and you too."

"Of course," he agreed easily. His gaze did a sweeping inspection of the room as if he'd noticed it for the first time. It reminded him of Maggie. Her presence was stamped in every piece of furniture, every corner. Suddenly, a tiredness stole into his bones. He was exhausted, mentally and physically. "Let's get ready for bed."

Maggie nodded, and some of her earlier apprehension faded. She wasn't completely comfortable sleeping with him after what had happened. Not when there was a chance he would take her in his arms, hold her close, kiss her, even make love to her, with another woman's name on his lips. "You go ahead, I've got a few odds and ends to take care of first."

Sitting at the oak desk in her office, Maggie lifted her long hair from her face and closed her eyes as weariness flooded her bones. She was tired—Glenn was tired. She was confused—Glenn was confused. They both wanted this marriage—they were both responsible for making it work. All right, there wasn't any reason to overreact. They'd share a bed and if he said "her" name in his sleep again, Maggie refused to be held responsible for her actions.

By the time Glenn returned from his shower, Maggie had gone back to the bedroom and changed into a sexless flannel pajama set that would have discouraged the most amorous male. She had slipped beneath the covers, and was sitting up reading, her back supported by thick feather pillows. Wary, uncertain eyes followed Glenn's movements when he reentered the bedroom.

He paused and allowed a tiny smile of satisfaction to touch his lips. He had half expected Maggie to linger in her office until he was asleep and was greatly pleased that she hadn't. Although she looked like a virgin intent on maintaining her chastity in that flannel outfit, he knew that this night wasn't the time to press for his husbandly rights. Things had gone badly. Tomorrow would be better, he promised himself.

Lifting back the thick quilt, Glenn slid his large frame into the queen-size bed and turned off the light that rested on the mahogany nightstand on his side of the bed.

"Good night." His voice was husky and low with only a trace of amusement. He thought she would probably sit up reading until she fell asleep with the light on.

"Good night," she answered softly, pretending to read. A few minutes later, Maggie battled to keep her lashes from drooping. Valiantly she struggled as her mind conjured up ways of resisting Glenn. The problem was that she didn't want to resist him. He would probably wait until she was relaxed and close to falling asleep, she theorized. When she was at her weakest point, he would reach for her and kiss her. Glenn was a wonderful kisser and she went warm at the memory of what had happened their first night together. He had held her as if he were dying of thirst and she was a cool shimmering pool in an oasis.

Gathering her resolve, Maggie clenched her teeth. Hell, the way her thoughts were going she'd lean over and kiss him any minute. Her hand rested on her abdomen and Maggie felt bare skin. Her pajamas might be sexless, but they also conveniently buttoned up the front so that if he wanted, there was easy access to her breasts. Again she recalled how good their lovemaking had been and how she had thrilled to his hands and mouth on her eager breasts. Her eyes drooped shut and with a start she forced them open. Lying completely still she listened, and after several long moments discovered that Glenn had turned away from her and was sound asleep.

An unexpected rush of disappointment filled her. He hadn't even tried to make love to her. Without a thought, he had turned onto his side and gone to sleep! Bunching up her pillow, Maggie rolled onto her stomach, feeling such frustration that she could have cried. He didn't want her, and as unreasonable as it sounded, Maggie felt discouraged and depressed. Her last thought as she turned out her light was that if Glenn reached for her in the night she would give him what he wanted . . . what she wanted.

Sometime in the middle of the night Maggie woke. She was sleeping on her side, but had moved to the middle of the bed. Her eyes fluttered open and she wondered what had caused her to wake when she felt so warm and comfortable. Glenn's even breathing sounded close to her ear and she realized that he was asleep, cuddling his body to hers. Contented and secure, she closed her eyes and a moment later a male hand slid over her ribs, just below her breasts. When he pulled her close, fitting his body to hers, Maggie's lashes fluttered open. Not for the first time, she was amazed at how perfectly their bodies fit together. Releasing a contented breath, Maggie shut her eyes and wandered back to sleep.

Glenn woke in the first light of dawn with a serenity that had escaped him for months. That morning he didn't mistake the warm body he was holding close. Maggie was responsible for his tranquillity of spirit, Glenn realized. He needed Maggie. During the night, her pajama top had ridden up and the urge to move his hand and trace the soft, womanly curves was almost overpowering. Maggie was all the woman he would ever want. She was everything he had ever hoped to find in a wife—a passionate, irresistible mistress with an intriguing mind and delectable body, who surrendered herself willingly to the fiery intensity of his need. Her passion had surprised and pleased him. She hadn't been shy, or embarrassed, abandoning herself to his demands with an eagerness that thrilled him every time he thought about it. She was more woman than he'd dared hope and he ached to take her again.

In her sleep, Maggie shifted and her breasts sprang free of the confining top and into Glenn's open hand. They were scrumptiously heavy, the perfect size, he determined, filling his palm, almost swelling at his touch. For an eternity he lay completely still until he couldn't resist touching her any longer. Lightly, his thumb massaged one dark nipple, which responded instantly by hardening. Glenn felt the heat building in his loins and gritted his teeth against the consuming need throbbing within him to arch his back and thrust his agonizing hardness into her. In his mind he pictured turning her onto her back and kissing her until her lips opened eagerly to his. With inhuman patience he would look into those dark beautiful eyes and wait until she told him how much she wanted him.

Groaning, he released her and rolled onto his back, taking deep breaths to control his frantic frustration. God only knew how long it would be before he would have the opportunity to make love to his wife again. Two weeks at least, maybe longer. Almost as overwhelming as the urge to make love to her was the one to cherish and protect her. She needed reassurance and he knew she needed time. Throwing back the blankets he marched into the bathroom and turned on the cold water.

Maggie woke at the sound of the shower running. Stirring, she turned onto her back and stared at the ceiling as the last dregs of sleep drained from her mind. She had been having the most pleasant erotic dream. One that caused her to blush from the roots of her dark hair to the ends of her toenails. Indecent dreams maybe, but excruciatingly sensual. Perhaps it was best that Glenn was gone when she woke, she thought. If he had been beside her she didn't know what she would have done. She could well have embarrassed them both by reaching for him and asking him to make love to her before he returned to Charleston...alone.

Taking advantage of the privacy, she dressed and hurriedly made the bed. By the time she had straightened the comforter across the mattress, Glenn reappeared.

"Good morning," he said as he paused just inside the bedroom, standing both alert and still as he studied her. "Did you sleep well?"

"Yes," she responded hastily, feeling like a specimen about to be analyzed, but a highly prized specimen, one that was cherished and valued. "What about you?" she asked to stop the meanderings of her mind.

The hesitation was barely noticeable, but Maggie noticed. "Like a rock."

"Good. Are you hungry?" Her eyes refused to meet his, afraid of what hers would tell him.

"Starved."

"Breakfast should be ready by the time you've finished dressing," she said as she left the room. Glenn had showered last night, she remembered; she couldn't recall him being overly fastidious. Shrugging, she moved down the long hall to the kitchen.

The bacon was sizzling in the skillet when Glenn reappeared, dressed in dark slacks and a thick pullover sweater. Maggie was reminded once again that he was devastatingly handsome and experienced, and with a burst of pride, she knew that he was hers. At least legally, he was hers. However, another woman owned the most vital part of him—his heart. In time, Maggie trusted, she would claim that as well.

The morning swam past in a blur; such was their pace. They began by contacting Maggie's attorney and were given an immediate appointment. Together they sat in his office, although it was Glenn who did most of the talking. Maggie was uncomfortable with the rewording of her will, but Glenn was adamant. He desired none of her money and he wanted it stated legally. When and if they had children, her inheritance would be passed on to them.

From the attorney's they stopped off at a prominent San Francisco jeweler. Maggie had never been one for flashy jewels. All too often her hands were in paint solvent or mixing clay and she didn't want to have to worry about losing expensive rings or valuable jewels. Knowing herself and her often thoughtless ways, Maggie was apt to misplace a diamond and she couldn't bear the thought of losing any ring Glenn gave her.

"You decide," Glenn insisted, his hand at the back of her neck. "Whatever one you want is fine."

Sensing a sure sale, the young jeweler set out a tray of exquisite diamonds, far larger than any Maggie had dreamed Glenn would want to purchase. Her gaze fell on a lovely marquise and her teeth worried her bottom lip. "I . . . was thinking maybe something with a smaller stone would be fine," she murmured, realizing that she should have explained her problems about a diamond to Glenn earlier.

He pinched his mouth closed with displeasure, resenting her concern that he couldn't afford to buy her a diamond large enough to weight her hand.

"Try on that one," he insisted, pointing to the marquise solitaire with the wide polished band that she had admired earlier. The diamond was the largest and most expensive on the tray.

Maggie paled, not knowing how to explain herself. The salesman beamed, exchanging pleased glances with Glenn.

"An excellent choice," the jeweler said, lifting Maggie's limp hand. The ring fit as if it was made for her slender finger. But the diamond was so heavy it felt bulky and unnatural. In her mind Maggie could picture the panic of looking for it once it was mislaid . . . and it would be.

"We'll take it."

"Glenn." Maggie placed her hand on his forearm. "Can I talk to you a minute? Please."

"I'll write up the sales order," the jeweler said, removing the tray of diamonds. "I'll be with the cashier when you've finished."

Maggie waited until the salesman was out of earshot before turning troubled eyes to Glenn. Her heart was in her eyes as she recognized the pride and irritation that glared back at her.

"What's the matter, Maggie?" he growled under his breath. "Are you afraid I can't afford a wedding ring for my wife? I may not own a fancy beach house, but be assured, I can afford a diamond."

Glenn's words smarted and it was all Maggie could do to bite back a flippant reply. "It's not that," she whispered fiercely, keeping her voice low so the jeweler wouldn't hear them arguing. "If you'd given me half a chance, I'd have explained. I'm an artist, remember? If you buy me that flashy diamond, I'll be constantly removing it for one reason or another."

"So? What are you suggesting? No ring at all?"

"No...I'm sorry I said anything. The ring is fine." Maggie backed down, aware that anything said now would be misconstrued. Somehow she would learn to be careful with the diamond. Purchasing it had become a matter of male pride and Maggie didn't want to cause any more problems than the ones already facing them.

"Would a plain gold band solve that?" he asked unexpectedly.

"Yes," she murmured, surprised. "Yes, it would." To her delight, Glenn also asked the jeweler to size a band for her. Maggie felt wonderful when they stepped outside. The question of the ring might have been only a minor problem, but together they had settled it without wounding each other's sensitive pride. They were making progress and it felt marvelous.

They ate lunch in Chinatown, feasting on hot, diced chicken stir-fried with fresh, crisp vegetables. All the time they were dining, Maggie was infinitely aware of two pressing items: the heavy feel of the ring on the third finger of her left hand, and the time. Within hours Glenn would be leaving for Charleston. A kaleidoscope of regrets and questions whirled through her mind. She wanted to go with him, but didn't feel she could make the suggestion. Glenn had to want her along, yet he hadn't said a word. Silence hung heavy and dark between them like a thick curtain of rain-filled clouds. He was going back to his lost love, and dread filled Maggie with each beat of her heart.

Glenn made several attempts at light conversation during their meal, but nothing seemed to ease the strained silence that had fallen over them. A glance at his watch reminded him that within a few hours he would be on a plane for Charleston. He didn't want to leave, but in some ways felt it was for the best. Maggie seemed to assume that she wouldn't be going with him and he was disappointed that she hadn't shown the willingness to travel with him. He might have made an issue of it if he hadn't thought a short separation would help them both become accustomed to their marriage without the issue of sleeping together. Those weeks would give Maggie the opportunity to settle things within her own mind. When he came back to her they would take up their lives as man and wife and perhaps she'd come to him willingly as she had that first night. God knew he wanted her enough.

The drive back to the house and then on to the airport seemed to take a lifetime. With each mile, Maggie felt her heart grow heavier. She was apprehensive and didn't know how to deal with it. She and Glenn had been together such a short time that separating now seemed terribly wrong. Unreasonable jealousy ate at her and Maggie had to assure herself repeatedly that Glenn probably wouldn't even be seeing the other woman. She was, after all, married to another man. But it didn't matter. Maggie didn't gain a whit's comfort from the knowledge. For the first time in memory, she found herself in a situation where money wasn't part of the solution.

As they left the airport parking garage, Glenn's hand took hers. "I won't be long," he promised. "I'll need to get everything settled at the office, list the condominium with a realtor and settle loose business ties—that kind of thing. I can't see it taking more than two weeks, three at the most."

"The weeks will fly by," she said on a falsely cheerful note. "Just about the time I clean out enough closet space for you, you'll be back."

"I wouldn't leave if it wasn't necessary," Glenn assured her as they approached the ticketing desk to check in his luggage.

"I know that." Maggie hugged her waist, feeling a sudden and unexpected chill. "I'm not worried." *Liar,* her mind tossed back.

Their shoes made a clicking sound as they walked to the departure gate. Unfortunately, the plane was on time so there wouldn't be any delays. The attendant was collecting the tickets for boarding the Boeing 767 by the time they arrived.

Maggie had the horrible feeling she was about to cry, which, she knew, was utterly ridiculous. She rarely cried, yet her throat felt raw and scratchy and her chest had tightened with pent-up emotion. All the things she wanted to say stuck in her throat and she found that she couldn't say a thing.

"Take care of yourself," Glenn murmured, holding her by the shoulders.

"I will," she promised and buried her hands deep within the pockets of her raincoat. Even those few words could barely escape.

Glenn fastened the top button of her coat and when he spoke his voice was softly gruff. "It looks like rain. Drive carefully."

"I always do. You'll note that you're here on time." She made a feeble attempt at humor.

Tiny laugh lines fanned out from his eyes. "Barely. I don't suppose you've noticed that most of the passengers have already boarded. Married two days and I'm already picking up your bad habits."

His observation prompted a soft smile. "You'll phone?" She turned soft, round eyes to him.

"Yes," he promised in a husky murmur. "And if you need me, don't hesitate to call." He had written down both his work and home numbers in case she had to get in touch with him.

"You'll phone tonight." It became immensely important that he did. She pulled her hands from her pockets and smoothed away an imaginary piece of lint from his shoulder. Her hand lingered there. "I'll miss you." Even now if he hinted that he wanted her with him, she'd step on that plane. Hell, she'd buy the stupid plane if necessary.

"I'll phone, but it'll be late because of the time change," Glenn explained.

"I don't mind.... I probably won't sleep anyway." She hadn't meant to admit that much and felt a rush of color creep up her neck and into her cheeks.

"Me either," he murmured. His hands tightened on her upper arms and he gently brought her against his bulky sweater. With unhurried ease his mouth moved toward hers. The kiss flooded her with a swell of emotions she had tasted only briefly in his arms. She was hot, on fire and cold as ice. Hot from his touch, cold with fear. His kiss sent a jolt rocketing through her and she fiercely wrapped her arms around his neck. Her mind whirled and still she clung, afraid that if Glenn ever released her she'd never fully recover from the fall. Dragging in a deep breath, Maggie buried her face in his neck.

Glenn wrapped his arms around her waist and half lifted her from the floor. "I'll be back soon," he promised.

She nodded because speaking was impossible.

The voice of the flight attendant was the intrusion that broke their embrace. Glenn's arms were wrapped around Maggie's waist, holding her loosely. His gaze was as gentle as a caress and as tender as a child's touch. Maggie offered him a feeble smile. Releasing her completely, Glenn turned up the collar of her coat. "Stay warm."

Again she nodded. "Phone me."

Tossing a glance over his shoulder at the attendant, who was beginning to walk into the jetway, Glenn claimed Maggie's lips again in a brief but surprisingly ardent kiss. "I'll call the minute I land."

She dropped her arms, pushing her hands in her pockets for fear she'd do something silly like reach out and ask him not to go, or beg him to ask her to come. "Hurry now, or you'll miss the flight."

Glenn took two steps backward. "The time will go fast."

"Yes," she said, not exactly sure what she was agreeing to.

"You're my wife, Maggie. I'm not going to forget that."

"You're my husband," she whispered and choked back the tears that filled her eyes and blurred her vision.

"Go on," she encouraged, not wanting him to see her cry. For all the emotion that was raging through her one would assume that Glenn was going off to war and was unlikely to return. Her stomach was in such tight knots that she couldn't move without pain. Rooted to the spot close to the gate, Maggie stood as she was until Glenn turned and ran into the jetway. When she could, she stepped to the window and whispered, "New rules for this marriage...don't ever leave me again."

The days passed in a blur. Not since art school had Maggie worked harder or longer. Denny phoned her twice. Once to thank her for the "loan" and later to talk to her about the top-notch lawyer he had on retainer. The attorney was exactly who he had hoped would pursue his case, and his spirits were high. Maggie was pleased for Denny and prayed that this would be the end of his problems.

Without Glenn, sound sleep was impossible. She'd drift off easily enough and then jerk awake a couple of hours later, wondering why the queen-size bed seemed so intolerably large. Usually she slept in the middle of the mattress, but she soon discovered that she rested more comfortably on the side where Glenn had slept. She missed him. The worst part was the unreasonableness of the situation. Glenn had spent less than twenty-four hours in her home, yet without him the beach house felt like a silent tomb.

As he promised, Glenn had phoned the night he arrived back in Charleston and again three days later. Maggie couldn't recall any three days that seemed longer. A thousand times she was convinced her mind had conjured up both Glenn and their marriage. The marquise diamond on her ring finger was the only tangible evidence that the whole situation hadn't been a fantasy and that they really were married. Because she was working so hard and long she removed it for safekeeping, but each night she slipped it on her finger. Maggie didn't mention the wedding to her parents or any of her friends, and Denny didn't notice anything was different about her. She didn't feel comfortable telling everyone she was married, and wouldn't until Glenn had moved in with her and they were confident that their marriage was on firm ground.

Glenn phoned again on the fifth day. Their conversation was all too brief and somewhat stilted. Neither of them seemed to want it to end, but after twenty minutes, there didn't seem to be anything more to say.

Replacing the receiver, Maggie had the urge to cry. She didn't, of course, but it was several minutes before she had composed herself enough to go on with her day.

Nothing held her interest. Television, music, solitaire—everything bored her. Even the housekeeper lamented that Maggie had lost her appetite and complained about cooking meals that Maggie barely touched. Glenn filled every waking thought and invaded her dreams. Each time they spoke she had to bite her tongue to keep from suggesting she join him; her pride wouldn't allow that. The invitation must come from him, she believed. Surely he must realize that.

As for Angie, the woman in Glenn's past, the more Maggie thought about the situation, the more angry she became with herself. Glenn hadn't deceived her. They both were bearing scars from the past. If it wasn't love that cemented their marriage then it was something equally as strong. Between them there was security and understanding.

The evening of the eighth day the phone rang just as Maggie was scrounging through the desk looking for an address. She stared at the telephone. Instantly she knew it was Glenn.

"Hello," she answered, happily leaning back in the swivel chair, anticipating a long conversation.

"Hi." His voice sounded vital and warm. "How's everything?"

"Fine. I'm a little bored." Maggie was astonished that she could sound so blasé about her traumatic week. "A little bored" soft-pedaled all her frustrations. "What about you?"

Glenn hesitated, then announced, "I've run into a small snag on my end of things." A small snag was the understatement of the century, he thought. Things had been in chaos from the minute he had returned. The company supervisor had paid a surprise visit to him

Thursday afternoon and had suggested an audit because of some irregularity in the books. The audit had gone smoothly enough, but Glenn had worked long hours and had been forced to reschedule several appointments. In addition, the realtor who listed the condominium offered little hope that it would sell quickly.

And worse, Glenn was miserable without Maggie. He wanted her with him. She was his wife, damn it. Pride dictated that he couldn't ask her. The suggestion would have to come from her. Even a hint would be enough. He would pick up on a hint, but she had to be one to give it.

"A small snag?" Her heart was pounding so hard and strong that she felt breathless.

"I've got several accounts here that have deals pending. I can't leave these people in the lurch. Things aren't going as smoothly as I'd like, Maggie," he admitted.

"I see." Maggie's vocabulary suddenly decreased to words of one syllable.

"I can't let them down." He sounded as frustrated as she felt. A deafening silence grated over the telephone line, and it was on the tip of Glenn's tongue to cast his stupid pride to the wind and ask her to join him.

"Don't worry, I understand," she said in an even tone, congratulating herself for maintaining firm control of her voice. On the inside she was crumbling to pieces. She wanted to be with him. He was her husband and her place was at his side. Closing her eyes she mentally pleaded with him to say the words—to ask her to come to Charleston. She wouldn't ask, couldn't ask. It had to come from Glenn.

"In addition there are several loose ends that are going to require more time than I originally planned." He sounded almost angry, an emotion that mirrored her own frustration.

"I think we were both naive to think you could make it back in such a short time."

"I suppose we were." *Come on, Maggie,* he pleaded silently. *If you miss me, say something. At least meet me halfway in this.*

The line went silent again, but Maggie didn't want to end the conversation. She waited endless hours for his calls. They would talk for ten minutes, hang up and immediately she'd start wondering how long it would be before he phoned again.

"The weather's been unseasonably cold. There's been some talk of freezing tempratures," Maggie said out of desperation to keep the conversation going.

"Don't catch cold." *Damn it, Maggie, I want you here, can't you hear it in my voice?*

"I won't," she promised. *Please,* she wanted to scream at him, *ask me to come to Charleston.* With her eyes shut, she mentally transmitted her need to have him ask her. "I've been too busy in the studio to venture outside."

"Brueghel or Frankenthaler?" Glenn questioned, his voice tinged with humor. "However, I'm sure that either one would be marvelous and wonderful." He smiled as he said it, wanting her with him all the more just to see what other crazy rules she'd come up with for their marriage.

"This one's a Margaret Kingsbury original," she said proudly. Maggie had worked hard on her latest project and felt confident that Glenn would approve.

"It can't be." Glenn stiffened and tried to disguise the irritation in his voice.

Maggie tensed, wondering what she had said wrong. He hadn't approved of her art, but surely he didn't begrudge her the time she spent on it when he was away.

"Your name's Lambert now," Glenn stated.

"I . . . forgot." *Remind me again,* she pleaded silently. *Ask me to come to Charleston.* "I haven't told anyone yet. . . . Have you?"

"No one," Glenn admitted.

"Not even your parents?" She hadn't told hers, either, but Glenn's family was in South Carolina. It only made sense that he'd say something to them before moving out west.

"That was something I thought we'd do together."

The sun burst through the heavy overcast and shed its golden rays on Maggie. He had offered her a way to Charleston and managed to salvage her pride. The tension flowed from her as her hand tightened around the receiver. "Glenn, don't you think they'll be offended if we wait much longer?"

"They might," he answered, unexpectedly agreeable. "I know it's an inconvenience, but maybe you should think about flying. . . ."

"I'll be on the first flight out tomorrow morning."

Chapter Six

Glenn was in the terminal waiting when Maggie walked off the plane late the following afternoon. He was tall, rugged and so male that it was all Maggie could do not to throw her arms around him. He looked wonderful and she wanted to hate him for it. For nine days she had been the most miserable woman alive and Glenn looked as if he'd relished their separation, thrived on it. Renewed doubts buzzed about her like swarming bees.

Stepping forward, Glenn took the carry-on bag from her hand and slipped an arm around her waist. "Welcome to Charleston."

Shamelessly, Maggie wanted him to take her in his arms and kiss her. She managed to disguise the yearning by lowering her gaze. "I didn't know if you'd be here."

She hadn't called and given him her flight number, and had later worried about that. If he wasn't home to receive her phone call when she arrived, Maggie wouldn't have had a way of getting into Glenn's condominium.

"You said the first plane out, so I took a chance and came down here."

"I'm glad you did." *Very glad,* her heart sang.

"How was the flight?"

"Just the way I like 'em," she said with a teasing smile. "Uneventful."

Glenn's features warmed and he grinned at her answer. Captivated by the tenderness in his eyes, Maggie felt her heart throb almost painfully. His eyes were dark, yet glowing with an intensely warm light. Although he hadn't said a word, Glenn's gaze told her he was pleased she was there.

"Your luggage is this way," he commented, pressing a hand to the middle of her back as he directed her down the wide concourse.

"I didn't bring much." "Not much" constituted two enormous suitcases and one cosmetics case that she had carried with her on the airplane. Maggie had spent half the night packing, discarding one outfit after another until her bedroom floor was littered with more clothes than a second-hand store. She wanted everything perfect for Glenn. She longed to be alluring and seductive, attractive without being blatant. She wanted his heart as well as his bed and only she realized how difficult that was going to be if Glenn was still in love with "her."

The more Maggie thought about the other woman who had claimed his heart the more she realized what an uphill struggle lay before her. Glenn wouldn't ever give his love lightly, and now that he had, it would take one hell of a struggle to replace her in his heart. Maggie yearned to know more of the details, but wouldn't pry. In the meantime, she planned to use every womanly wile she knew and a few she planned to invent.

The leather strap of her purse slid off her shoulder and Maggie straightened it. As she did, Glenn stopped in midstride, nearly knocking her off balance.

"Where's your diamond?" he asked, taking her hand. Surprise mingled with disappointment and disbelief. "I thought you said the only time you wouldn't wear it was when you were working. You aren't painting now."

Maggie's mind whirled frantically. She had removed the diamond the morning before the phone call and placed it in safekeeping the way she always did. Then in her excitement about meeting Glenn in Charleston, she had forgotten to put it back on her finger.

"Maggie?"

Her fingers curled around the strap of her purse. "Oh, Glenn..."

He took her hand and examined the plain gold band that he had bought her with the marquise.

Maggie wanted to shout with frustration. From the moment they'd ended their phone conversation she had been carefully planning this reunion. Each detail had been shaped in her mind from the instant he picked her up until they dressed for bed.

"Maggie, where is the diamond?" he repeated.

"I forgot it, but don't worry...it's in my suitcase." Her voice rose with her agitation. They hadn't so much as collected her luggage and already they were headed for a fight.

"You mean to tell me you packed a seven-thousand-dollar diamond with your underwear?" His voice was a mixture of incredulity and anger.

"I didn't do it on purpose, I... forgot I wasn't wearing it." Somehow that seemed even worse.

Glenn's stride increased to a quick-paced clip that left Maggie half trotting in an effort to keep up. "Glenn," she protested, refusing to run through airports. She wasn't O.J. Simpson and she wasn't renting a car.

He threw an angry glare over his shoulder. "Forgive me for being overly concerned, but I work damn hard for my money."

The implication being, she thought, that she didn't work and the ring meant nothing to her. Little did he realize how much it did mean.

Maggie stopped cold as waves of unbelievable pain hit her. Few words could have hurt her more. She was so angry that for several minutes she couldn't speak. Nothing was going as she had planned. She'd had such wonderful images of Glenn sweeping her into his arms, holding her close and exclaiming that after the way he'd missed her, they'd never be separated again. He was supposed to tell her how miserable he'd been. Instead, he'd insulted her in a way that would hurt her the most.

Apparently he was angry because she had forgotten to slip on the diamond ring he'd gotten her, finding her casualness with the diamond a sign of irresponsibility. She had the ring; she knew where it was.

Glenn was standing outside the baggage-handling system, waiting for it to unload the suitcases from her flight, when she joined him.

"If you'd give me a second I'll ..."

"Talk to me after you've gotten your suitcase, Maggie. At the moment I'm worried about losing an expensive diamond."

"And you work hard for your money. Right? At least that's what you claim. I don't doubt it. It's said that those who marry for it usually do."

Although he continued to look straight ahead, a nerve jumped convulsively in his clenched jaw, and Maggie was instantly aware of just how angry that remark had made him. Good, she meant it to do exactly that. If he wanted to hurl insults at her, then she could give as well as take.

"Can I have my cosmetics bag?"

Without a word, he handed it to her. He studied the baggage conveyor belt as if it were the center of his world. Maggie wasn't fooled. Glenn was simply too outraged to even look at her.

Maggie knelt down on the floor and flipped open the lid. Her small jewelry case was inside and the ring was tucked safely in that. With a brooding sense of unhappiness, Maggie located the marquise diamond and slipped it on her finger beside the plain gold band. Snapping the suitcase closed, she stood.

"I hope to hell you didn't mean that about me marrying you for your money."

Maggie regarded him coolly before answering. "I didn't," she admitted. "I was reacting to your comment about not working for my money."

"I didn't mean that."

"I know." His hand claimed hers and when he noticed the diamond was on her ring finger, he arched one brow expressively. "You had it with you all the time?"

"Yes."

He nodded, and groaned inwardly. He had been wanting Maggie for days, longing for her. And now things were picking up right where they'd left off, with misunderstandings and sharp words. He had wanted things perfect for her, and once again this bad start had been his own doing.

His fingers tightened over hers. "Can I make a new rule for this marriage?" he asked her with serious eyes.

"Of course."

"I want you to wear your wedding set all the time."

"But ..."

"I know that may sound unreasonable," he interrupted, "and I'm not even entirely sure why my feelings are so strong. I guess it's important to me that your wedding bands mean as much to you as our marriage."

Slowly, thoughtfully, Maggie nodded. "I'll never remove them again."

Looking in her eyes, Glenn felt the overwhelming urge to take her in his arms and apologize for having started on the wrong foot once again. But the airport wasn't the place and now wasn't the time. From here on, he promised himself, he'd be more patient with her, court her the way he should have in the beginning.

They didn't say a word until the luggage was dispensed. Maggie pointed out her suitcases and gave Glenn her tickets so that he could collect them.

He mumbled something unintelligible under his breath and Maggie realized he was grumbling about the fact she claimed to have packed light for this trip. But he didn't complain strenuously.

The deafening quiet in the car was one neither seemed willing to wade into. Maggie wanted to initiate a brilliant conversation, but nothing came to mind and she almost cried with frustration. Their meeting wasn't supposed to happen this way. She sat uncomfortably next to a man she'd known most of her life and whom, she was discovering, she didn't know at all.

Glenn's condominium was situated just outside historic Charleston with a view of Colonial Lake. Maggie knew little about the area. Her head flooded with questions about the city that Glenn had made his home for a decade, but she asked none. While he took care of her luggage, she wandered into the living room to admire the view. The scenery below revealed magnificent eighteenth-century homes, large public buildings and meticulously kept gardens. The gentle toll of church bells sounded, and Maggie strained to hear more. Charleston was definitely a city of grace, beauty and charm. Yet Glenn was willing to sacrifice it all—his home, his family, his job, maybe even his career to move to San Francisco.

He must have suffered a great deal of mental anguish to be willing to leave all this, Maggie determined, experiencing an attack of insecurity. Glenn had told her so little about this other woman, and Maggie had the feeling he wouldn't have told her that if it hadn't been for the unfortunate scene the morning after their wedding. He was an intensely personal man.

The condominium was far more spacious than what Maggie had assumed. The living room led into a formal dining area and from there to a spacious kitchen with plenty of cupboards and a pantry. A library/den was separated from the living room by open double-width doors that revealed floor-to-ceiling bookcases and a large oak rolltop desk. She hadn't seen the bedrooms yet, but guessed that there were three, possibly four. The condo was much larger than what a single man would require. Her eyes rounded with an indescribable feeling that bordered on pain. Glenn had purchased this home for Angie.

"Are you hungry?" he asked, halfway into the living room, standing several feet from her.

Maggie unbuttoned her coat and slipped the scarf from her neck. "No thanks, I ate on the plane, but you go ahead." The lie was a small, white one. The stewardess had served the meal, but Maggie had declined. She had not been too anxious to eat when she was hours from meeting Glenn.

He hesitated, turned, then whirled back around so that he was facing her again. "I regret this whole business with the ring, Maggie."

A shiver of gladness raced through her at his offhand apology. He cared enough to clear the air between them. "It's forgotten."

Something close to a smile quirked his mouth. "I'm glad you're here."

"I'm glad to be here."

He leaned around the kitchen door. "Are you sure you're not hungry?"

A small smile claimed her mouth. "On second thought, maybe I am at that."

A sense of relief flooded through Glenn's tense muscles. He hadn't meant to make such an issue of the diamond. For days he'd been longing for Maggie, decrying his earlier decision to leave her in San Francisco. They had so few days together that he'd thought the separation would give her the necessary time to adjust mentally to her new life. Unfortunately, it was he who had faced the adjustment…to his days…and nights without her. Now that she was here, all he wanted was to take her in his arms and make love to her. The level of physical desire she aroused in him was a definite shock. He hadn't expected to experience such overwhelming desire. All he had thought about since he'd known she was coming was getting her into his bed. He'd dreamed of kissing her, holding her and burying himself so deep inside her that he'd touch her soul. She was his wife and he'd waited a long time for the privileges due a husband. He doubted that Maggie had any conception of how deep his anger had cut when she had suggested that he'd married her for her money. That was a problem he had anticipated early on and it was the very reason he had insisted they see a lawyer as soon as possible.

Working together they cooked their dinner. Maggie made the salad while Glenn broiled thick steaks. Glenn didn't have a housekeeper to prepare his meals and for that matter, Maggie surmised, he might not even have someone in to do the housework. Now that she was here, she decided, she would take over those duties. Surprisingly, Maggie discovered she looked forward to being a wife. Glenn's wife.

Later, while he placed the few dirty plates in the dishwasher, Maggie decided to unpack her bags. She located the master bedroom without a problem and gave a sigh of relief when she noticed that Glenn fully intended that she would sleep with him. It was what she wanted, what she had planned, but after their shaky beginning, Maggie hadn't known what to think. A soft smile worked its way across her face, bright-

ening her dark eyes. Glenn longed for their marriage
to work as much as she did, she thought. What they
both needed to do was quit trying so damn hard.

When Maggie had finished unpacking, she joined
Glenn in the living room. It amazed her how unsettled they were around each other still. Glenn suggested they turn on the late-night news. Readily,
Maggie agreed. She supposed that this time could be
thought of as their honeymoon. They were probably
the only couple in America to watch television when
they could be doing other . . . things.

After the newscast, Glenn yawned. Once again
Maggie was reminded that his daily schedule was set
with the routine of his job. Staying awake until two or
three in the morning, watching a late late movie or
reading would only cause problems the following
morning. She would need to adjust her sleeping habits as well, although she had become a night person
these past few years, often enjoying the peace and
tranquillity of the early-morning hours to paint. Glenn
didn't live a life of leisure and she couldn't any longer,
either.

Funny, Maggie thought, that the realization that she
must now live according to a clock didn't depress her.
She was willing to get up with him in the morning and
cook his breakfast and even do the dishes. She didn't
know how long this "domesticated" eagerness would
continue, and vowed to take advantage of it while it
lasted. In the morning, she would stand at the front
door, hand him a packed lunch and send him off to
the office with a juicy kiss. But from the frowning
look he was giving the television, Maggie had the
impression the goodbye kiss in the morning would be
all the kissing she was going to get.

Glenn's thoughts were heavy. Maggie was sitting at his side and he hadn't so much as put his arm around her. He felt as though he were stretched out on a rack, every muscle strained to the limit of his endurance. It was pure torture to have her so close and not haul her into his arms and make love to her. If she could read only half of what was going through his mind, she would start running back to California, he thought dryly. No, he wouldn't take her that night. He'd bide his time, show her how empty his life was without her, how much he needed a woman's tenderness. Then, in time, she would come to him willingly and desire him, maybe even as keenly as he did her.

"Don't you think we should go to bed? It's after eleven." Maggie broached the subject with all the subtlety of a locomotive. Sitting next to him was torture. They had hardly said two words all night. The thick, unnatural silence made the words all the more profound.

Smoothly rolling to his feet, Glenn nodded. He hadn't noticed that the news was over. For that matter, he couldn't recall the headlines or anything that had been reported. Not even the weather forecast, which he listened for each night. "I imagine you're tired," he finally answered.

"Dead on my feet," she confirmed, walking with him toward the hallway and the master bedroom. *You're wide awake,* her mind accused. She was on Pacific time and it was barely after eight in San Francisco.

Following a leisurely scented bath, Maggie joined him wearing a black nightshirt that buttoned up the front and hit her at midthigh with deep side slits that went halfway up to her hip. The satin top was the most feminine piece of sleepwear Maggie owned. The two top buttons were unfastened and she stretched her hands high above her head in a fake yawn, granting him a full glimpse of her upper thighs.

Glenn was in bed, propped against thick feather pillows, reading a spy thriller. One look at her in the black satin and the book nearly tumbled from his hands. Tension knotted his stomach and he all but groaned at the agony that crashed through him with the turbulence of a tidal wave. But witnessing her beauty and wanting her was torture he endured willingly.

The mattress dipped slightly as she lifted back the sheet and slipped inside. Glenn set his novel aside and reached for the lamp switch. The room went dark with only the shimmering rays of the distant moon dancing across the far walls.

Neither moved. Only a few inches separated them, but for all the good it did to be sleeping with her husband, Maggie could well have been in San Francisco, she decided.

"Good night, Glenn," Maggie whispered after several stifled moments. If he didn't reach for her soon she'd clobber him over the head. Maybe she should say something to encourage him—let him know her feelings. But what? Listen, Glenn, I've reconsidered and although I realize that you may still be in love with another woman I've decided it doesn't matter. We're married. I'm your wife.... Disheartened, Maggie realized she couldn't do it. Not so soon, and not in a condominium he probably bought with "her" in mind.

Glenn interrupted Maggie's dark thoughts with a deep, quiet voice. "Good night." With that he rolled onto his side away from her.

Gallantly, she resisted the urge to smash the pillow over the top of his head, pull a blanket from the mattress and storm into the living room to sleep. She didn't know how any man could be so unbelievably dense.

Maggie fell easily into a light, untroubled slumber. Although asleep, lying on her side, her back to him, she was ever conscious of the movements of the man who was sharing the bed. Apparently, Glenn was having more difficulty falling asleep, tossing to one side and then to another, seeking a comfortable position. Once his hand inadvertently fell onto her hip and for a moment he went completely still. Content now, Maggie smiled inwardly and welcomed the calm. Sleeping with him was like being in a rowboat wrestling with a storm at sea.

With unhurried ease the hand that rested against her bare hip climbed upward, stopping at her ribs. Shifting his position, Glenn scooted closer and gathered her into his embrace. As if he couldn't help himself, his hand sought and found a firm breast. Maggie's eyes flew open and she swallowed down a soft moan of unexpected pleasure. Gently he kneaded the pliant flesh and she bit into her bottom lip at the sensations that swirled through her. His touch was doing insane things to her equilibrium and she was encompassed in a gentle, sweet warmth. Savoring the moment, Maggie bit into her bottom lip as he slowly, tantalizingly, caressed the hard tips of her breasts until she thought she'd moan audibly and give herself away.

Glenn was in agony. He had thought that he would wait and follow all the plans he'd made for courting his wife. But each minute grew more torturous than the one just past. He couldn't sleep; even breathing normally was impossible when she lay just within his grasp. He hadn't meant to touch her, but once his hand lightly grazed her rounded hip he couldn't stop his mind from venturing to rounder, softer curves and the memory of the way her breast had fit perfectly into the palm of his hand. Before he could stop, his fingers sought to explore her ripe body. He resisted the overwhelming urge to arch closer so she could feel his desire and know beyond a doubt his hunger for her.

Maggie remained completely still, waiting patiently for him to roll her onto her back and take her with all the force of his ardor. When he didn't move and she suspected that he might not ease the painful longing throbbing within her, she rolled onto her back and linked her arms around his neck.

"Kiss me," she pleaded.

"Maggie." He ground out her name like a man possessed, and hungrily devoured her lips with deep, slow, hot kisses that drove him to the brink of insanity. Groaning, he buried his face in her hair and he drew deep gulps of oxygen into his parched lungs. Again he kissed her, tasting her willingness, reveling in her eagerness. Only when her hips slowly began to rotate against him in an age-old rhythm did Glenn free her from the confining folds of the satin top. His hand pushed aside the material and his lips sought her breasts, kissing, sucking and caressing each nipple until they strained upward, hard and throbbing. Just when she felt she couldn't endure any more of the sweet rapture, Glenn switched tactics, tantalizing both breasts with his tongue, flickering, circling, teasing her until a moan slipped from her lips.

Her hands rumpled the dark thickness of his hair while she repeated his name again and again in fevered need. Hungry for the taste of him, Maggie urged his mouth to hers, but his devouring kiss only increased the aching in her loins.

"I want you," he groaned, breathing in sharply.

"Yes," she murmured, kissing the hollow of his throat and arching against him so that the fiery tips of her breasts seared his bare chest.

Led by his own towering desire, Glenn parted her legs, taking an infinite amount of time to enter the warm, tight sheath that throbbed in eager welcome.

"Oh, Glenn," Maggie groaned in a harsh whisper. "What took you so long?" The sensation was so blissfully exultant that she felt she could have died from sheer ecstasy.

With every ounce of his will, Glenn refused to move, savoring these few moments of intense pleasure after the long hours of abject agony. "Took me so long?" he repeated and groaned harshly. "You wanted me to make love to you?"

Looping her arms around his neck, Maggie strained upward and planted a long, hot kiss on his parted mouth. "How can any man be so blind?"

"Next time, hit me over the head." He arched forward then, thrusting himself deep within her heated flesh.

Maggie moaned and rotated her hips to better receive him. "I will. Oh, Glenn, I will," she cried, rolling her head to one side and surrendering to the pleasure that stabbed sweetly through her ripe body.

He took her quickly, driving into her, unable to bear slow torture. Their bodies fused in a glorious union of heart with soul, of man with woman, of Maggie with Glenn. They strained together, giving, receiving until their hearts beat in a paired tempo that left them breathless, giddy and spent.

Glenn gathered her in his arms and rolled onto his side, taking her with him. Her head rested in the crook of his shoulder, their legs entwined as if reluctant to release the moment.

Maggie felt the pressure of his mouth on her hair and snuggled closer into his embrace, relishing the feel of his strong arms wrapped securely around her.

Brushing a wayward curl from her cheek, Glenn's hand lingered to lightly stroke the side of her face. Maggie smiled gently up at him, the contented smile of a satisfied woman.

"Do you think you'll be able to sleep now?" she teased.

Glenn chuckled, his warm breath fanning her forehead. "Did my tossing and turning keep you awake?"

"Not really.... I was only half-asleep." Maggie lowered her chin and covered her mouth in an attempt to stifle a yawn. "Good night, Mr. Lambert," she whispered, dragging out the words as she swallowed back another yawn.

"Mrs. Lambert," he murmured huskily, kissing the crown of her head.

Maggie's last thought before slipping into an easy slumber was that she wasn't ever going to allow another woman's ghost to come between them again. This man was her husband and she loved him ... yes, loved him with a ferocity she was only beginning to understand. Together they were going to make this marriage work. One hundred Angies weren't going to stand in the way of their happiness. Maggie wouldn't allow it.

Within minutes Maggie was asleep. Still awake, Glenn propped up his head with one hand and took delight in peacefully watching the woman who had become everything to him in such a shockingly short time. She was his friend, his lover, his wife, and he had the feeling he had only skimmed the surface of who and what Maggie would be in his life. His finger lightly traced the delicate line of her cheek and the hollow of her throat. As impulsive as their marriage had been, there wasn't a second when Glenn regretted having pledged his life to Maggie. She was fresh and warm, a loving, free spirit. And he adored her. She had come to him with an ardor he had only dreamed of finding in a woman. She was stubborn, impulsive, head-strong: a rare and exquisite jewel. His jewel. His woman. His wife.

The low, melodious sound of a Neil Diamond ballad startled Maggie out of a sound sleep.

"Good morning, Sleeping Beauty," Glenn said as he sat on the edge of the mattress and kissed her lightly. He finished buttoning his shirt and flipped up the collar as he straightened the silk tie around his neck.

"You're dressed," she said, struggling to a sitting position and wiping the sleep from her eyes. She had wanted to get up with him, but must have missed the alarm.

"Would you like to undress me?"

Leaning against the thick fullness of the down pillow, Maggie crossed her arms and smiled beguilingly up at him. "What would you do if I said yes?"

Glenn's fingers quit working the silk tie. "Don't tempt me, Maggie, I'm running late already."

"I tempt you?" He'd never said anything more beautiful.

"Oh, dear God, if only you knew."

"I hope you'll show me." She wrapped her arms around her bent knees and leaned forward. "It . . . it was wonderful last night." She felt shy talking about their lovemaking, but it was imperative that he realize how much he pleased her.

"Yes it was," he whispered, taking her hand and kissing her knuckles. "I never expected anything so good between us."

"Me neither," she murmured and kissed his hand. "I wish you'd gotten me up earlier."

"Why?" He looked surprised.

Tossing back the covers, Maggie climbed out of bed and slipped into a matching black satin housecoat that she hadn't bothered to put on the night before—for obvious reasons. "I wanted to do the wifely thing and cook your breakfast."

"I haven't got time this morning." He paused, thinking he'd never seen any woman more beautiful. Her tousled hair fell to her shoulders, her face was free of any cosmetics, but no siren had ever been more alluring.

"Is there anything you'd like me to do while you're gone?" she offered. The day stretched before her and they hadn't made plans.

"Yes, in fact there are several things. I'll make a list." He reached for a pad and paper on his nightstand and spent the next few minutes giving her directions and instructions. "And don't plan dinner tonight," he added. "I phoned my parents yesterday and told them I had a surprise and to expect two for dinner.''

Maggie sat on the bed beside him and unconsciously her shoulders slouched slightly. This was the very reason she'd come to Charleston, yet she was afraid. ''Will they think we've gone crazy?''

''Probably,'' he returned with a short chuckle. ''But they'll be delighted. Don't worry about it; they know you and have always liked you. Mom and Dad will be happy for us.''

''I'm happy, Glenn.'' She wanted to reassure him that she had no regrets in this venture.

The smile faded from his dark eyes and his gaze held her immobile. ''I am, too, for the first time since I can remember. We're going to make it, Maggie.''

A grandfather clock in the den chimed the hour and reluctantly Glenn stood. ''I've got to leave.''

''Glenn.'' Maggie stopped him, then lowered her gaze, almost afraid of what she had to say. Waiting until the last minute to tell him wasn't the smartest thing to do.

''Yes?'' he prompted.

''I'm... Listen, I think you should probably know that I'm not using any birth control.''

His index finger lifted her chin so that her uncertain gaze met his. ''That's fine. I want a family.''

A sigh of relief washed through her and she beamed him a brilliant smile. ''I probably should warn you, though, my mother claims the Kingsbury clan is a fertile one. We could be starting our family sooner than you expect.''

''Don't worry about it; I'm not going to. When a baby comes, you can be assured of a warm welcome.''

Maggie experienced an outpouring of love far too powerful to be voiced with simple words. Nodding demanded an incredible effort.

"I'll leave the car keys with you and I'll take the bus. If you're in the neighborhood around noon stop into the office and I'll introduce you and take you to lunch."

"Maybe tomorrow," she said, stepping onto her tiptoes to kiss him goodbye. There was barely enough time to do everything she had to and be ready for dinner with his parents that evening.

A minute later Glenn was out the door. The condo seemed an empty shell without him. Maggie wandered into the kitchen with her list of errands, then poured a cup of coffee and carried it to the round table. She pulled out a chair and sat, drawing her legs under her. The first place she needed to stop was the bank to sign the forms that would add her name to the checking account. When she was there, Glenn had asked her to make a deposit for him.

She glanced at the front page of the paper he had left on the table and worked the crossword puzzle, then finished her coffee and dressed. The day held purpose. If she was going to see his parents it might not be a bad idea to find someplace where she could have her hair done.

With a jaunty step, Maggie found the deposit envelope Glenn had mentioned on the top of his desk. The room emanated his essence and she paused to drink it in. As she turned, Maggie caught a glimpse of a frame sticking above the rim of his wastepaper basket. What an unusual thing to do to a picture, she thought. As an artist, her sense of indignation rose until she lifted the frame from out of the basket and saw the multitude of small pictures with faces smiling back at her. Her breath clogged in her lungs and the room crowded in on her, pressing at her with a strangling sensation. *So this was Angie.*

Chapter Seven

The first thought that came to Maggie was how beautiful Angie was. With thick, coffee-dark hair and intense brown eyes that seemed to mirror her soul, Angie had the ethereal look of a woman meant to be cherished, loved and protected. There was an inner glow, a delicate beauty to her that Maggie could never match. Angie was a woman meant to be loved and nurtured. It was little wonder what Glenn loved her so profoundly. One glance at the woman who claimed his heart told Maggie that by comparison she was a poor second.

The frame contained a series of matted pictures that had obviously been taken over a period of several months. There was Angie on a sailboat, her wind-blown hair flying behind her as she smiled into the camera; Angie leaning over a barbecue, wearing an apron that said Kiss The Cook; Angie standing, surrounded by floral bouquets, in what looked like a flower shop, with her arms outstretched as though to signal this was hers. And more…so much more. Each picture revealed the rare beauty of the woman who claimed Glenn's heart.

A sickening knot tightened Maggie's stomach and she placed a hand on her abdomen and slowly released her breath to ease the physical discomfort. Although most of the photos were of Angie alone, two of them showed Glenn and Angie together. If recognizing the other woman's inner and outer beauty wasn't devastating enough, then the happiness radiating from Glenn was. Maggie had never seen him more animated. He seemed to glow with love. In all the years Maggie had known Glenn, she had never seen him look more content. He was at peace with his world, and so in love that it shone like a polished badge from every part of him. In comparison, the Glenn who had arrived in San Francisco was a sullen, doleful imitation.

Pushing the hair off her forehead, Maggie leaned against a filing cabinet and briefly closed her eyes. As early as the night before, she'd thought to banish Angie's ghost from their marriage. She had been a fool to believe it would be that easy. With a feeling of dread, she placed the frame back where she'd found it. Building a firm foundation for their marriage wasn't going to be easy, not nearly as easy as she'd thought. But then, nothing worthwhile ever was. Maggie loved her husband. Physically, he wanted her and for now that would suffice. Someday Glenn would look at her with the same lambent glow of happiness that Angie could evoke, she vowed. Someday his love for her would be there for all the world to witness. Someday...

Glancing at her wristwatch, Maggie hurried from the bathroom into the bedroom. In a few hours she and Glenn were having dinner with his parents, Charlotte and Mel, people she'd known and liked all her life. Family friends, former neighbors, good people. Yet Maggie had never been less sure of herself. Already she had changed dresses twice. This outfit will have to do, she decided. There wasn't time to change her mind again. As she put the finishing touches on her makeup, Maggie muttered disparaging remarks over the sprinkling of freckles across the bridge of her nose; wanted to know why her lashes couldn't be longer and her mouth fuller. Mentally she had reviewed her body: her breasts looked like cantaloupes, her hips like a barge; her legs were too short, her arms too long. Maggie could see every imperfection. Finally she had been forced to admit that no amount of cosmetics was going to make her as lovely as Angie. She had to stop thinking of Charlotte and Mel as the mother- and father-in-law who would compare her to their son's first choice and remember them instead as the friends she knew them to be.

Perhaps if she'd had more time to prepare mentally for this dinner, she thought defensively. As it was, the list of errands had taken most of the day and Maggie had been grateful to have something to occupy her time and her mind. Instead of concentrating on being bright and witty for her meeting with Glenn's parents, her thoughts had returned again and again to the discarded series of photographs. If she had found those photos, she reasoned, then there were probably other pictures around. The realization that Angie could be a silent occupant of the condominium was an intolerable conjecture.

When Glenn had walked in the door that afternoon and kissed her, Maggie had toyed with the idea of confronting him with the pictures. Sanity had returned just in time. He had obviously intended to throw them away, but surely must have realized that she would stumble upon them. Maybe it was cowardly of her, but Maggie had decided to ignore the fact that the pictures were in the other room, and pretended she hadn't seen them. For the first time since their marriage, things were going right and she didn't want to do anything to ruin that.

"Maggie, are you ready?" Glenn sauntered into the bedroom and hesitated when he saw her. "I thought you were wearing a blue dress."

"I...was," she answered slowly, turning and squaring her shoulders. "Do I look all right?"

"You're lovely." He placed a hand on each of her shoulders. "Maggie, I wish you'd stop worrying. Mom and Dad are going to be thrilled for us."

"I know." Absently she brushed her hand across the skirt of her black-and-red-print crepe dress and slowly released her breath. "I've always been Muffie to them and I'm...I'm not sure they'll be able to accept me as your wife."

Glenn's chuckle echoed through the bedroom. "Maggie, how can they not accept you? You're my wife. Mother's been after me for years to marry and settle down. She'll be grateful I finally took the plunge."

"That's encouraging," she mumbled sarcastically. "So you were desperate to placate your mother and

decided I'd do nicely as a wife. Is that supposed to reassure me?"

The muscles of his face tightened and a dark frown
marred his wide brow as he dropped his hands to his
side. "That's not true and you know it."

Ashamed, Maggie lowered her head and nodded.
"I'm sorry, I didn't mean that. My stomach feels like
a thousand bumblebees have set up camp. Even my
hands are clammy." She held them out, palms up, for
him to inspect. "Wait until we visit my parents, then
you'll know how I feel."

Slipping an arm around her trim waist, Glenn led
Maggie into the living room. "If you're worried, stick
to my side and I'll answer all the questions."

"I had no intention of leaving your side," she returned, slightly miffed.

A faint smile touched his mouth.

The ride to Glenn's parents' did little to settle her
nerves. Maggie thought she would be glad when the
day was over. When Glenn turned off the main road
and into a narrow street lined with family homes,
Maggie tensed. Two blocks later he slowed and turned
into a cement driveway.

Before Maggie was out of the car the front door
opened and Mel and Charlotte Lambert were standing on the wide porch. Maggie was surprised by how
little they'd changed. Glenn's father's hair was completely gray now and his hairline had receded, but he
stood proud and broad shouldered just as Maggie remembered him. Glenn's mother was a little rounder,
and wearing a dress. She had always worn dresses, although she wasn't the least bit formal or stuffy. As a
child, Maggie knew she was always welcome at the
Lamberts' kitchen. Charlotte had claimed it was a

pleasure having another woman around since she lived with a house full of men. Maggie had dropped over regularly when Dale, the youngest Lambert, was born. She had been at the age to appreciate babies and had loved to help feed and bathe him.

"Muffie!" Charlotte exclaimed, her bright eyes shining with genuine pleasure. "What a pleasant surprise. I had no idea you were in town."

Glenn joined Maggie and draped his arm around her shoulders as he boldly met his parents' gaze. To be honest, he had been dreading this confrontation himself. His parents would be pleased for him and Maggie, and do their best to hide their shock. But his father was bound to say something about Angie when they had a private moment. He might even suspect that Glenn had married on the rebound. He hadn't. Glenn tried not to think of Angie and ignored the nip of emotional pain associated with her name. His parents had loved her and encouraged him to marry her. Their disappointment had been keen when he told them she'd married Simon.

"Are you visiting from California?" Charlotte asked with a faint tinge of longing. "I do miss that old neighborhood. If we had a hundred years, we'd never find any better place to raise our family." Taking Maggie by the elbow, she led her into the house. "What's the matter with us, standing on the porch and talking when there's plenty of comfortable chairs inside."

Maggie tossed a pleading glance over her shoulder to Glenn, hoping he wouldn't leave the explaining to her.

The screen door closed with a bang as they entered the house. The small living room managed to hold a

recliner, a sofa and an overstuffed chair and otto-
man. In addition, a rocking chair sat in one corner.
The fireplace mantel was lined with pictures of the
three sons and the grandchildren.

"Mom, Dad," Glenn began, his expression sober as
he met their curious faces. His arm slipped around
Maggie as he stood stiffly at her side. He didn't know
any better way to say it than right out. "Maggie is my
wife. We've been married nearly two weeks."

"Married? Two weeks?" Charlotte echoed in a
stunned whisper.

Mel Lambert recovered quickly and reached across
the room to pump Glenn's hand. "Congratulations,
son." Cupping Maggie's shoulders he gently kissed her
cheek. "Welcome to the family, Muffie."

"Thank you." Her voice was both weak and weary.
This was worse than she'd thought. Glenn's mother
stood with a hand pressed over her heart and an ab-
surd look of shock written across her face, which she
was trying desperately to disguise.

"You two married," Charlotte whispered, apparently having recovered. "This is wonderful news. Mel,
you open that bottle of wine we've been saving all
these years and I'll get the goblets." Within seconds
they had both disappeared.

Glenn took Maggie's hand and led her to the sofa
where they both sat. "See, I told you it wouldn't be so
bad." His hand squeezed hers and his eyes smiled
confidently into hers. He smoothed a strand of hair
from her temple with his forefinger in a light caress.

"How can you say that?" she hissed under her
breath. "Your mother damn near fainted." To further her unease she could hear hushed whispers coming from the kitchen. The barely audible word

"rebound" heightened the embarrassed flush in Maggie's red cheeks. She pretended not to hear, as did Glenn.

Glenn's handsome face broke into a scowl. It was a mistake not to have said something to his parents earlier. His better judgment had prompted him to tell them. But he had made such an issue of the necessity of Maggie and him confronting them together that he couldn't change his plans. Informing his parents of their marriage had been what it took to get Maggie to join him in Charleston, and he would never regret that.

Mel and Charlotte reappeared simultaneously. Charlotte carried four shining crystal goblets on a silver tray and Mel had a wine bottle and corkscrew in one hand.

"Before leaving California," Mel explained as he pulled open the corkscrew, "Charlotte and I took a drive through the Napa Valley and bought some of the finest wines available. That was thirteen years ago now and we only open those bottles on the most special occasions."

"Let me see, the last time we opened our California wine was..." Charlotte paused and a network of fine lines knitted her face as she concentrated.

Glenn tensed and his hand squeezed Maggie's so tightly that she almost yelped at the unexpected pain. Gradually he relaxed his punishing grip, and Maggie realized that the last special occasion in the Lambert family had been shared with Angie and Glenn.

"Wasn't it when Erica was born?" Mel inserted hastily.

"No, no," Charlotte dismissed the suggestion with an impatient wave of her hand. "It was more recent than that... I think it was..." Flustered, she swallowed and reached for a wineglass to hide her discomfort. "I do believe you're right, dear, it was when Erica was born. It just seems more recent is all."

The tension flowed from Glenn, and even Maggie breathed easier. Mel finished opening the bottle and nimbly filled the four goblets. Handing Maggie and Glenn their wineglasses, he proposed a toast. "To many years of genuine wedded happiness."

"Many years," Charlotte echoed.

Later Maggie helped Charlotte set the table, carrying out the serving dishes while Glenn and his father chatted companionably in the living room. At dinner, the announcement that Glenn would be moving to San Francisco was met with a strained moment of disappointment.

"We'll miss you, son," was all that was said.

Unreasonably, Maggie experienced a flood of guilt. It hadn't been her idea to leave Charleston. She would make her home wherever Glenn wished, but apparently he wanted out of South Carolina.

"We'll visit often," Glenn assured his parents and catching Maggie's eye, he winked. "Especially after the children come."

Mel and Charlotte exchanged meaningful glances, making Maggie want to jump up and assure them she wasn't pregnant.

The meal was saved only because everyone felt the need to chat and cover the disconcerting silence. Maggie did her share, catching the Lamberts up on what had been happening with her parents and skimming over Denny's misfortunes, giving them only a brief outline of his life. In return, Charlotte proudly spoke of each of her three grandchildren, and while they cleared the table the older woman proudly brought out snapshots of them. Maggie examined each small smiling face, realizing for the first time that these little ones were now her nieces and nephew.

While Maggie wiped off the table, Charlotte ran sudsy water into the kitchen sink. "There was a time that I despaired of having a daughter," Charlotte began awkwardly.

"I remember," Maggie responded, recalling all the afternoons she had sat with Mrs. Lambert.

"And now I have three daughters. Each one of my sons have married well. I couldn't be more pleased with the daughters they've given me."

Maggie's hand pushed the rag with unnecessary vigor across the tabletop. "Thank you. I realize our marriage must come as a shock to you, but I want you to know, Mrs. Lambert, I love Glenn and I plan to be a good wife to him."

The dark eyes softened perceptively. "I can see that, Muffie. No woman can look at a man the way you look at Glenn and not love him." Hesitantly, she wiped her wet hands on her apron and turned toward Maggie. Her gaze drifted into the living room and she frowned slightly. "Are you free for lunch tomorrow? I think we should talk."

"Yes, I'd enjoy that."

Maggie didn't inform Glenn of her arrangement with his mother until the following morning. She woke with him and put on the coffee while he showered. When he joined her in the kitchen, Maggie had fried bacon and eggs, which was about the limit of her breakfast skills. Learning to cook was something she planned to do soon. Rosa, her housekeeper at the beach house, would gladly teach her. Thoughts of

California brought back a mental image of her brother, and Maggie sighed expressively. She had left instructions with her secretary that only Denny was to contact her when she was in Charleston. He needed her and she didn't want him to worry while she was out of town.

"I'll need the car again today; do you mind?" Maggie asked Glenn, turning her thoughts from the unhappy subject of Denny.

Glenn glanced up from the morning paper. "Do you want to do some shopping?"

"No . . . I'm meeting your mother for lunch." With a forced air of calm she scooted out the chair across from him. Her hands cupped the coffee mug, absorbing its warmth. She was worried about letting Glenn know she was meeting his mother. "You don't mind, do you . . . I mean, about me using the car?"

"No." He pushed his half-eaten breakfast aside, darting a concerned look toward Maggie. "I don't mind." Damn! he thought vehemently. What the hell was his mother going to tell her? If Maggie heard the details of his relationship with Angie, he'd prefer that they came from him, not his mother.

"Good." Despite his aloofness, Maggie had the impression that he wasn't altogether pleased. He didn't have to be—she was going and she sensed they both knew what would be the main subject of the luncheon conversation.

"Would you like to meet me at the health club afterward?" Glenn asked, but his attention didn't waver from the newspaper. "I try to work out two, sometimes three times a week."

It pleased Maggie that he was including her. "Sure, but let me warn you I'm terrible at handball, average at tennis and a killer on the basketball court."

"I'll reserve a tennis court," Glenn informed her, a smile curling up one side of his mouth. "And don't bother about dinner tonight. We'll eat at the club."

The morning passed quickly. Since she was meeting Glenn later, Maggie dressed casually in white linen slacks and a pink silk blouse, checking her appearance several times. All morning, Maggie avoided going near Glenn's den. She wouldn't torment herself by looking at the pictures again; stumbling upon them once had been more than enough. For all she knew, Glenn could have tossed them out with the garbage, but Maggie hadn't the courage to look, fearing that he hadn't.

Allowing herself extra time in case she got lost, Maggie left early for her luncheon date with Charlotte. She had some difficulty finding the elder Lamberts' home, and regretted not having paid closer attention to the route Glenn had taken the night before. As it turned out, when she pulled into the driveway it was precisely noon, their agreed time.

Charlotte met her at the door and briefly hugged her. "I got to thinking later that I should have met you someplace. You hardly know your way around yet."

"It wasn't any problem," Maggie fibbed, following the older woman into the kitchen. A quiche was cooling on the countertop, filling the room with the delicious smell of egg, cheese and spices.

"Sit down and I'll get you a cup of coffee."

Maggie did as requested, not knowing how to say that she didn't want to be thought of as company. Charlotte took the chair beside her. "The reason I asked you here today is to apologize for the way I behaved last night."

"No, please." Maggie's hand rested on her mother-in-law's forearm. "I understand. Our news must have come as a shock. Glenn and I were wrong not to have told you earlier."

"Yes, I'll admit that keeping it a secret for nearly two weeks was as much of a surprise as the deed." She lifted the delicate china cup to her mouth and took a sip. Glenn had always been close to his family; for him to have married without letting them know immediately was completely out of character. For that matter, their rushed marriage wasn't his style either. Maggie didn't need to be reminded that Glenn was a thorough person who weighed each decision, studied each circumstance. It was one reason he was such an excellent stockbroker.

"You have to understand," Maggie said, wanting to defend him. "We were as surprised as anyone. Glenn arrived for Steve and Janelle's wedding and everything seemed so right between us that we flew to Reno that night."

"The night of the wedding?" Charlotte did a poor job of hiding her astonishment. "Why, he'd only arrived in San Francisco..."

"Less than twenty-four hours before the wedding." Maggie confirmed her mother-in-law's observation. "And we hadn't seen each other in twelve—thirteen years. It sounds impulsive and foolish, doesn't it?" Maggie wouldn't minimize the circumstances surrounding their marriage.

"Not that... Glenn's never done anything impulsive in his life. He knew exactly what he was doing when he married you, Maggie. Don't ever doubt that."

"I don't. But I know that Glenn was engaged to someone else recently and that he loved her a great deal."

Obviously flustered, Charlotte shook her head, her face reddening. "You don't need to worry any about her."

"I have, though," Maggie confirmed honestly. "Glenn hasn't told me much."

"He will in time," Charlotte stated with confidence. The older woman's brow was furrowed with unasked questions, and Maggie nearly laughed aloud at how crazy the situation must sound to someone else. Glenn and Maggie had grown up fighting like brother and sister, had moved apart for more than a decade and on the basis of a few hours' reacquaintance, had decided to get married.

"I think I always knew there was something special between you and Glenn. He wasn't too concerned about girls during high school. Sports and his grades seemed more important. But he was at ease with you. If there was something troubling him, it wasn't me or his father he discussed it with, but you. I suppose a few people will be surprised at this sudden marriage, but don't let that bother you. The two of you are perfect together."

"I won't." Maggie swallowed, the words nervously tripping over her tongue. "Neither of us came into this marriage the way normal couples do, but we're both determined to make it work. I'd been hurt, perhaps not as deeply as Glenn, but for the past few years I've been lonely and miserable. Glenn's still...hurting, but

I've staked our future together on the conviction that time will heal those wounds.''

"I'm pleased he told you about Angie." The look of relief relaxed Charlotte's strong face.

"Only a little. He loved her very much, didn't he?" Just saying the words caused a pain to stab at Maggie's sensitive heart, but she successfully disguised a grimace.

"I won't deny it. Glenn did love her," Charlotte answered, then added to qualify her statement, "More than she deserved."

Maggie had guessed as much already. When Glenn committed himself to someone or something there would never be any doubts. He had loved her, but by his own words, he had no intention of pining away the rest of his life because she married another man. With their wedding vows, Glenn had pledged himself to Maggie. At moments like these and the one yesterday when she discovered the photos, this knowledge of his determination was the only thing that kept her from drowning in frustration.

"I think I always knew that Angie wasn't the right woman for Glenn. Something in my mother's heart told me things were wrong for them. However, it wasn't my place to intrude in his life. He seemed to love her so much."

This time Maggie was unable to hide the small pain that stabbed at her with Charlotte's words. She felt the blood drain from her face and lowered her eyes, not wanting her mother-in-law to know how tender her heart was.

"Oh dear, I've said the wrong thing again. Forgive me." Shaking her head as if silently scolding herself, Mrs. Lambert added, "That came out all wrong. He was happy, yes, but that happiness wouldn't have lasted and I suspect that even Glenn knew that." Charlotte stood and brought the quiche to the table along with two place settings.

"No, please continue," Maggie urged, needing to know everything about the situation she had married into.

Seeming to understand Maggie's curiosity, Charlotte rejoined her at the kitchen table. "Glenn cared enough for Angie to wait a year for her to decide she'd marry him. I've never seen Glenn so happy as the night she agreed to be his wife. We'd met Angie, of course, several times. She has the roundest, darkest eyes I've ever seen. She's an intense girl, quiet, a little withdrawn, exceptionally loyal, and although she's hurt Glenn terribly, I'm afraid I can't be angry with her. Ultimately she made the right decision. It would have been wrong for her to have married Glenn when she was in love with another man."

The irony of the situation was more than Maggie could stand. It was wrong for Angie to have married Glenn in those circumstances, yet he had done exactly that when he married her. Apparently, Charlotte didn't see it that way. For that matter, Maggie was convinced that had she known beforehand, she probably would have married him anyway.

"And she never did take the ring," Charlotte finished.

"The ring?"

"My mother's," the older woman explained. "She willed it to me as part of my inheritance, and when Glenn graduated from college I opted to make it his. It's a lovely thing, antique with several small diamonds, but of course, you've seen it."

Maggie thrust an expectant look at her mother-in-law. "No...I haven't. Glenn's never mentioned any ring."

Charlotte dismissed the information with a light shrug. "I wouldn't worry about it, you'll receive it soon enough. As I recall, Glenn had it sized and cleaned when he and Angie decided..." Realizing her mistake, Charlotte lowered her gaze and fidgeted with her coffee cup. "He's probably having it resized and is keeping it as a surprise for Christmas. As it is I've probably ruined that. I apologize, Maggie."

The racket slammed against the tennis ball with a vengeance and Maggie returned it to Glenn's side of the court with astonishing accuracy. So he had his grandmother's antique ring that was to go to his wife. She was his wife. Where the hell was the ring? *Slam*. She returned the tennis ball a second time, stretching as far as she could reach to make the volley. Not expecting her return, Glenn lost the point.

Maggie's serve. She aced the first shot, making his return impossible. Fueled by her anger, she had never played a better match. The first two games were hers, and Glenn's jaw sagged open as he went into mild shock. He rallied in the third, and their fourth and fifth games were heated contests.

"I don't recall you ever being this good," he shouted from the other side of the court.

She tossed the ball into the air, and fully extending her body, wielded the racket forward, bending her upper torso in half.

"There are a lot of things you don't know about me, Lambert," she shouted back, dashing to the far end of the court to return the volley. She felt like a pogo stick hopping from one end of the clay surface to the other with a quickness she didn't know she possessed. At the end of the first set, Maggie was so exhausted that she was shaking. Good grief, she thought, she had a tennis court at the beach house that she never used. This match was a misrepresentation of her skill.

Wiping the perspiration from her face with a thick white towel, Maggie sagged onto the bench. Glenn joined her, taking a seat beside her. "You should have told me you were this good. I've never had to work this hard to win."

Her breath came in deep gasps. "That was quite a workout." She hoped he didn't suggest another one soon. A repeat performance of this magnitude was unlikely. The match had helped her vent her frustrations over the issue of his grandmother's ring—her normal game was far less aggressive.

Taking his mother's words at face value, Maggie decided the best thing she could do was patiently wait. Glenn had originally intended the ring would go to Angie, but he'd married Maggie. When he felt comfortable with the idea he'd present her with the ring, not before. Christmas was less than seven weeks away, and Charlotte was probably right. He'd give it to her then. Maybe.

Regaining his breath, Glenn leaned forward and placed his elbows on his knees. "What did you and my mother have to talk about?" The question wasn't an idle one. His brows were drawn into a single tense line. All afternoon he had worried about that luncheon date. Maggie had a right to know everything, but he didn't want the information coming from his mother. If anyone was going to tell her, it would come best from him. He had thought to call and talk to his mother, and discreetly explain as much, but the morning had been hectic and by the time he was out of the board meeting, it had been too late.

Wickedly, Maggie fluttered her thick, dark lashes. "I imagine you'd love to know what tales she carried, but I'm not breaking any confidences."

"Did she give you her recipe for my favorite dinner?"

"What makes you think we discussed you?" Maggie tilted her flushed face to one side and grinned up at him, her smile growing broader.

"It only seems natural that the two women in my life would talk of little else." He placed his arm around her shoulder and helped her stand, carrying her tennis racket for her.

Maggie placed her arm around his waist, pleased with the way he linked her with his mother. "If your favorite meal is beef Stroganoff, then you're in luck."

"The luckiest day of my life was when you agreed to be my wife," Glenn murmured as he looked down on her with a haunting look so intense that Maggie's heart throbbed painfully. Her visit with his mother hadn't been easy for him, she realized. He had probably spent the entire day worrying about what she'd say afterwards.

Her voice grew husky with emotion. "What an amazing coincidence, that's my favorite day, too."

The longing in his eyes grew all the more poignant as Glenn weighed her words. If they'd been anyplace else, Maggie was convinced he would have tossed their tennis rackets aside and pulled her into his arms.

"Come on," she chided lovingly. "If you're going to beat me when I've played my best game, then the least you can do is feed me."

Laughing, Glenn kissed the top of her head and led her toward the restaurant.

His good mood continued when they reached the condominium. Maggie was bushed, and although she had taken a quick shower at Glenn's club, she couldn't resist a leisurely soak in a hot tub to soothe the aching cries of unused tendons. This day had been their best yet. The tension eased from her sore muscles and her heart. The matter with the ring no longer bothered her. When Glenn decided to give it to her, she'd know that it came from his heart and she need never doubt again.

With her hair pinned up, and a terry-cloth bathrobe wrapped around her, Maggie walked into the living room, looking for her husband.

"Glenn."

"In here." His voice came from the den.

Remembering the photographs inside, Maggie paused in the doorway. Threads of tension shot through her nerves, although she struggled to appear outwardly composed. With monumental effort she kept her gaze from the large garbage can beside his desk.

"What are you doing?" She was exhausted and it was late. She'd have thought that after a workout on the courts he'd be ready for bed.

"I've got a few odds and ends to finish up here. I'll only be a few minutes," he answered without looking up, scribbling across the top of a computer sheet. When he did glance up he was surprised to find Maggie standing in the doorway as if she were afraid to come into the room. "I'd appreciate a cup of coffee."

Maggie shrugged. "Sure."

"Maggie." Glenn stopped her. "Is anything wrong?"

"Wrong?" she echoed. "What could possibly be wrong?" *Just that I'm such a coward I can't bear to look and see if those snapshots are still there,* she chastised herself, turning toward the kitchen.

"I don't know." Glenn's puzzled voice followed her.

The instant coffee only took a minute to make. Maggie stood in the kitchen, waiting for the water to heat and told herself she was behaving like an idiot.

She pasted a smile on her lips as she carried the cup into his den and set it on the edge of the desk. "Here you go."

"Thanks," Glenn murmured, busily working.

Maggie straightened and took a step backward. As she did, her gaze fell to the empty garbage can. Relief washed over her in rippling waves. He had gotten rid of them. She wanted to dance around the room and sing.

"Glenn." She moved behind his chair and slid her arms around his neck.

"Hmm..."

"How late did you say you'd be?" She dipped her head and nuzzled the side of his neck, darting her tongue in and out of his ear.

Glenn could feel the hot blood stirring within him. "Not long, why?"

"Why?" she shot back, giggling. "You need me to tell you why?"

Scooting the chair around, Glenn gripped her by the waist and pulled her into his lap. A brilliant smile curved her lips as she slid her hands around his neck.

Glenn's mouth twisted wryly as he studied her. He didn't know what had gotten into Maggie today. First she had surprised the hell out of him on the tennis court. Then she had behaved like a shy virgin outside his door, looking in as if his office was a den of iniquity. And now she was a bewitching temptress who came to him with eyes that were filled with passion. Good Lord, he'd never get enough of this woman.

Maggie's fingers fumbled with the buttons of his shirt so that she had the freedom to run her hands over his dark chest. She reveled in the sensuous enjoyment of simply touching him, and pulled the shirt free of his shoulders. The hard muscles rippled as she slowly slid her hands upward to either side of his neck. Unhurried, she branded him with a kiss so hot it stole his breath.

"Maggie," he whispered hoarsely, intimately sliding his hands between her legs and stroking her bare thigh. "Maybe I haven't got so much paperwork to do after all."

Smiling dreamily, Maggie directed his mouth back to hers. "Good."

Chapter Eight

Two weeks passed and Maggie grew more at ease with her marriage. She realized that a silent observer to their world would have assumed that they had been married for several years. Externally, there was nothing to show that their marriage wasn't the product of a long, satisfying courtship. It didn't seem to matter that Glenn hadn't declared his love. He respected her, enjoyed her wit, encouraged her talent. They were happy... and it showed.

Maggie greeted each day with enthusiasm, eager to discover what lay in store for her. She purchased several cookbooks and experimented, putting her creativity to work in the kitchen. Glenn praised her efforts and accepted her failures, often helping her laugh when it would have been easy to be angry at her own inefficiency. In the early afternoons, if there was time, Maggie explored Charleston with Glenn's mother and came to appreciate anew what a wonderful woman Charlotte Lambert was. They never spoke of Angie again.

South Carolina was everything Maggie had known it would be, and more than she'd ever expected. She was thrilled by the eighteenth- and nineteenth-century paintings that displayed regional history in the Gibbes Art Gallery and explored the Calhoun Mansion and even the Confederate Museum, examining for the first time the Civil War from the Confederate point of view. One hundred and twenty years after the last battles of the war had been waged, Maggie felt the anguish of the South and tasted its defeat.

Her fingers longed to hold a paintbrush, but she satisfied her urgings with a pen and pad, sketching the ideas that came to her. Charlotte was amazed at her daughter-in-law's talent, and Maggie often gave Glenn's mother her pencil sketches. At Sunday dinner with his family, Maggie was embarrassed to find those careless drawings framed and hanging on the living room wall. Proudly, Glenn's eyes had met hers. They didn't often speak of her art, and Maggie basked in the warm glow of his approval.

For his part, Glenn was happy, happier than he ever imagined he'd be. In the afternoons he rushed home from the office, knowing Maggie would be there waiting for him. Maybe he hadn't married her for the right reasons, maybe what they had done was half-crazy, but, he thought tenderly, he wouldn't have it any different now, and he thanked God that he'd acted on the impulse. Maggie was his and she gave his life purpose. In the afternoons she would be there waiting. And the minute he walked in the door, she'd smile. Not an ordinary smile, but a soft feminine one that lit up her dark eyes and curved the smooth edges of her mouth in a sultry way that sent hot need coursing through him. In his lifetime, Glenn never hoped to see another woman smile the way Maggie did. Often he barely made it inside the door before he knew he had to kiss her. He would have preferred to react casually to his desire for her, but discovered it was impossible. Some days he couldn't get home fast enough, using every ounce of self-control he'd ever possessed not to burst in the door, wrap his arms around her and carry her into their bedroom. He couldn't touch, or taste, or hold her enough. And when he exploded deep inside her, Glenn felt he'd choose death rather than a life without her. Angie might have possessed his heart, but Maggie had laid claim to his soul.

He wondered sometimes if she had even an inkling of what she did to him physically. He doubted it. If she wasn't pregnant soon, he mused, it would be a miracle. The thought of Maggie heavy with his child, her breasts swollen, her stomach protruding, produced such a shocking desire within him that it was almost painful. The feeling left him weak with wonder and pride. They'd have exceptionally beautiful children.

For the first time, Glenn understood his brothers' pride in and awe of their children. At thirty, Glenn hadn't given much thought to a family. Someday, he had always thought, he'd want children, but he hadn't put faces or names to those who would fill his life. With Maggie he envisioned a tall son and a beautiful daughter. Every man wanted an heir, and now he yearned for a son until some nights he couldn't sleep thinking about the children Maggie would give him. On those evenings, late, when his world was at peace, Glenn would press his hand over her satiny smooth stomach, praying her body was nurturing his seed. A child would cement Maggie and him so firmly together that only death would ever separate them.

Their evenings were filled with contentment. Only rarely did he bring work home, lingering instead in front of the television, using that as an excuse to have Maggie at his side, to watch her. If he did need to deal with some paperwork, she sat quietly in his den, curled up in a chair reading. It was as though they couldn't be separated any longer than necessary and every moment apart was painful.

Maggie enjoyed watching Glenn in his office more than any other place. He sat with simple authority at his desk while she pretended absorption in a novel, when actually she was studying him. Now and then he would look up and they'd exchange warm, lingering glances that left her wondering how long it would be until they could go to bed.

When they did head toward the bedroom, it was ridiculously early. The instant the light went off Glenn reached for her with such passion that she wondered if he would ever get his fill of her—then promptly prayed he wouldn't. Their nights became a celebration for all the words stored in their hearts that had yet to be spoken. Never shy nor embarrassed, Maggie came to him without reserve, holding nothing back. She was his temptress and mistress. Bewitching and bewitched. Seduced and seducer.

Maggie had assumed that the fiery storm of physical satisfaction their bodies gave each other would fade with time, not increase. But as the days passed, she was pleased that Glenn's constant need equaled her desire for him. Each time they made love, Maggie would lie in his arms thinking that their appetite for each other would surely diminish, and knew immediately that it wouldn't.

In the mornings when she woke to the clock radio, Maggie was securely wrapped in Glenn's arms. He held her close and so tight she wondered how she had managed to sleep. Some mornings Maggie felt the tension leave Glenn as he emerged from the last dregs of slumber and realized she remained with him. It was as though he feared she would be gone. Once assured she was at his side, Glenn would relax. As far as Maggie could tell, this insecurity was the only part of his relationship with Angie that continued to haunt him. One hundred times each day, in everything she did, every place she went, Maggie set out to prove she would never willingly leave him.

Life fell into a comfortable pattern and the third full week after Maggie arrived in Charleston, the condominium sold. Maggie met Glenn at the door with the news.

"The realtor was by with an offer," she said, draping her arms around his neck and pressing her lithe body to his.

Glenn held her hips and placed his large hands on her buttocks, thrusting her even closer as he kissed her hungrily. "As far as I can see we should be able to make the move within a week, two at the most," he commented a few minutes later, as he curled an arm around her shoulder and deposited his briefcase in the den.

"A week?" Now that she was here, Maggie would have welcomed the opportunity to settle in South Carolina. California, Denny, the beach house seemed a million miles away, light-years from the life she shared with Glenn here.

"You sound like you don't want to move." He leaned against the edge of his desk, crossing his long legs at the ankles.

"South Carolina is lovely."

"So is California," Glenn countered. "You don't mind the change, do you?"

In some ways she did. Their time in Charleston was like a romantic interlude—the honeymoon they'd never gotten. They were protected from the outside world. No one knew who Maggie was, or cared. For the first time in several years she was a regular person and she loved it. In Charleston she had blossomed into a woman who boldly met a passerby's glance. She explored the art galleries without fear that someone would recognize her. No one came to her with "get rich quick" schemes, seeking naive investors. No one rushed to wait on her or gain her attention or her gratitude. However, Maggie was wise enough to know that those things would follow in time.

"No," she told Glenn soberly. "I don't mind the move."

He turned, sorting through the stack of mail she had set on the desk top, smiling wryly. Maggie wanted to stay in Charleston for the same reasons he wanted to move to San Francisco. They were each looking for an escape to problems they would need to face sooner or later. For his part, Glenn chose the West Coast more for nostalgia than any need to escape. San Francisco felt right and Charleston held too many painful memories.

"Will you want to live at the beach house?" Maggie's one concern was that Glenn might not like her home. Her own feelings toward the house were ambivalent. On some days, it was her sanctuary and on others, her prison. She liked the house; she was comfortable there, but she didn't know that Glenn would be.

"Sure. Is there any reason you'd want to move?"

"No, it's just that..." The telephone rang and Maggie paused as Glenn lifted the receiver.

After a moment he handed it to her. "It's for you."

"Me?" She felt her heart rate accelerate. She'd given specific instructions that she wasn't to be contacted except for her brother. And Denny would only call if he was in financial trouble.

"Hello." Her voice was wispy with apprehension.

"Who was that?"

"Denny, are you all right?"

"I asked you a question first. It's not often I call my sister and a man answers the phone. Something's going on. Who is it, Maggie?"

"I'm with Glenn Lambert."

A low chuckle followed, but Maggie couldn't tell if her brother was pleased or abashed. "So you and Glenn are together. Be careful, Maggie, I don't want to see you hurt again." He hesitated, as though he didn't want to continue. "Are you living with him?"

"Denny," Maggie had been foolish not to have told her family sooner. "Glenn and I are married."

"Married," he echoed in shock. "When did this happen?"

"Several weeks ago."

A short, stunned silence followed. "That's sudden, isn't it? Linda and I would have liked to have been there."

"We decided this was what we wanted and didn't stop to question it."

"That's not like you."

"It wasn't like either of us. I'm happy, Denny, really happy. You know what it's been like the past few years. Now don't worry about me. I'm a big girl. I know what I'm doing."

"I just don't want to see you get hurt."

"I won't," she assured him.

"Do Mom and Dad know?"

Denny had her there. "Not yet. We're planning to tell them once we're back in San Francisco."

"And when will that be?" His words were slow as if he were still thinking.

"A couple of weeks."

He didn't respond and the silence seemed to pound over the great echoing canyon of the telephone wire. Denny hadn't done a good job of disguising his reservations. Once he saw how good this marriage was for her, she was sure, he'd share her happiness. Her brother had been her anchor when she broke up with Dirk. He had seen firsthand the effects of one painful relationship and sought to protect her from another. Only Glenn wasn't Dirk, and when they arrived back in San Francisco Denny would see that.

"Is there a reason you phoned, Denny?"

"Oh, yeah." His voice softened. "Listen, I hate to trouble you but there's been some minor complications and the lawyer has to charge me extra fees. Also, Linda's been sick and the kids aren't feeling that well, either...."

"How much do you need?"

"I hate having to come to my sister like a pauper. But I swear as soon as everything's straightened out I'll repay every penny."

"Denny, don't worry about it. You're my brother, I'm happy to give you whatever you need. You know that.'' She couldn't refuse her own brother no matter what the reason.

"I know and appreciate it, Sis. I really do."

"You wouldn't ask if it wasn't necessary." She had hoped to make this difficult time in Denny's life smoother but sometimes wondered if she contributed more to the problem. Yet she couldn't say no. "I'll instruct Shirley to write you a check."

Once he had gotten what he wanted the conversation ended quickly. Maggie replaced the receiver and forced a smile to her lips. "That was my brother," she announced, turning back to Glenn.

"Who's Shirley?" he asked starkly.

"My money manager." She lowered her gaze to the lush carpet, feeling her husband's censure. Glenn didn't understand the circumstances that had led to Denny's problems. They had both received a large inheritance. Maggie had received half of her great-aunt's fortune; her parents and Denny had split the other half. Everything had gone smoothly until Denny had invested in public works bonds that went defunct. Now his money—or what was left of it—was tied up in litigation.

"Does Denny need her name often?"

"Not really," she lied. "He's been having some cash flow problems lately." As in not having any, her mind added. "We were talking about the move to California when the phone buzzed, weren't we?"

"You don't want to discuss Denny, is that it?"

"That's it." Glenn couldn't tell her anything she didn't already know. She was in a no-win situation with her brother. She couldn't abandon him, nor could she continue to feed his dependence on her.

"Okay, if that's the way you want it." His eyes and voice silently accused her as he turned back and sorted through the mail.

"California will be good for us," Maggie said, hoping to lighten the sullen atmosphere.

"Yes, it will," Glenn agreed almost absently, without looking up. "Before I forget, the office is having a farewell party for me Friday night. We don't have any plans, do we?"

Maggie had met Glenn's staff and seen for herself the respect his management had earned him. One afternoon when she had met him for lunch, Maggie had witnessed anew the quiet authority in his voice as he spoke to his associates. He was decisive and sure, calm and reassuring, and the office had thrived under his care. It went without saying that he was a popular manager and would be greatly missed.

Friday night Maggie dressed carefully, choosing a flattering cream-colored creation and pale blue designer nylons. She had never been one to enjoy parties, especially when they involved people she barely knew. This one shouldn't be so bad though, she reasoned. The focus would be on Glenn, not her.

"Am I underdressed?" she asked him, slowly rotating for his inspection. Not having attended this kind of function previously put her at a disadvantage. She didn't know how the other wives would dress and had chosen something conservative.

Glenn stood, straightening his dark blue silk tie. His warm chuckle filled their bedroom as he examined his wife. "As far as I'm concerned you're overdressed. But I'll take care of that later myself." His eyes met hers in the mirror and filled with sweet promise.

After inserting dangly gold earrings into her ear-lobes, Maggie joined Glenn in the living room. He was pouring them a drink and Maggie watched her hus-band with renewed respect. He was tall, athletic and unbearably handsome. Her heart swelled with the surge of love that raced through her. She hadn't been looking forward to the party; in fact, she had been dreading it from the moment Glenn had mentioned it. Early on, she had reconciled herself to being a good stockbroker's wife, and that meant that she'd be at-tending plenty of functions over the years. It would be to her advantage to adapt to them now. Although he hadn't said anything, Maggie was confident Glenn knew she was determined to make the best of this eve-ning.

They arrived precisely at eight at the home of Glenn's regional manager, Gary Weir. Already the living room was filled with smoke, and from the look of things the drinks had been flowing freely. As Glenn and Maggie walked in the front door, spirited cheers of welcome greeted them. Maggie painted a bright smile on her lips as they moved around the room, mingling with the guests. Everyone, it seemed, was in a good mood. Everyone, that is, except Maggie.

She didn't know how to explain her uneasiness. There wasn't anything she could put a name to and she mentally chastised herself. Glenn's friends and asso-ciates appeared to be going out of their way to make her feel welcome. Her hostess, Pamela Weir, Gary's wife, was warm and gracious, if a bit reserved. Yet a cold persistence nagged at Maggie that something wasn't right. Glenn stayed at her side, smiling down on her now and then. Once her eyes fell upon two women whispering with their heads close together. They sat on the far side of the room and there wasn't any possibility that Maggie could hear their murmured discussion, but something inside told Maggie they were talking about her. A chill went up her spine and she gripped Glenn's elbow, feeling ridiculous and calling herself every kind of idiot. Lightly, she shook her head, hoping to toss aside those crazy insecurities.

A few minutes later Glenn was pulled into a conversation with some of the men and Maggie was left to her own devices. Seeing Maggie alone, Pamela Weir strolled over.

"It was such a pleasant surprise when Glenn announced he had married," Pamela said.

Maggie took a sip of her martini to disguise her lack of attention. Glenn was involved with his friends and moved to another section of the crowded room. "Yes, I imagine it was. But we've known each other almost all our lives."

"That was what Glenn was saying." Pamela gave her a funny look and then smiled quickly. "For a long time Gary was worried that Glenn wanted the transfer because of a problem at the office."

Maggie forced a smile. "We decided when we married that we'd live in San Francisco," she explained to the tall, elegant woman at her side. "We were both raised there."

"Yes, Glenn explained that too."

Maggie's throat constricted and she made an effort to ease the strange tension she felt. "Although I've only been in Charleston a few weeks, I'm impressed with your city. It's lovely."

Pamela nodded and her eyes revealed her pride in Charleston. "We do love it."

"I know Glenn will miss it."

"We'll miss him."

Silence. Maggie could think of nothing more to comment upon. "You have a lovely home," she said and faltered slightly. "Glenn and I both appreciate the trouble you've gone to for this evening."

"It's no bother. Glenn has always been special to the firm. We're just sick to lose him." The delicate hands rotated the stem of the crystal goblet. "I don't mind telling you that Glenn is the best manager Gary has. In fact—" she paused and gave Maggie a falsely cheerful smile "—Gary had been hoping to move Glenn higher into management. Of course that won't be possible now."

As with his parents, Maggie was again put on the defensive. Leaving Charleston hadn't been her idea and she didn't like being made the scapegoat. Swallowing back a heated retort, Maggie lowered her gaze and said, "I'm sure Glenn will do just as well in San Francisco."

"We all hope he does," Pamela said with a note of censure.

Glenn's gaze found Maggie several moments later. She stood stiff and uneasy on the other side of the room, holding her drink and talking to Pamela Weir. He watched her reach for a cigarette and light up. The action surprised him—Maggie only smoked when she was upset or irritated. Now she appeared to be both and he couldn't understand why. He had known from the beginning that she hadn't been looking forward to this party. He wasn't all that fond of this sort of affair himself. But since the party had been given in his honor, he couldn't refuse the invitation. Maggie's attitude troubled him. Earlier in the evening, he had stayed at her side, but eventually he'd been drawn away for one reason or another. Good grief, he thought, he shouldn't have to baby-sit her. The longer he watched her actions with Pamela, the darker his scowl became. She wasn't even making eye contact with Pamela and when his supervisor's wife moved away, Glenn felt a surge of irritation. With determined strides he crossed the room to Maggie's side.

She lifted her gaze to his and Glenn was shocked at the look of anger she sent him.

"What's wrong?" he demanded.

She met his gaze with a determined lift to her chin. She was upset, more upset than she'd been since the first morning of their marriage. Glenn had let her walk into the party, knowing the resentment his co-workers felt toward her because he was leaving. "When we arrived tonight I kept feeling these weird vibes that people didn't like me. Now I know why...."

"You're being ridiculous," Glenn muttered, his hand tightening around his drink. "These are my friends and they accept you as my wife."

Glenn was on the defensive and clearly unwilling to listen to her. With restrained force, she smashed out the cigarette in a glass ashtray. "They don't, Glenn," she murmured, "and with good reason. We'll talk about it later."

A tense muscle flexed in his clenched jaw, but Glenn said nothing. The discordant sound of someone banging a teaspoon against the side of a glass interrupted their discussion.

"Attention everyone," Gary Weir called as he came to stand beside Glenn and Maggie. With dull blue eyes that revealed several drinks too many, Gary motioned with his arms that he wanted everyone to gather around.

Maggie felt like a statue with a frozen smile curving her mouth as she watched the party crowding around them. Glenn placed an arm at her neck, but his touch felt cold and impersonal.

Ceremoniously clearing his throat, Gary continued. "As you're all aware, tonight's party is being given in honor of Glenn and his—" he faltered momentarily, and seemed to have forgotten Maggie's name "—bride." A red blush attacked the cheeks of the supervisor and he reached for his drink and took a large swallow.

"As we know," he said, glancing over his shoulder to Glenn and Maggie, "Glenn has recently announced that he's transferring to California." Gary was interrupted with several low boos until he sliced the air, cutting off his associates. "Needless to say, everyone is going to miss him. Glenn has been a positive force within our company. We've all come to appreciate him and it goes without saying that he'll be sorely missed. But being good sports, we want to wish him the best in San Francisco." A polite round of applause followed.

"In addition," Gary went on, his voice gaining volume with each word, "Glenn has taken a wife." He turned and beamed a proud smile at the two of them. "All of us felt that we couldn't send you away without a wedding gift. So we took up a collection and got you this." He turned around and lifted a gaily wrapped gift from behind a chair, holding it out to Glenn and Maggie.

Clearing his throat, Gary finished by saying, "This gift is a token of our appreciation and well wishes. We'd all like to wish Glen and Angie many years of happiness."

Maggie felt as if she'd been slapped in the face and her eyes widened with the unexpectedness of it. An embarrassed hush fell over the room and Maggie felt Glenn stiffen with outrage. Not realizing his mistake, Gary flashed a troubled look to his wife who was mouthing Maggie's name.

To cover the awkward moment, Maggie stepped forward and took the gift from Gary's hand. He gave her an apologetic look and fumbled, obviously flustered and deeply embarrassed.

"Glenn and I would like to thank you, Larry."

"Gary," he corrected instantly, some color seeping back into his pale face.

A slow smile grew across Maggie's tight features. "We both seem to be having problems with names tonight, don't we?"

The party loved it, laughing spontaneously at the way she had aptly turned the tables on their superior. Laughing himself, Gary briefly hugged her and pumped Glenn's hand.

Not until they were on their way home did Glenn comment on the mishap. "Thank you," he said as they headed toward the freeway.

"For what?"

"For the way you handled that." He didn't need to explain what "that" was. Maggie knew. Rarely in his life had Glenn felt such outrage and anger. He had wanted to throw Gary against the wall and demand that he apologize to Maggie for embarrassing her that way. Of course, the slip hadn't been intentional, but it hadn't seemed to matter.

Several times in the past few weeks, Glenn had questioned whether he was making the right decision leaving Charleston. Maggie had blossomed here and seemed to genuinely love the city. Now he knew beyond a shadow of a doubt that leaving was best. Angie would haunt them here. He had been a fool not to realize why Maggie had been so miserable at the party. The thought that his co-workers would confuse her with Angie hadn't crossed his mind. It seemed impossible that only a few months back he had been planning to marry her. He even had trouble picturing Angie anymore and seldom tried. Angie would always hold a special place in his heart. He wished her a long and happy life with Simon. But he had Maggie now, and thanked God for the woman beside him. He might not have courted her the way he should have, the way she deserved, but he desperately needed her in his life.

He loved her. Simply. Profoundly. Utterly. He'd tell her soon. Not tonight though, he thought or she'd think the mistake at the party had prompted the admission. Glenn wanted to choose the time carefully. For several weeks now, he had realized she loved him. Yet she hadn't said anything. He couldn't blame her. Things would straighten themselves out once they were in San Francisco. The sooner they left Charleston the better. In California, Maggie need never worry that someone would bring up Angie's name again.

"Gary's mistake was an honest one. He didn't mean to embarrass anyone." Without a problem, Maggie excused Glenn's friend.

"I know," Glenn murmured, concentrating on his driving.

They didn't talk again until they were home and then only in polite phrases. They undressed in silence and when they lifted the covers and climbed into bed, Glenn gathered her close in his arms, kissing her softly. He was asleep long before she was and rolled away from her. Maggie lay staring at the ceiling, unable to shake what had happened earlier from her mind. The flickering moon shadows seemed to taunt her. All they had been doing for the past few weeks was pretending. The two of them had been so intent on making believe that there had never been another woman in Glenn's life that the incident tonight had nearly devastated them. That was the problem with fantasies—they were so easily shattered. Maggie didn't need to be told that Glenn had been equally disturbed. Angie was present in their lives; she loomed between them like an uninvited guest. With a heavy heart, Maggie rolled over and tried to sleep, but she couldn't. Not until Glenn's arms found her and he pulled her into the loving circle of his embrace. But he had been asleep, and for all she knew, Maggie thought bitterly, he could have been dreaming it was "her" he was holding.

Monday morning after Glenn left for work, Maggie sat lingering over a cup of coffee, working the crossword puzzle. The first thing she should do was get dressed, but she had trouble shaking off a feeling of melancholy. No matter how hard she tried, she hadn't been able to forget what had happened Friday night. They hadn't spoken about it again, choosing to ignore it. For now the puzzle filled her time. Her pen ran out of ink and after giving it several hard shakes, she tossed it in the garbage. Glenn kept a dozen or more in his desk.

Standing, Maggie headed toward his office. One thing they had decided over the weekend was that Maggie would fly ahead of Glenn to California. Like a fool Maggie had suggested it on the pretense that she

had several items that required her attention waiting
for her. She had hoped that Glenn would tell her he
wanted them to arrive together. But he had agreed all
too readily and she'd been miserable for the remainder of the day.

Pulling open Glenn's drawer, she found what she
needed and started to close the desk drawer. As she did
it made a light, scraping sound. Her first inclination
was to shove it closed. Instead, she carefully pulled the
drawer free and discovered an envelope tucked away
in the back that had been forced upward when she'd
gotten the pen.

It wasn't the normal place for Glenn to keep his
mail, and she examined the envelope curiously. The
even, smooth flowing strokes of the handwriting attracted her artist's eye. This was a woman's handwriting—Angie's handwriting. Maggie felt the room sway
as she sank onto the corner of the swivel chair, her
knees giving out. The postmark revealed that the letter had been mailed a week before Steve and Janelle's
wedding.

Perspiration broke out across Maggie's upper lip
and she placed a hand over her mouth. Her heart
hammered so loudly she was sure it rocked the room.
The letter must have meant a great deal to Glenn for
him to have saved it. Although she hadn't searched
through the condominium, she had felt confident that
he'd destroyed everything that would remind him of
the other woman. Yet the letter remained.

Half of her wanted to stuff it back inside the drawer
and pretend she'd never found it. The other half knew
that if she didn't know the contents of the letter she
would always wonder. Glenn had told her so little. She
was his wife. She had a right to know. He should have

explained the entire situation long ago and he hadn't, choosing instead to leave her curious and wondering. If she looked, it would be his own fault, she argued with herself. He had driven her to it.

It was wrong; Maggie knew it was wrong, but she couldn't help herself. Slowly, each inch pounding in the nails of her guilt, she withdrew the scented paper from the envelope.

Chapter Nine

Carefully Maggie unfolded the letter and was again struck by the smoothly flowing lines of the even handwriting. Angie's soulful dark eyes flashed in Maggie's memory from the time she'd seen the other woman's photograph. The handwriting matched the woman.

Dear Glenn,

I hope that I am doing the right thing by mailing you this letter. I've hurt you so terribly, and yet I owe you so much. I'm asking that you find it in your heart to forgive me, Glenn. I realize the pain I've caused you must run deep. Knowing that I've hurt you is my only regret.

Glenn, I don't believe that I'll ever be able to adequately thank you for your love. It changed my life and gave Simon back to me. Simon and I

were destined to be man and wife. I can find no
other way to explain it. I love him, Glenn, and
would have always loved him. You and I were
foolish to believe I could have forgotten Simon.

My hope is that someday you will find a
woman who will love you as much as I love Simon. You deserve happiness. Simon and I will
never forget you. We both want to thank you for
the sacrifice you made for us. Be happy, dear
Glenn. Be very happy.

With a heart full of gratitude,
Angie

With trembling hands, Maggie refolded the letter
and placed it back inside Glenn's drawer. If she had
hoped to satisfy her curiosity regarding Angie, the
letter only raised more questions. Angie had mentioned a sacrifice Glenn had made on her behalf. But
what? He was like that, noble and sensitive, even self-
sacrificing. Angie's marrying Simon must have devastated him.

All day the letter troubled Maggie, until she decided that if she were to help Glenn bury the past, she
had to understand it. That night she would do the very
thing she had promised she wouldn't: she would ask
Glenn to tell her about Angie.

No day had ever seemed so long. She didn't leave
the house, didn't even comb her hair until the
afternoon, and when she did, her mirrored reflection
revealed troubled, weary eyes and tight, compressed
lips. If Glenn could talk this out with her, their
chances of happiness would be greatly increased. He
had saved the letter, risked her finding it. Although he
might not be willing to admit it, he was holding on to

Angie, hugging the memory. The time had come to let go.

With her arms cradling her middle, Maggie paced the living room carpet, waiting for Glenn to come home from work. The questions were outlined in her mind. She had no desire to hurt or embarrass him. She wanted him to tell her honestly and freely what had happened with Angie and why he had stepped aside for Angie to marry Simon.

Yet for all her preparedness, when Glenn walked in the door Maggie turned abruptly toward him with wide, apprehensive eyes, her brain numb.

"Hello, Glenn." She managed to greet him calmly and walked across the room to give him a perfunctory kiss. She felt comfortable, but her cheeks and hands were cold. Earlier she had decided not to mention finding the letter, not wanting Glenn to know she had stooped so low as to read it. However, if he asked, she couldn't . . . wouldn't lie.

His hands found her waist and he paused to study her. "Maggie, what's wrong, you're as cold as an iceberg."

She felt ridiculously close to tears and nibbled at her lower lip before answering. This was far more difficult than she'd thought it would be. "Glenn, we need to talk."

"I can see that. Do you have another rule for our marriage?"

Absently, she rubbed the palms of her hands together. "No."

He followed her into the living room and took a seat while she poured him a drink. "Do you think I'm going to need that?" He didn't know what was troubling Maggie, but he had never seen her this way. She

looked almost as if she were afraid, which was ludicrous. There was nothing she had to fear from him.
He was her husband, and she should always feel comfortable coming to him.

Maybe she was pregnant. His pulse leaped eagerly
at the thought. A baby would be the answer to his
prayers. A feeling of tenderness overcame him. Maggie was carrying his child.

"Maggie," he asked gently, "are you pregnant?"

She whirled around, sloshing some of the bourbon
over the side of the tumbler, her eyes wide with astonishment. "No, what makes you ask?"

Disappointed, Glenn slowly shook his head. "No
reason. Won't you tell me what's troubling you?"

She handed him the drink, but didn't take a seat,
knowing she would never be able to sit comfortably in
one position. She was too nervous. Hands poised, her
body tense, she stood by the window and looked down
at the street far below. "I've been waiting to talk to
you all day."

Damn, he thought, he wished she'd get to the point.
He had never seen her this edgy. She resembled a child
who had come to her parent to admit a great fault. "If
it was so important, why didn't you phone me at the
office?"

"I . . . couldn't. This was something that had to be
done in person, Glenn," she said, then swallowed,
clenching and unclenching her fists as she ignored the
impatience in his eyes. "This isn't easy." She resisted
the urge to dry her clammy palms on the pockets of
her navy-blue slacks.

"I can see that," he said gently. Whatever it was had
caused her a hell of a lot of anxiety. Rushing her
would do no good, he knew, so he relaxed as much as

possible, crossed his legs and leaned back against the thick cushions of the chair.

"I thought for a long time I'd wait until you were comfortable about this...this subject. Now I feel like a fool, forcing it all out in the open. I wish I were a stronger person for you, but I'm not. I'm weak, really." Slowly she turned and hesitantly raised her eyes to his. "Glenn, I'm your wife. Getting married the way we did may have been a crazy thing to do, but I have no regrets. None. I'm happy being married to you. But as your wife, I'm asking you to tell me about Angie." Helpless, Maggie watched as surprise mingled with frustration and grew across his face.

"Why now?" Angie was the last subject he had expected Maggie to force upon him. As far as he was concerned, his relationship with her was over. He wouldn't deny that he had been hurt, but he had no wish to rip open the wounds of his pride. And that was what had suffered most. Even when he had known he'd lost her, he had continued to make excuses to see and be with Angie. Something perverse within himself had forced him to go back again and again even when he had recognized that there wasn't any possibility of her marrying him. For weeks he had refused to let go of her even though he'd known he'd lost her and she would never be his.

Now was the opportunity to explain that she'd found the letter, Maggie thought. But she couldn't admit that she'd stooped so low as to read the extremely personal letter. "I . . . wanted to know. . . . It's just that . . ."

"Is it because of what happened the other night?"

Glenn offered her an excuse that Maggie readily accepted. "Yes."

Glenn's mouth tightened, not with impatience, but confused frustration. After everything they had shared, he couldn't believe that she'd be so insecure now. No good would come from dredging up the past. "Whatever there was between us is over. Angie has nothing to do with you and me."

"But ultimately she does," Maggie countered swiftly. "You wouldn't have married me if your engagement hadn't been broken."

"Now you're being ridiculous. We wouldn't have married if I hadn't attended Steve and Janelle's wedding, either."

"You know what I mean."

"Maggie, trust me. There's nothing to discuss." The words came at her sharply, cutting at her sensitive heart.

Previously when Glenn was angry, Maggie had marveled at his control. He rarely raised his voice, and never at her. Until now. The only evidence she had ever had of his fury was a telltale leap of muscle in his jaw. He moved from his chair to the far side of the room.

"But, Glenn," she ventured. "I don't understand why you're so reluctant to discuss her. Is it because I've never told you about Dirk? I would have gladly, but you see, you've never asked. If there's anything you want to know, I'll be happy to explain."

"No, I don't care to hear the sorry details of your relationship with another man, and in return I expect the same courtesy."

Her hand on the back of the davenport steadied her. All these weeks, she'd been kidding herself, living in a dreamer's world. As Glenn's wife, she would fill the void left when Angie married Simon, but now she knew she would never be anything more than a substitute. These glorious days in Charleston had been an illusion. She had thought they'd traveled so far and yet they'd only been walking in place, stirring up the roadway dust so that it clouded their vision and their perspective. Oh, she would cook his meals, keep his house and bear his children, and love him until her heart would break. But she would never be anything more than second best.

"All right, Glenn," she murmured, casting her eyes to the carpet. "I'll never mention her name again."

His eyes narrowed as if he didn't believe her. But he had asked her not to, and she wouldn't. She had swallowed her pride, and come to him when he must have known how difficult it had been for her. That meant nothing to him, she realized. It didn't matter what she said or did; Glenn wasn't going to tell her anything.

Purposefully, Maggie moved into the kitchen and started to prepare their evening meal. She was both hurt and disillusioned. She realized that Glenn hadn't been angry, not really. The displeasure he had shown had been a reaction to the fact that he'd been unable to deal with his feelings for Angie. But he must, and she prayed he realized it soon. Only when he acknowledged his feelings and sorted it out in his troubled mind would he be truly free to love Maggie.

It took Glenn several minutes to analyze his indignation. Of all the subjects in the world, the last thing he wanted to discuss was the past. He had handled it badly. Maggie was upset, and he regretted that, but it was necessary. The damn farewell party was responsible for this sudden curiosity, he thought, and cursed. He should have realized earlier the repercussions. Damn Gary, damn them all.

Glenn made his way to the kitchen and pretended to read the evening paper, all the while studying Maggie as she worked, tearing lettuce leaves for a salad. *Someday soon he'd make it up to her and she'd know how important she was in his life...how much he loved her and needed her.*

In bed that night, the entire Alaska tundra might as well have lain between them. Glenn was on his side of the bed, his eyes closed, trying to sleep. He had wanted to make love and reassure Maggie, but she had begged off, claiming a headache. He was disappointed in her. The least she could do was be more original than that.

Other than polite conversation, Maggie hadn't said a word to him all evening. She cooked their dinner, but didn't bother to eat any of it. For his part, he could hardly stomach the fresh crab salad, although generally Maggie was a good cook and he enjoyed their meals together. Cleaning the kitchen afterward seemed to take her hours, and when she returned to the living room he had guiltily searched her face for evidence of tears. She hadn't cried, and Glenn was relieved, regretting everything. Maggie was a wonderful woman and he knew he was lucky to have her. He hadn't meant to raise his voice at her.

For a full ten minutes Glenn was tempted to wake Maggie and tell her he would answer any questions she had. Maggie was right. She did deserve to know and it was only his pride that prevented him from explaining everything. But she was asleep by then and he decided to see how things went in the morning. If Maggie was still troubled, then he'd do as she had asked. But deep down, Glenn hoped that Maggie would put the subject out of her mind so they could go on with their lives.

Maggie lay stiffly on her side of the bed, unable to sleep. That stupid comment about having a headache had been just that—stupid. Now she longed for the comfort of Glenn's body and the warmth of his embrace. He had hurt her, and refusing to make love had been her way of getting back. Now it seemed unbelievably childish, especially when she had never needed him more. Her heart felt as if a block of concrete were weighing it down.

The pain of his refusal had faded, and now she experienced a surge of genuine anger. She was his wife and yet he withheld from her an important aspect of his life. Glenn was denying her his trust. Their marriage was only a thin shell of what it was meant to be. If Glenn wouldn't tell her about his relationship with Angie, then he left her no option. Maggie decided she would find Angie and ask her what had happened. From the pieces of information she'd gathered, locating the other woman wouldn't be difficult.

In the long, sleepless hours of the night, Maggie mentally debated the pros and cons of such an action. What she might discover could ruin her marriage and her life. Yet what she didn't know was, in essence, doing the same thing. The thought of Glenn making love with the other woman caused such an intense physical pain that it felt as if something were cutting into her heart. Unable to bear the agony, she tried to blot the picture from her mind, but no matter how she tried, the fuzzy image stayed with her, taunting her.

By the early hours of the morning, Maggie had devised her plan. It worked with surprising ease.

Two days later Charlotte Lambert dropped Maggie off at the airport for a flight scheduled for San Francisco. As Glenn had agreed earlier, Maggie was going to fly ahead and take care of necessary business that awaited her. From the wistful look Glenn gave her that morning when she brought out her suitcases, she realized that he regretted having consented that she return before him. Some of the terrible tension between them had lessened in the two days before the flight. With Maggie's plan had come a release. Glenn wouldn't tell her what she wanted to know, but she'd soon learn on her own.

The Delta 747 left Charleston for San Francisco on time, but Maggie wasn't on the flight. Instead, she boarded a small commuter plane that was scheduled to land in Groves Point. The same afternoon she would take another commuter plane and connect with a flight to Atlanta. If everything went according to schedule, Maggie would arrive in California only three and a half hours later than her original flight.

Groves Point was a charming community. The man at the rental car agency gave her directions into town, and Maggie paused at the city park and looked at the statue of the Civil War heroes. She gazed at the drawn sword of the man standing beside the cannon and knew that if Glenn ever found out what she was doing then her fate would be as sure as the South's was to the North.

The man at the corner service station, wearing greasy coveralls and a friendly smile, gave her directions to Simon Canfield's home. Maggie drove onto the highway past the truck stop, as instructed. She would have missed the turnoff from the highway if she hadn't been watching for it. The tires kicked up gravel as the car wound its way along the curved driveway, and she slowed to a crawl, studying the long, rambling house. Somehow, having Angie live in an ordinary house was incongruous with the mental image Maggie had conjured up. Angie should live in a castle with knights fighting to protect and serve her.

A sleek black dog was alert and barking from the front step and Maggie hesitated before getting out of the car. She wasn't fond of angry dogs, but she'd come too far to be put off by a loud bark. Cautiously she opened the car door and stepped out, pressing her back against the side of the compact vehicle as she inched forward.

"Prince. Quiet." The dark-haired woman wearing a maternity top opened the back door and stepped onto the porch.

Instantly the dog went silent and Maggie's gaze riveted to the woman. Maggie stood, stunned. The photos hadn't done Angie's ethereal beauty justice. No woman had the right to look that radiant, lovely and serene. Angie was everything Glenn's silence had implied—and more. Her face glowed with her happiness, although she wasn't smiling now, but was regarding Maggie curiously. Maggie had been prepared to feel antagonistic toward her, and was shocked to realize that disliking the woman would be impossible.

"Can I help you?" Angie called from the top step, holding the dog by the collar.

All Maggie's energy went toward moving her head in a simple nod. Angie's voice was soft and lilting with an engaging Southern drawl.

"Bob phoned and said a woman had stopped in and asked directions to the house."

Apparently Bob was the man at the gas station. Putting on a plastic smile, Maggie took a step forward. "I'm Maggie Lambert."

"Are you related to Glenn?"

Again it was all Maggie could do to nod.

"I didn't know Glenn had any sisters."

Forcing herself to maintain an air of calm, Maggie met the gentle gaze of the woman whom Glenn had loved so fiercely. "He doesn't. I'm his wife."

If Angie was surprised she did an admirable job of not showing it. "Please, won't you come inside."

After traveling so far, devising the plan behind her husband's back and, worse, following through with it—Maggie stood cemented to the spot. After all that, without allowing anything to dissuade her from her idea, she was suddenly amazed at the audacity of her actions. Wild uncertainty, fear and unhappiness all collided into each other in her bemused mind until she was unable to move, struck by one thought: *it was wrong for her to have come here.*

"Maggie?" Angie moved down the steps with the dog loyally traipsing behind. "Are you all right?"

Maggie tasted bitter regret at the gentleness in Angie's eyes. No wonder Glenn loved her so much, she thought. This wasn't a mere woman. Maggie hadn't known what to expect, but it hadn't been this. Angie was the type of woman a man yearned to love and protect. More disturbing to Maggie was the innate knowledge that Angie's inner beauty far surpassed any outer loveliness. And she was gorgeous. Not in the way the fashion models portrayed beauty, with sleek bodies and gaudy cosmetics. Angie was soft and gentle and sweet—a madonna, meant to be cherished and loved. All of this flashed through Maggie's mind in the brief moment it took for Angie to reach her.

"Are you feeling ill?" Angie asked, placing a hand on Maggie's shoulder.

"I . . . I don't think so."

"Here," she said softly, leading her toward the house. "Come inside and I'll give you a glass of water. You look as if you're about to faint."

Maggie felt that a strong gust of wind would have blown her over. Mechanically, she allowed Angie to direct her through the back door and into the kitchen. Angie pulled out a chair at the table and Maggie sank into it, feeling more wretched than she had ever felt in her life. Tears were perilously close and she shut her eyes in an effort to forestall them. Maggie could hear Angie scurrying around for a glass of water.

She brought it to the table and sat across from Maggie. "Should I call the doctor? You're so pale."

"No, I . . . I'm fine. I apologize for putting you to all this trouble." Her wavering voice gained stability as she opened her dry eyes.

A few awkward seconds passed. "I'm pleased that Glenn married. He's a good man."

Maggie nodded. Everything she had wanted to say had been set in her mind, but all her well-thought-out questions had vanished.

"How long have you been married?" Angie broached the subject carefully.

"Five weeks." Holding the water glass gave Maggie something to do with her hands.

"Glenn must have told you about me?"

"No," Maggie took a sip of water. The cool liquid helped relieve the parched feeling in her throat. "He won't talk about you. He's married to me, but he's still in love with you."

A sad smile touched the expressive dark eyes as Angie straightened in the chair. "How well do you know Glenn?"

"We grew up together," Maggie responded somewhat defensively. "I...I thought I knew him, but I realized recently that I don't."

"Do you love him?" Angie asked, then offered Maggie a faint smile of apology. "Forgive me for even asking. You must. Otherwise you wouldn't be here."

"Yes, I love him." Words couldn't adequately express the depth of her emotion. "But that love is hurting me because I don't know how to help him forget you. He won't talk about what happened."

"Of course he wouldn't," Angie said with a sweet, melodic laugh. "His pride's at stake and as I recall, Glenn is a proud man."

"Very."

The dark eyes twinkled with encouragement. "First, let me assure you that Glenn isn't in love with me."

Maggie opened her mouth to contradict her, but Angie cut her off by sharply shaking her head.

"He isn't, not really," Angie continued. "Oh, he may think he is, but I sincerely doubt even that. For one thing, Glenn would never marry a woman without loving her. He holds his vows too sacred. He could have married me a hundred times after I first saw Simon again, but he wouldn't. Glenn was wise enough to recognize that if we did marry I would always wonder about Simon. Glenn's a gambler, and he gambled on my love. At the time I don't think I realized what it must have cost him to give me the freedom to choose between the two of them."

"You mean you would have married Glenn?"

"At the drop of a hat," Angie assured her. "Glenn Lambert was the best thing to come into my life for twelve years and I knew it. I cared deeply for him, too, but that wasn't good enough for Glenn. He wanted me to settle my past, and heal all the old wounds before we made a life together. It was Glenn who led me by the hand back to the most difficult days of my life. Glenn's love gave me back Simon and I'll always be grateful to him for that. Both Simon and I will. We realize how dearly it cost Glenn to step aside so I could marry Simon."

Maggie grimaced at Angie's affirmation of love for Glenn and briefly closed her eyes to the pain. So this was the sacrifice Angie had mentioned in the letter.

"Knowing this, Maggie, you couldn't possibly believe that Glenn would take his vows lightly."

She made it all sound so reasonable and sure, Maggie thought uncertainly. "But . . . but if he was so strongly convinced that you should settle your past, then why is he leaving his own open like a festering wound?"

"Pride." There wasn't even a trace of hesitation in Angie's voice. "I doubt that Glenn continues to have any deep feelings for me. What happened between us is a painful time in his life he'd prefer to forget. Be patient with him."

Maggie realized that she had rammed heads with Glenn's fierce male pride when she'd asked him to tell her about Angie. His indomitable spirit had been challenged, and admitting any part of his pain to her went against the grain of his personality. Logically, knowing Glenn, it made sense.

"Glenn deserves a woman who will give him all the love he craves," Angie continued. "I could never have loved him like that. But he's found what he needs in you. Be good to him, Maggie, he needs you."

They talked nonstop for two hours, sometimes laughing, other times crying. Angie told Maggie of her own love story with Simon and their hopes and dreams for the child she carried. When it came time for Maggie to leave, Angie followed her to the airport and hugged her before she boarded her flight.

"You're a special lady, Maggie Lambert," Angie stated with conviction. "I'm confident Glenn realizes that. If he doesn't, then he's not the same man I remember."

Impulsively Maggie hugged Angie back. "I'll write once we've settled. Let me know when you have the baby."

"I will. Take care now, you hear?"

"Thank you, Angie, thank you so much. For everything."

Maggie's throat filled with emotion. There were so many things she wanted to say. Glenn had given Angie her Simon, and in return Maggie now had Glenn. She could leave now and there would no longer be any doubts to plague her. Angie would always be someone special in Glenn's life, and Maggie wouldn't begrudge him that. She would leave him with his memories intact, and never mention her name. Angie was no longer a threat to their happiness. Maggie understood the past and was content to leave it undisturbed.

The flight from Groves Point to Atlanta and the connection from Atlanta to San Francisco went surprisingly well. Although before Maggie would have worried that each mile took her farther from Glenn, she didn't view the trip in those terms anymore. She was in love with her husband and the minute she touched down in San Francisco she planned to let him know that.

A smile beamed from her contented face when she landed in the city of her birth. She took a taxi directly to the beach house, set her bags in the entryway and headed for the kitchen and the phone. She had to talk to Glenn; she burned with the need to tell him of her love. In some ways she was concerned. There was a better time and place, but she couldn't wait a second more.

His phone rang and she glanced at the clock. With the time difference between the East and the West Coast it was well after midnight in Charleston. Discouraged, she fingered the opening of her silk blouse, wondering if she should hang it up and wait until morning.

Glenn answered on the second ring. "Maggie?" The anger in his voice was like a bucket of cold water dumped over her head, sobering her instantly. Somehow, he had found out that she'd gone to Groves Point and talked to Angie.

"Yes," she returned meekly.

"Where the hell have you been? I've been half out of my mind worrying about you. Your flight landed four hours ago. Why did you have to wait so long to call me? You must have known I was waiting to hear from you." The anger in his voice had lessened, diluted with relief from his worries.

Maggie sagged with relief onto the bar stool positioned by the phone. He didn't know. "To be honest, I wasn't sure if you wanted me to phone or not."

"Not phone?" He sounded shocked. "All I can say is that it's a damn good thing you did." His voice grew loud and slightly husky. "It's like a tomb around here without you."

Maggie tried to suppress the happiness that made her want to laugh. *He missed her.* He was miserable without her and she hadn't even been away twenty-four hours.

"Whose idea was it for you to leave early anyway?"

"Mine," she admitted ruefully. "But who agreed, and said I should?"

"A fool, that's who. Believe me, it won't happen again. We belong together, Maggie." He made the concession willingly.

From the moment she had left that morning, he'd been filled with regrets. He should never have let her go, he had realized. He'd tried phoning an hour after her plane touched ground in California. At first it didn't bother him that she wasn't home. There were any number of things that could take up her time. She's probably gone to Denny's, he had assured himself earlier. Later, when he hadn't been able to get hold of her, Glenn assumed she had unplugged the phone and taken a nap. After a time his worry had grown to alarm, and from alarm to near panic. If she hadn't called him when she did—he hadn't been teasing—he would well have gone crazy. His feelings were unreasonable, Glenn knew that. His reaction was probably part of his lingering fear that he'd lose Maggie, he rationalized. But there was no denying it: the past few hours had been miserable.

Glenn said they belonged together with such meaning that it took a moment before Maggie could speak. "Glenn," she finally whispered, surprised at how low her voice dropped. "There's something you should know, something I should have told you long before now."

"Yes?" His voice didn't sound any more confident than her own.

"I love you, Glenn. I don't know when it happened, I can't put a time to it. But it's true. It probably embarrasses you to have me tell you like this, there are better times and places—"

"Maggie." He interrupted her with a gentle laugh. "You don't need to tell me that, I already know."

"You know?" All these weeks she'd kept her emotions bottled up inside, afraid to reveal how she felt—and he'd known!

"Maggie, it was all too obvious. You're an artist, remember? You don't do a good job of hiding your emotions."

"I see." She swallowed down the bitter disappointment. Although eager to tell him of her feelings, she had wondered how he'd react. In her mind she had pictured a wildly romantic scene in which he'd tenderly admit his own feelings. Instead, Glenn acted as if she were discussing the weather.

"Well, listen, it's late here, I think I'll go to bed." She tried to make her voice light and airy, but a soft sob escaped and she bit into her lower lip to hold back another.

"Maggie, what's wrong?"

"Nothing. I'll talk to you tomorrow. Maybe. There's lots to do and—"

"Damn it, Maggie, you're crying. You never cry. I want to know why. What did I say?"

The insensitive boor, she silently fumed, if he couldn't figure it out, she wasn't going to tell him. "Nothing," she choked out in reply. "It doesn't matter. Okay?"

"No, it's not all right. Tell me what's wrong."

Maggie pretended she didn't hear. "I'll phone tomorrow night."

"Damn it, Maggie," he shouted. "Either you tell me what's wrong or I'm going to become violent."

"Nothing's wrong." Her heart was breaking. She'd just told her husband she loved him for the first time, and he'd practically yawned in her face.

"Listen, we're both tired. I'll talk to you tomorrow," she finished. Before he could argue, she gently replaced the receiver. The phone rang again almost immediately and Maggie simply unplugged it, refusing to talk to Glenn again that night. For a full five minutes she didn't move. She had left Atlanta with such high expectations, confident that she could create a wonderful life with Glenn. There was enough love in her heart to build any bridge necessary in their marriage. A half hour after landing in San Francisco, she was miserable and in tears. So much for banishing her insecurities.

Maggie slept late, waking around eleven the next morning. She felt restless and desolate. Early that afternoon, she forced herself to dress and deal with her mail. By evening her desk was cleared and she phoned Denny. She was half-tempted to paint, but realized it would be useless with her mind in turmoil. Glenn would be furious with her for disconnecting the phone, and she had yet to deal with him. He might not have appreciated her actions, but it was better than saying things she was sure to regret later.

By early evening she had worked up her courage enough to dial his number. When he didn't answer she wasn't concerned. He was probably at the health club, she thought. An hour later she tried phoning again. By ten, Pacific Coast time, she was feeling discouraged. Where was he? She toyed with the idea of phoning his family and casually inquiring, but she didn't want to alarm them.

A noise in the front of the house alerted her to the fact that someone was at the door. She left her office and was halfway into the living room when she discovered Glenn standing in the entryway, setting his suitcases on the floor.

He straightened just in time to see her. Time went still as he covered the short space between them and reached for her, crushing her in his arms. "You crazy fool. If you'd given me half a chance I would have told you how much I love you."

"You love me?"

"Oh God, yes," he whispered into her hair.

With a smothered moan of delight, Maggie twined her arms around his neck and was lifted off the floor as his mouth came down hungrily on hers.

Chapter Ten

Why didn't you say something earlier?" Maggie cried and covered Glenn's face with eager kisses, locking her arms around his neck.

"Why didn't you?" She was lifted half off the ground so that their gazes were level, his arms wrapped around her waist.

Maggie could hardly believe he was with her and stared at him in silent wonder, still afraid it could all be part of some fanciful dream. She couldn't very well admit that it had been her conversation with Angie that had convinced her that Glenn needed to know what was in her heart. The time had come to quit playing games with each other. The shock had come when he'd already known how she felt. Well, what did she expect? She'd never been good at disguising things and something as important as love shouldn't be concealed.

"I take it you're pleased to see me?"

Happiness sparkled from her eyes as she raised her hands and lovingly traced the handsome contours of his face. "Very."

His hold on her tightened. He hadn't slept in thirty hours. The first ten of those hours had been spent in abject frustration. He had tried countless times to get her to answer the phone until he realized she must have unplugged it. In the beginning he hadn't understood why she had resorted to tears. He relived every word of their conversation and as far as he could see she was behaving like a lunatic. She had told him she loved him and immediately shocked him by crying. Maggie wasn't a crier. Several times in the first weeks of their marriage he would have expected a lot more than tears and outrage from her. God knew he'd given her enough reason. But Maggie had proudly held up her head and met each challenge head-on, not relinquishing a whit of her pride. Yet she had been reduced to tears when she so dramatically confessed her love— something he'd known for weeks. For heaven's sake, he had thought, he couldn't help but be aware that Maggie loved him.

With startling clarity it had come to him in the early-morning hours. Maggie had expected him to declare his own love. What an idiot he'd been. Of course he loved her. He didn't know why she could ever question it. He had realized he felt something profound for Maggie the minute she had walked down the aisle at Steve and Janelle's wedding. She'd been vulnerable, proud and so lovely that Glenn went weak with the memory. He had originally assumed that his friends' wedding followed the lowest point of his life, but one look at Maggie and he'd nearly been blown over. She had lived next door to him for most of his life and he'd blithely gone on his way not recognizing what was before his own eyes. Love her? He loved her so much a lifetime together wouldn't be enough time to show her.

Maggie shared his name and his devotion and, God willing, later she would bear his children. How could she possibly think he didn't love her? Just as amazing was the knowledge that he'd never told her. Glenn was astonished at his own stupidity. He would phone her as soon as she would talk to him, he had decided, and never again in her life would he give her reason to doubt.

In theory, Glenn had felt, his plan sounded reasonable, but as the hours fled, and a rosy dawn dappled the horizon, he began to worry. In her frame of mind, Maggie might consider doing something stupid.

The first thing the following morning, Glenn decided not to jeopardize this marriage more than he had already. He would fly to Maggie on the first plane he could catch. When he tried phoning several times, and there wasn't any answer, he fretted all the more. For caring as much as he did he'd done one hell of a job messing things up.

Now that he was looking at her face flushed with a brilliant happiness, Glenn realized that he had done the right thing.

"Do you have to go back?"

"I probably should, but I won't." Her smile was back, he noticed. Lord, he loved that smile. "I don't deserve you, Maggie."

"I know."

Tipping back her head, she laughed and his heart was warmed by the sound. Maggie made his heart sing. Being around her was like lying in the sun on a glorious day and soaking up energy. She was all warmth and vitality, both springtime and Christmas, and he couldn't imagine his life without her. Twisting her around in his embrace, he supported her with an arm under her legs and carried her down the long hall that led to the master bedroom.

"My dear Mr. Lambert, just where are you taking me?"

"Can't you guess?"

"Oh, yes," she said and her lips brushed his, enjoying the instant reaction she felt from his body when her tongue made lazy, wet circles outlining his mouth.

"Maggie," he groaned. "You're going to pay for that."

"Good, I'm looking forward to it. Very forward."

She couldn't undress fast enough. When Maggie's fingers fumbled with the buttons of her blouse in her eagerness, Glenn stopped her, placing her hand aside. Slowly, provocatively, he unfastened each one. As the new area of her skin was exposed, Glenn's finger lovingly trailed the perfection until he finally slipped the smooth material of her blouse from her shoulders and down her arms, letting it fall to the carpet. With equal patience, he released the clasp that held her bra. When her breasts sprang free from the confining lace, he felt his loins tighten. For a long moment he did nothing but drink in the sight before him. Gently, he cupped each breast in the palm of his hand as if weighing it. The nipples hardened with the lightest flick of his thumb. He continued to make slow, tantalizing circles until her rosy buds peaked and strained against his finger.

Maggie felt an exhilarating sense of power at the awe reflected in her husband's eyes. Her breasts yearned for the gentle touch of his lips, but she stood proud and silent, knowing Glenn would give her what she wanted and more. Impatience played no role in their lovemaking. Glenn had taught her the importance of self-control. The excruciating wait seemed only to enhance their pleasure; the disciplined pauses served to heighten their eagerness. Maggie was a willing pupil.

As if he couldn't deny himself a second longer, Glenn wrapped her in his arms and in one sweeping motion buried his mouth over hers.

What had begun with impatient eagerness slowed to a breathless anticipation. When they moved, it was with one accord. They broke apart and finished undressing, then lay together on the thick, soft quilt. Glenn gathered her in his arms and kissed her, exploring her body an inch at a time with a husband's familiarity.

Then slowly, so slowly that they both found they were holding their breaths, they joined, and began to move. Maggie looked up at this man she loved more than life itself and slid her arms around his bare back.

"I love you," she whispered, arching upward to receive him again and again in the rhythmic ebb and flow of their lovemaking. "Please love me," she cried, surprised to hear her own voice.

"I do," Glenn breathed. "Always."

A searing, breath-stealing fire swept through her until she wanted to cry out with the joy of it.

With one final, gigantic thrust he buried himself deep within her and wrapping his arms around her, he went still.

Blissfully content, Maggie spread eager kisses over his face. Briefly she wondered if this exhilaration, this heartfelt elation would always stay with them. She wondered if twenty years from now she would still experience a thrill when Glenn made love to her. Somehow, Maggie doubted that this aspect of their marriage would ever change.

Glenn shifted positions so that Maggie was lovingly cradled in his arms and his fingers lightly stroked the length of her arm. Her fingers played at his chest, curling the fine dark hairs that were abundant there. A feeling of overpowering tenderness rocked him. He reveled in the emotion of loving and being loved, and knew what they shared would last forever. He was tired, more than tired—exhausted. He looked down and discovered Maggie asleep in his arms. Everything was going to work out, he thought sleepily. He wasn't going to lose her.... Slowly, his eyes drifted closed.... Maggie was his.

The following morning Maggie woke and studied her husband as he slept. A trace of a smile curved his mouth and her heart thrilled with the knowledge that she had placed it there. He must have been worried, terribly worried, she thought, to have dropped everything and flown to her. Surely, he couldn't believe that she'd ever leave him. A woman didn't love as strongly as she did and surrender without a fierce battle. Glenn's arrival had proved that Angie was right.... Glenn took his vows far too seriously to have married her or anyone when he was in love with another woman. Maggie didn't know what Glenn felt for the other woman anymore, but it wasn't love. Utterly content, Maggie silently slipped from the bed and dressed, eager for the new day.

Glenn woke with a smile as Maggie's sweet lips brushed his in a feather-light kiss. "Morning," he whispered, reaching up to wrap his arms around her waist.

"Morning," she returned brightly. "I wondered how long it'd take for you to join the living."

Glenn eased upright, using his elbow for support. "What time is it?"

"Noon."

"Noon!" he cried, rubbing the sleep from his face as he came fully upright. "Good grief, why didn't you wake me?"

Giggling, Maggie sat on the edge of the mattress and looped her arms around his strong neck. "I just did."

"You've been painting," he said, noticing that Maggie was in her smock.

"It felt good to get back to it. Charleston was wonderful, but it's great to be home and back into my regular schedule."

A light knock against the bedroom door attracted Maggie's attention. "Phone for you, Maggie," Rosa, the older Hispanic woman who was Maggie's housekeeper, announced from the other side. "It's your brother."

"Tell him I'll be right there," Maggie said, and planted a tender kiss on Glenn's forehead. "Unfortunately, duty calls."

"Maggie." Glenn's hand reached for her wrist, stopping her. His eyes were questioning her as though he didn't like the idea of releasing her even to her own brother. "Never mind."

"I shouldn't be more than a few minutes. Do you want to wait for me here?"

He shook his head, already tossing aside the blankets as he climbed from the bed. "I'll be out by the time you've finished."

True to his word, Glenn was leaning his hip against the kitchen counter, sipping coffee from a mug and chatting easily to Rosa when Maggie reappeared.

"I see that you two have introduced yourselves," Maggie said, sliding her arms around Glenn's waist.

"*Sí,*" Rosa said with a nod, her dark eyes gleaming. "You marry good man. You have lots of healthy *muchachos.*"

Maggie agreed with a broad grin, turning her eyes to her husband. "Rosa is going to teach me to cook, isn't that right?"

"*Sí.* Every wife needs to know how to make her man happy," Rosa insisted as she went about cleaning the kitchen. "I teach Maggie everything about cooking."

"Not quite everything," Glenn whispered near Maggie's ear, mussing the tiny curls that grew at her temple. "In fact you wouldn't even need to go near a kitchen to keep me happy."

"Glenn," she whispered, hiding a giggle. "Quiet, or Rosa will wonder."

"Let her." His hold tightened as the housekeeper proceeded to chatter happily in a mixture of Spanish and English, scrubbing down already spotless counters as she spoke.

The lazy November day was marvelous. They took a dip in the heated pool and splashed and dunked each other like feisty teenagers at a beach party. Later, as they dried out in the sauna, Glenn carefully broached the subject of Maggie's brother.

"Was that Denny this morning?"

"Yes. He and Linda have invited us to Thanksgiving dinner. I didn't think you'd mind if I accepted."

"That'll be fine. How is Denny?"

Maggie wiped a thick layer of perspiration from her cheeks using both hands, biding time while she formed her thoughts. "Fine. What makes you ask?"

"He seems to call you often enough. Didn't you get a couple of calls from him when we were in Charleston?"

"Yes. He's been through some rough times lately."

"How rough?"

Wrapping the towel around her neck, Maggie stood and paced the small enclosure while the heavy heat pounded in around her. "As you probably know, Denny and my parents inherited a portion of Great-aunt Margaret's money. Denny made some bad investment choices."

"What happened?" As a stockbroker, Glenn felt his curiosity piqued.

"It's a long, involved story not worth repeating. Simply put, Denny invested heavily in what he felt were safe public works bonds that went defunct. Everything's being decided in the courts now, but it looks like he'll only get a dime back on every dollar invested."

"So you're bailing him out a thousand at a time." The statement was loaded with censure.

Maggie had to bite her tongue to keep from lashing out at Glenn for being so insensitive. He should know that litigation and lawyers are damned expensive, she thought self-righteously. She was only doing what any sister would do in similar circumstances. "Listen, what's between my brother and me is private. You don't want to talk about certain things in your life, and I don't, either. We're both entitled to that."

"Don't you think you're being overly defensive?"

Maggie looked at him sharply. "So what? Denny's my brother. I'll give him money any time I please."

Glenn was taken back by her bluntness. "Fine." He wouldn't bring up the subject again . . . at least not for a while.

Thanksgiving arrived and Maggie's parents flew out from Florida. The elder Kingsburys had reacted with the same pleased surprise as Glenn's family had when Maggie phoned to announce that she and Glenn had married. The gathering at Denny and Linda's was a spirited but happy one. Neither of Maggie's parents mentioned how brief her and Glenn's courtship had been, nor that they were shocked at the suddenness of the ceremony. The questions were in their eyes, but Maggie was so radiantly happy that no one voiced any doubts.

The traditional turkey was placed in the oven to be ready to serve at the end of the San Francisco 49'ers football game. They ate until they were stuffed, played cards, ate again and watched an old movie on television until Maggie yawned and Glenn suggested they head home. The day had been wonderful and Maggie looked forward to Christmas for the first time since moving to the beach house.

Glenn's days were filled. He started work at Lindsey & McNaught Brokerage the Monday after his arrival in San Francisco, and continued to work long hours to build up his clientele. More often than not, it was well past seven before he arrived home. Maggie didn't mind the hours Glenn put in away from home. She understood his need to secure his position with the company branch. The competition was stiff and as a new boy on the block, the odds were against him.

"How are things going at the office?" she asked him one evening the first week of December.

"Fine," he responded absently as he sorted through the mail. "How about a game of tennis? I need to work out some of my frustrations."

"Everything's fine at the office, but you want to use me as a whipping boy?" she joked lovingly.

Glenn raised his gaze to hers and met the teasing glimmer mingled with truth in her eyes.

"Are you sorry we're here?" she asked on a tentative note. In Charleston, Glenn had held more than forty million dollars in assets for his firm, a figure that was impressive enough for him to have quickly worked his way into a managerial position. In San Francisco, he was struggling to get his name out and establish himself with a new set of clients. From the hours he was putting in during the day and several long evenings, the task must be a formidable one.

"No," he said gently. "Where you and I are concerned, I have no regrets. Now," he added, releasing a slow breath, "are we going to play tennis or stand here and chat?"

Just as he finished speaking the telephone rang. "Saved by the bell," Maggie mumbled as she moved across the room to answer it. "Hello."

"Hi, Maggie," Denny said in the low, almost whiny voice she had come to know well.

"Hi. What's up?" She didn't want to encourage Denny to drag out the conversation when Glenn was in the room. Denny was a subject they avoided. She knew her husband disapproved of her handing over large sums of money to Denny, but she didn't know what else she could do—Denny needed her. The money wasn't doing her any good, and if she could help her only brother, then why not?

The argument was one Maggie had waged with herself countless times. As long as she was available to lean upon, the opposing argument went, then Denny would be content to do exactly that. He hadn't accomplished anything worthwhile in months. From conversations with her sister-in-law, Linda, Maggie had learned that Denny did little except decry his misfortune and plot ways of regaining his loses. Yet Maggie could understand his circumstances well enough to realize he was in an impossible position. He didn't like it, she didn't like it, but there was nothing that either of them could do until the court case was settled.

"I just wanted you to know that I'll be meeting with the lawyers tomorrow afternoon."

"Good luck," she murmured.

A silence followed. "What's the matter? Can't you talk now?"

"That about sizes up the situation." Glenn was studying her and Maggie realized her stalling tactics weren't fooling him. He knew exactly whom she was talking to and did nothing to make the conversation any easier by leaving the room.

"Maybe I should phone you tomorrow," Denny suggested.

"That would be better." Maggie forced a carefree note into her tone. "I'll talk to you tomorrow then."

"Okay." Denny sounded disappointed, but there wasn't anything Maggie could do. She wanted to avoid another confrontation with Glenn regarding Denny.

Replacing the receiver, she met her husband's gaze. "You said something about tennis?" Her voice was remarkably steady for all the turmoil going on inside her.

"You're not helping him any, you know," Glenn said calmly.

It was on the tip of her tongue to tell him that she was aware of that. She had seen it all herself, but she was caught in a vicious trap where Denny was concerned. "He needs me," she countered defensively.

"He needs a job and some self-worth."

"I thought you were a stockbroker, not a psychologist."

Maggie could tell by the tightness in his jaw that she had angered Glenn. "Look, I'm sorry, I didn't mean to snap at you. Denny's in trouble. I can't let him down when he needs me the most. If you recall, I did ask you to stay out of it."

"Have it your way," he mumbled and handed her a tennis racket.

Their game wasn't much of a contest. Glenn overpowered her easily in straight sets, making her work harder than ever. Maggie didn't know if he was venting his frustrations from the office or if he was angry because of Denny. It didn't matter; she was exhausted. By the time he had finished showering, she was in bed half-asleep. Glenn's pulling the covers over her shoulders and gently kissing the top of her head were the last things Maggie remembered.

With the approach of the Christmas holidays, Maggie felt a renewed sense of rightness. She was in love with her husband, they were together and her world seemed in perfect balance. Glenn worked hard and so did she, spending hours in her studio doing what she enjoyed most—painting. With her marriage, Maggie had discovered that there was a new depth to her art. She had once told Glenn that color was mood and brushwork emotion. Now with Glenn's love, her brush painted bold strokes that revealed a maturity in her scenes that had been missing before their wedding. She was happy, truly happy, and it showed in ways she'd never expected.

Maggie didn't mention Glenn's grandmother's antique ring, confident that he'd gift her with it on Christmas morning. And she would react with the proper amount of surprised pleasure.

She wore her wedding ring continually now, even when she worked. Glenn glanced at her hand occasionally to be sure it was there. It was an odd quirk of his, but she didn't really mind. The ring meant as much to her as their marriage vows and that was all he wanted. They had come a long way from the night she'd arrived in Charleston.

For their first Christmas, Maggie wanted to buy Glenn a special gift, something that would show the depth of her love and appreciation for the good life they shared. But what? For days she mulled over the problem. She could give him one of her paintings for his office, but he had already asked her for one. She couldn't refuse him by telling him that that was what she planned to give him for Christmas. He took one of her seascapes and she was left without an idea. And she so wanted their first Christmas together to be special.

For the first time in years Maggie went Christmas shopping in stores. Usually she ordered through the mail or by the telephone, but she feared missing the perfect gift that would please Glenn most. In the beginning, she was apprehensive that someone would recognize her. No one did and her confidence rose. Janelle joined her one day, surprised at the changes in Maggie.

"What changes?"

"You're so happy," Janelle claimed.

"I really am, you know."

"I can tell. You positively glow with it."

The remark pleased Maggie so much that she repeated it for Glenn later that evening.

"So you were out Christmas shopping. Did you buy me anything?"

How she wished. Nothing seemed special enough. She had viewed a hundred jewelry display cases, visited the most elite men's stores and even gone to obscure bookstores, seeking rare volumes of Glenn's favorite novels. A sense of panic was beginning to fill her.

"You'll have to wait until Christmas morning to find out," she told him, coyly batting her long lashes.

With so many relatives on their list, Glenn and Maggie were in and out of more department stores the following Saturday than Maggie cared to count. Soft music filled the stores and bells chimed on the street corners, reminding them to be generous to those less fortunate. The crowds were heavy, but everyone seemed to expect that and took the long waits at the cash registers in stride.

While Maggie stood in line buying a toy farm set for Glenn's nephew, Glenn wandered over to the furniture department. Lovingly, Maggie's gaze followed him as he looked over cherrywood bookcases in a rich, deep-red color. Bookcases? Glenn wanted something as simple as bookcases? Maggie couldn't believe it. After days of looking at the latest gadgets and solid-gold toys, she stared in utter disbelief that he could be interested in something as simple as this. When the salesman approached, Glenn asked several questions and ran his hand over the polished surface.

"Did you see something?" she asked conversationally when he returned to her side. He wanted those bookcases, but she doubted that he'd mention it to her.

"Not really," he replied, but Maggie noted the way his gaze returned and lingered over the cases.

Maggie's heartbeat raced with excitement. At the first opportunity she'd return and buy Glenn those bookcases.

"You're looking pleased about something," Glenn commented over dinner Wednesday evening.

His comment caught her off guard and she lightly shook her head. "Sorry, I was deep in thought. What did you say?"

"I could tell," he said with a chuckle. Standing, he carried his clean plate to the sink. "Do you want to talk about it, or is this some deep dark secret you're hiding from your husband?"

"Some deep dark secret."

"What did you do today?" he asked, appreciating anew how beautiful his wife had become. She was a different woman from the frightened one who'd met him at the airport months ago.

"What did I do today?" Maggie repeated, her dark eyes rounding with shock. Swallowing back her unease, she cast her gaze to her plate. "Christmas cards." The truth nearly stuck in her throat. She had written Christmas cards, but in addition she had penned a long letter to Angie, thanking her for everything she had shared the day of their brief visit. In the letter, Maggie told Angie how improved her marriage was now that she'd told Glenn how much she loved him, and was confident that he loved her in return.

As impractical as it sounded, Maggie would have liked to continue the friendship with Angie. Rarely had Maggie experienced such an immediate kinship with another woman. Impractical and illogical. Of all the people in the world, Maggie would have thought she'd despise Angie Canfield. But she didn't. Now, weeks later, Maggie felt the need to write the other woman and extend her appreciation for their afternoon together and to wish her and Simon the warmest of holiday greetings. The letter had been interrupted by Glenn's homecoming and she had safely tucked it away from the other cards she kept on top of her desk.

"I still have several things that need to be done before Christmas," she said quickly to hide her discomfort.

Glenn was silent for a moment. "You look guilty about something. I bet you went out shopping today and couldn't resist buying yourself something."

"I didn't!" she declared with a cheery laugh.

Later, in the den, when Glenn was looking over some figures, Maggie joined him. She sat in the chair opposite his desk. When Maggie glanced up she found her husband regarding her lazily with a masked expression, and she wondered at his thoughts.

On the other side of the desk, Glenn studied his wife, thinking that she was more beautiful that night than he ever remembered. Her eyes shone with a translucent happiness and a familiar sensation tugged at his heart. Something was troubling her to-night...no, troubling was too strong a word. She was hiding something from him. Which was natural, he supposed. It was Christmastime and she had probably cooked up some scheme for his gift, yet Glenn had the feeling this had nothing to do with the holiday season.

Convinced he shouldn't go looking for trouble, he shook his mind free of the brooding sensation. Whatever it was probably involved Denny, and it was just as well that he didn't know. It would only anger him.

Glenn pushed back his chair and stood. "I'll be right back. I'm going to need a cup of coffee to keep these figures straight. Do you want one?"

Maggie glanced up from the book she was reading and shook her head. The caffeine would keep her awake. "No, thanks," she said as he left the room.

The phone rang and Glenn called out that he'd answer it. The information didn't faze Maggie until she realized that he had probably gone into her office since the phone was closer there.

He returned a minute later, strolling into the room with deceptive casualness. "It's your leeching brother," he told her.

Chapter Eleven

Glenn, what a nasty thing to say.'' Maggie couldn't help knowing that Glenn disapproved of the way she gave Denny money, but she hadn't expected him to be so blunt or openly rude. "I hope Denny didn't hear you," she murmured, coming to her feet. "He feels terrible about the way things have turned out.''

"If he honestly felt that, he wouldn't continue to come running to you at every opportunity.''

Straightening her shoulders to a military stiffness, Maggie marched from the room and picked up the telephone. "Hello, Denny.''

A short silence followed. "Hi. I take it I should call back another time.''

"No," she contradicted firmly. She wasn't going to let Glenn intimidate her out of speaking to her own brother. "I can talk now.''

"I just wanted to tell you that my lawyer didn't have anything new to tell me regarding our case. It looks like this thing could be tied up in the courts for years. I'm telling you, Maggie, this whole mess is really getting me down. Who could have guessed that a state would default on public works bonds?"

"No one," she offered sympathetically. "But you don't need to worry, I'm here to help you."

"But Glenn..."

"What I do with my money is none of his concern." In her heart Maggie knew that Glenn was right, but Glenn was a naturally strong person, and her brother wasn't to be blamed if he was weak. They had to make allowances for Denny, help him.

"You honestly mean that about helping, don't you?" Denny murmured, relief and appreciation brightening his voice.

"You know I do."

Ten minutes later Maggie rejoined her husband. Myriad emotions were coming at her. She was angry with Glenn for being so unsympathetic to her brother's troubles, infuriated with Denny because he pushed all the right buttons with her, and filled with self-derision because she gave in to Denny without so much as a thoughtful pause. Denny had only to give his now familiar whine and she handed him a signed check.

"Well?" Glenn glanced up at her.

"Well what?"

"He asked for money, didn't he?"

"Yes," she snapped.

"And you're giving it to him?"

"I don't have much choice. Denny is my brother."

"But you're not helping him, Maggie, don't you honestly see that?"

"No," she cried, and to her horror tears welled in the dark depths of her eyes, spilled onto her thick lashes and wove a wet path down her pale cheeks. It was so unlike her to cry over something so trivial that Maggie had trouble finding her breath, which caused her to weep all the louder.

Glenn stood and gently pulled her into his arms. "Maggie, what is it?"

"You...Denny...me," she sobbed and dramatically shook her hands. "This court case might take years to decide. He needs money. You don't want me to lend him any, and I'm caught right in the middle."

"Honey, listen." Glenn stood and gently placed his arms around her. "Will you do something for me?"

"Of course," she responded on a hiccupping sob. "What?"

"Call Denny back and tell him he can't have the money...."

"I can't do that," she objected, shaking his arms free. She hugged her waist and moved into the living room where a small blaze burned in the fireplace. The warmth of the fire chased the chill from her arms.

"Hear me out," Glenn said, following her. "Have Denny give me a call at the office in the morning. If he needs money, I'll loan it to him."

Maggie was skeptical. "But why...?"

"I don't want him troubling you anymore. I don't like what he's doing to you, and worse, what he's doing to himself." He paused, letting her assimilate his words. "Agreed?"

She offered him a watery smile and nodded.

With Glenn standing at her side, Maggie phoned Denny back and gave the phone over to her husband a few minutes later. Naturally, Denny didn't seem overly pleased with the prospect of having to go through Glenn, but he had no choice. Maggie should have been relieved that Glenn was handling the difficult situation, but she wasn't.

In the morning, Maggie woke feeling slightly sick to her stomach. She lay in bed long after Glenn had left for the office, wondering if she could be pregnant. The tears the evening before had been uncharacteristic and she'd had a terrible craving for Chinese food lately that was driving her crazy. For three days in a row she had eaten lunch in Chinatown. None of the symptoms on their own was enough for her to make the connection until this morning.

A smile formed as Maggie placed a hand on her flat stomach and slowly closed her eyes. A baby. Glenn would be so very pleased. He'd be a wonderful father. She'd watched him with Denny's girls on Thanksgiving and had been astonished at his patience and gentleness. A tear of happiness slid from between her closed eyelids. The ironic part was all these weeks she'd been frantically searching for just the right Christmas gift for Glenn, and all along she'd been nurturing his child in her womb. They both wanted children so much. Oh, she'd get him the bookcases he had admired, but she'd keep the gift he'd prize most a secret until Christmas morning.

Not wanting to be overconfident without a doctor's confirmation, Maggie made an appointment for that afternoon, and her condition was confirmed in a matter of minutes. Afterward she was bursting with excitement. Her greatest problem would be keeping it from Glenn when she wanted to sing and dance with the knowledge.

When Maggie returned to the beach house Rosa had left a message that Denny had phoned. Maggie returned his call immediately.

"How did everything go with Glenn?" she asked him brightly. Nothing would dim the brilliance of her good news, not even Denny's sullen voice.

"Fine, I guess."

"There isn't any problem with the money, is there?" Glenn wouldn't be so cruel to refuse to make the loan when he'd assured her he'd help her brother. Maggie was confident he wouldn't do anything like that. Glenn understood the situation.

"Yes and no."

Her hand tightened around the receiver. "How do you mean? He's giving you the money, isn't he?"

"He's lending me the money, but he's got a bunch of papers he wants me to sign and in addition he's set up a job interview for me. He actually wants me to go to work."

By the time Denny finished with his sorry tale, Maggie was so furious she could barely speak. Lending him the money—making him sign for it—a job interview. Glenn had told her he was going to help her brother. Instead he was stripping Denny of what little pride he had left.

By the time Glenn arrived home that evening, he found Maggie pacing the floor. Sparks of anger flashed from her dark eyes as she spun around to face him.

"What's wrong? You're looking at me like I was Jack the Ripper."

"Did you honestly tell Denny that he couldn't borrow the money unless he got a job?" she said in accusation. Her hands were placed defiantly on her hips, challenging Glenn to contradict her.

Unhurriedly, Glenn removed his raincoat one arm at a time and hung it in the hall closet. "Is there something wrong with an honest day's toil?"

"It's humiliating to Denny. He's... accustomed to a certain life-style now.... He can't lower himself to take a job like everyone else and..."

Maggie could tell by the way Glenn's eyes narrowed that he was struggling to maintain his own irritation. "I live in a fancy beach house with you and somehow manage to suffer the humiliation."

"Glenn," she cried. "It's different with Denny."

"How's that?"

Unable to remain still, Maggie continued to stalk the tiled entryway like a lion confined to a cage. "Don't you understand how degrading that would be to him?"

"No," Glenn returned starkly. "I can't. Denny made a mistake. Any fool knows better than to place the majority of his funds in one investment no matter how secure it appears. The time has come for your brother to own up to the fact he goofed, and pay the consequences of his actions. I can't and won't allow him to sponge off you any longer, Maggie."

The tears sprang readily to the surface. Lord, she hated to cry and speculated that she would probably be like this the entire pregnancy. "But don't you understand?" she blubbered, her words barely intelligible. "I inherited twice the money Denny did."

"And he's made you feel guilty about that."

"No," she shouted. "He's never said a word."

"He hasn't had to. You feel guilty enough about it, but love, trust me. Denny will feel better about you, about himself, about life in general. You can't give him the self-worth he needs by handing him a check every time he asks for it."

"You don't understand my brother," Maggie cried. "I can't let you do this to him. I...I told you once that I wanted you to stay out of this."

"Maggie—"

"No, you listen to me. I'm giving Denny the money he wants. I told him that he didn't need to sign anything, and he doesn't need to get a job. He's my brother and I'm not going to turn my back on him. Understand?"

Silence crackled in the room like the deadly calm before an electrical storm. A muscle leaped in Glenn's jaw, twisting convulsively.

"If that's the way you want it." His voice was both tight and angry.

"It is," she whispered.

What Maggie didn't want was the silent treatment that followed. Glenn barely spoke to her the remainder of the evening, and when he did his tone was hardly civil. It was clear that Glenn considered her actions a personal affront. Maybe it looked that way to him, she reasoned, but she'd explained long ago that she preferred to handle her brother herself. Glenn had interfered and now they were both miserable.

When morning arrived to lighten the dismal winter sky, Maggie rolled onto her back and stared at the ceiling, realizing she was alone. The oppressive gray light of those early hours invaded the bedroom and a heaviness settled onto Maggie's heart. She climbed from the bed and felt sick and dizzy once again, but her symptoms were more pronounced this morning. Her mouth felt like dry, scratchy cotton.

Glenn had already left for the office and the only evidence of his presence was an empty coffee cup in the kitchen sink. Even Rosa looked at Maggie accusingly and for one crazy instant Maggie wondered how the housekeeper knew that she and Glenn had argued. That was the crazy part—they hadn't really fought. Maybe if they had, the air would have been cleared.

The crossword puzzle didn't help occupy her mind and Maggie sat at the kitchen table for an hour, drinking cup after cup of watered-down apple juice while sorting through her thoughts. With a hand rubbing her throbbing temple, Maggie tried to recall how Glenn had been as a youth when he was angry with someone. She couldn't recall that he had ever held a grudge or been furious with anyone for long. That was a good sign.

Tonight she'd talk to him, she decided, try to make him understand why she had to do this for Denny. If the situation was reversed and it was either of his brothers, Glenn would do exactly the same thing. Maggie was sure of it.

Because of the Christmas holidays, the stock market was traditionally slow, and Glenn had been home before six every night for the past week. He wasn't that night. Nor was he home at seven, or eight. He must be unbelievably angry, she thought, and a part of Maggie wondered if he'd ever be able to completely understand her actions. Apparently, he found it easier to blame her than to realize that he'd forced her into the situation. Maggie spent a miserable hour watching a television program she normally disliked.

The front door clicked open and Maggie pivoted sharply in her chair, hoping Glenn's gaze would tell her that they'd talk and clear up the air between them.

Glenn shrugged off his coat and hung it in the hall closet. Without a word he moved into his den and closed the door, leaving Maggie standing alone and miserable.

Desolate, she sat in the darkened living room and waited. She hadn't eaten, couldn't sleep. Leaving the house was impossible, looking and feeling the way she did. Her only companion was constant self-recrimination and doubt. There wasn't anything she could do until Glenn was ready to talk.

When he reappeared, Maggie slowly came to her feet. Her throat felt thick and uncooperative. Her hands were clenched so tightly together that the blood flow to her fingers was restricted. "Would you like some dinner?" The question was inane when she wanted to tell him they were both being silly. Arguing over Denny was the last thing she wanted to do.

"I'm not hungry," he answered starkly without looking at her. His features tightened.

Undaunted, Maggie asked again. "Can we at least talk about this? I don't want to fight."

He ignored her and turned toward the hallway. "You said everything I needed to hear last night."

"Damn it, Glenn," she shouted after him. "What do you want from me? Are you so insensitive that you can't see what an intolerable situation you placed me in?"

"I asked you to trust me with Denny."

"You were stripping him of his pride."

"I was trying to give it back to him," he flared back. "And speaking of intolerable positions, do you realize that's exactly what you've done to me?"

"You . . . How . . . ?"

"You've asked me to sit by and turn a blind eye while your brother bleeds you half to death. I'm your husband. It's my duty to protect you, but I can't do that when you won't let me, when you resent, contradict and question my intention."

"Glenn, please," she pleaded softly. "I love you. I don't want to fight. Not over Denny—not over anything. It's Christmas, a time of peace and goodwill. Can't we place this behind us?"

Glenn looked as weary as she felt. "It's a matter of trust too, Maggie."

"It's not. I trust you completely."

"You don't," Glenn announced and turned away from her, which only served to fuel Maggie's anger.

Maggie slept in the guest bedroom that night, praying Glenn would insist she share his bed. She didn't know what she had thought sleeping apart would accomplish. It took everything within Maggie not to swallow her considerable pride and return to the master bedroom. A part of her was dying a slow and painful death.

Maggie couldn't understand why Glenn was behaving like he was. Only once had he even raised his voice to her in all the weeks they'd been married. But now the tension stretched between the two bedrooms was so thick Maggie could have sliced it with a dull knife. Glenn was so disillusioned with her that even talking to her was more than he could tolerate. He wasn't punishing her with the silent treatment, Maggie realized. He was protecting her. If he spoke it would be to vent his frustration and say things he'd later regret.

Instead of dwelling on the negative, Maggie recalled the wonderful love-filled nights when they had lain side by side and been unable to stay out of each other's arms. The instant the light was out, Glenn would reach for her with the urgency of a condemned man offered a last chance at life. And when he'd kissed her and loved her, Maggie felt as though she was the most precious being in the world. Glenn's world. He was a magnificent lover. She closed her eyes to the compelling images that crowded her mind, feeling sick at heart and thoroughly miserable.

In the other room Glenn lay on his back staring at the ceiling. The dark void of night surrounded him. The sharp edges of his anger had dulled, but the bitterness that had consumed him earlier had yet to fade. In all his life he had never been more disappointed and more hurt—yes, hurt, that his wife couldn't trust him to handle a delicate situation and protect her. He wasn't out to get Denny; he sincerely wanted to help the man.

Morning arrived and Maggie couldn't remember sleeping although she must have closed her eyes sometime during the long, tedious night. The alarm rang and she heard Glenn stirring in the other room.

While he dressed, Maggie moved into the kitchen and put on a pot of coffee. Ten minutes later, he joined her in the spacious room and hesitated, his gaze falling from her wide, sad eyes to the outline of her jutting breasts through the thin silk gown. Purposely he jerked his eyes away. There was no way around it. He had missed her last night. A hundred times he had had to stop himself from going into the bedroom and hauling her to his bed where she belonged. He wouldn't tolerate her trick another night.

Now she stood not three feet from him in a sexy gown and his senses were filled with her. He should be aware of the freshly brewed coffee, but he discovered the elusive perfumed scent of Maggie instead. Silently he poured himself a cup of coffee and pulled out a kitchen chair. He tried to concentrate on something other than his wife standing before him in a sheer nightgown. He reached for the newspaper and focused his attention on that. But mentally he was undressing her, kissing her, caressing her with his hands and mouth until his blood stirred so hotly that it took every ounce of his will not to crush her in his arms and make love to her right in their kitchen.

Sensing Glenn's thoughts, Maggie modestly tied her bathrobe closed. Sexual attraction wasn't her motive. She wanted to end their torment.

Propping up the newspaper against the napkin holder, Glenn hid behind the front page, not wanting to look at Maggie for fear she'd read his thoughts. Yet he couldn't keep his eyes from the bold outline of her lush body in her revealing outfit. Even now in his bitterness, her body had the power to stir his loins.

"Will you be home for dinner?" Maggie forced the question out. Leaning against the kitchen counter, her fingers bit into the tiled surface as she waited for his answer.

"I've been home for dinner every night since we've been married. Why should tonight be different?"

Maggie had only been trying to make idle conversation and break down the ice shield positioned between them. "No reason," she murmured and turned back to the stove.

A few minutes later Glenn left for the office with little more than a casual farewell.

By noon Maggie was convinced she couldn't spend another day locked inside the confines of the beach house. Even the studio that had been her pride now became her torture chamber. One more hour alone and she'd go stir-crazy.

Aimlessly, she wandered from room to room, seeking confirmation that she had done the right thing by Denny and finding none. She took a long, uninterrupted walk along the beach where gusts of ocean air carelessly whipped her hair across her face and lightened her mood perceptibly. Christmas was only a week away, and there were a hundred things she should be doing. But Maggie hadn't the heart for even one.

Recently she had been filled with such high expectations for this marriage. Now she realized how naive she'd been. She had always thought that love conquered all. What a farce that was. She had been unhappy before marrying Glenn; now she was in love, pregnant, and utterly miserable. And why? Because she'd stood by her brother when he needed her. It hardly seemed fair.

A light drizzle began to fall and she walked until her face felt numb with cold. She trekked up to the house, fixed herself something hot to drink and decided to go for a drive.

The ride into the city was sluggish due to heavy traffic. She parked on the outskirts of Fisherman's Wharf and took a stroll. A multitude of shops and touristy places had sprung up since her last visit—but that had been years ago, she realized. She dropped into a few places and shopped around, finding nothing to buy. An art gallery caught her eye and she paused to look in the window at the painting on display. A card tucked in the ornate frame revealed the name of the painting was *The Small Woman*. The artist had used a black line to outline the painting, like lead surrounding the panes in a stained-glass window. The colors were bold, the setting elaborate. The simple woman, however, was strangely frail and pathetic, detached from the setting as though she were a sacrifice to be offered to the gods in some primitive culture. Examining the painting, Maggie saw herself in the tired woman and didn't like the reflection.

A blast of chilling wind whipped her coat around her legs, and to escape the unexpected cold, Maggie opened the glass door and entered the gallery. The room was deceptively large, with a wide variety of oil paintings, some watercolors, small sculptures and other artworks in opulent display.

"Can I help you?"

Maggie turned toward the voice to find a tall, slender woman dressed in a plaid wool skirt and creamy white silk blouse. She appeared to be studying Maggie closely, causing Maggie to wonder at her appearance. The wind had played havoc with her hair and...

"Maggie?"

Maggie blinked twice. She didn't recognize the woman. "Pardon?"

"Are you Maggie Kingsbury?"

"Yes... my married name is Lambert. Do I know you?"

The woman's laugh was light and sweetly musical. "I'm Jan Baker Hammersmith. Don't you remember we attended..."

The name clicked instantly. "Jan Baker." The two had been casual friends when Maggie was attending art school. "I haven't seen you in years. The last I heard, you were married."

"I'm divorced now."

Maggie dropped her gaze, desperately afraid that she would be adding that identical phrase someday when meeting old friends. "I'm sorry to hear that."

"I am, too," Jan said with a heavy sadness. "But it was for the best. Tell me, are you still painting?" Maggie noted how Jan quickly diverted the subject from herself.

"Occasionally. Not as much since I married."

Jan strolled around the gallery with proud comfort. "I can still remember one of your paintings—a beach scene. The detail you'd put into it was marvelous. Whatever happened to that?"

"It's hanging in our living room."

"I can understand why you'd never want to sell that." Jan's eyes were sincere. "Rarely have I seen a painting with such vivid clarity and color."

"It would sell?" Maggie was surprised. Ridiculous as it seemed, she'd never tried to sell any of her paintings. There hadn't been any reason to try. She gave them away as gifts and to charities for auctions but she didn't have any reason to sell them. She didn't need the money and inwardly she feared people would buy them simply because of who she was. Her artwork was for her own pleasure. The scenes painted by her brush had been the panacea for an empty life within the gilded cage.

"It'd sell in a minute," Jan stated confidently. "Do you think you'd consider letting the gallery represent you?"

Maggie hedged, uncertain. "Let me think about it."

"Do, Maggie, and get back to me. I have a customer I know who'd be interested in a painting similar to the beachscape, if you have one. Take my card." They spoke for several minutes more and Maggie described some of her other works. Again Jan encouraged her to bring in a few of her canvases. Maggie noted that Jan didn't make any promises, which was reasonable.

Sometime later, Maggie returned to her car. Meeting Jan had been just the uplift she'd needed. Already her mind was buzzing with possibilities. There wasn't any reason she shouldn't sell her work. No one would recognize the name Maggie Lambert.

Glenn's car was in the driveway when she returned and she pulled to a stop in front of the house and parked there. A glance at her watch told her that it was later than she suspected. Her spirits were lighter than at any time during the past two days, but she didn't hurry toward the house.

"Where have you been?" Glenn demanded the minute she walked in the door. Not granting her the opportunity to respond, he continued. "You made an issue of asking me if I was going to be home for dinner and then you're gone."

Carelessly, Maggie tossed her coat over an armchair. "I lost track of the time," she explained on her way into the kitchen. Glenn was only a step behind. From the grim set of his mouth, Maggie recognized that once again she had irritated him. Everything she'd done the past few days seemed to fuel his indignation.

He didn't say another word as she worked, dishing up the meal of baked pork chops and scalloped potatoes Rosa had prepared for them. Maggie could feel his gaze on her defeated shoulders, studying her. He looked for a moment as if he wanted to say something, but apparently changed his mind.

"I was in an art gallery today," she told him conversationally.

"Oh."

"I'm thinking of taking in some of my work."

"You should, Maggie."

Silence followed. This was the first time they'd been civil to each other since she'd sided with her brother against him.

Their dinner was awkward, each trying to find a way to put their lives into focus. Glenn sat across from her, cheerless and somber. Neither ate much.

"Did the mail come?" Maggie asked, setting the dinner dishes aside.

"It's in your office," Glenn answered without looking up. "Would you like me to bring it in to you?"

"Please. I'll finish up here in a minute." Well, at least they were speaking to each other, she thought. It was a start. Together they'd work things out. The situation with Denny was probably the first of many disagreements and misunderstandings they would face through the years. It might take time, she told herself, but they'd work it out. They loved each other too much to allow anything to wedge a space between them for long. They had both behaved badly over this issue with Denny, but if she'd bend a little, Glenn would, too.

When Glenn returned to the living room, he said her name with such fervor that her head came up. He stalked into the room and stood over her, intimidating her. Unconsciously Maggie pressed farther back into the thick cushions of her chair, utterly stunned by the look that flashed from her husband's eyes. She could think of nothing that would cause him such anger.

"Explain this," he said and thrust her letter to Angie in front of Maggie's shocked face.

Chapter Twelve

Maggie's mind was in complete turmoil. She'd known it was a risk to write Angie, and later had regretted it. She hadn't mailed the card. Yet she'd left the letter on top of her desk for Glenn to find. Perhaps subconsciously she had wanted him to discover what she'd done.

Threads of tension shot along her nerves as she struggled to appear outwardly calm. Lifting the chatty letter Glenn handed her, she examined it as if seeing it for the first time, amazed at her detachment. Whatever she wished, consciously or subconsciously, Glenn had found it and the timing couldn't be worse. They were just coming to terms with one argument and were about to come to loggerheads over another. Only this issue was potentially far more dangerous to the security of their marriage. Going behind Glenn's back had never been right and Maggie had regretted her deception a hundred times since. And yet it had been necessary. Long ago Maggie had admitted that Glenn had forced her into the decisive action. She had asked him about Angie and he'd refused to discuss the other woman. Maggie was his wife and she loved him; she had a right to know. But all the rationalization in the world wasn't going to help now.

"How do you explain this?" His voice went deep and low, as though he couldn't believe what he'd found. Maggie hadn't trusted him to help her brother, he thought, somewhat dazed, and now he'd learned that she had betrayed his trust as well. Glenn knew he should be furious. Outraged. But he wasn't. His emotions were confused—he felt shocked, hurt and discouraged. Guilt was penned all over Maggie's pale face as she sat looking up at him, trying to come up with some explanation. There could be none. None. Feeling sick with defeat, he turned away from her.

Maggie's heartbeat quickened at the pained look in Glenn's dark eyes. Squarely she met his gaze. She wouldn't back away from his anger, nor would she lie. "I met Angie."

"When?" he asked, still hardly able to comprehend what she was saying. He paced the area in front of her in clipped militarylike steps as if standing in one place were intolerable.

Maggie had never seen any man's features more troubled. "The...the day I flew to San Francisco...I took a commuter plane to Groves Point."

If possible Glenn went even more pale.

"I asked you to tell me about the two of you but—" Maggie attempted to explain and was quickly cut off.

"How did you know where she lived?"

Admitting everything she had done made it sound all the more sordid and deceitful. She hesitated.

"How did you know where she lived?" he repeated, his rising voice controlled and deliberate. Maggie was pressed as far back against the chair cushion as possible as dread settled firmly over her.

"I found her letter to you...and read it." She wouldn't minimize her wrongdoing. The letter had been addressed to him and she had purposely taken it from the envelope and read each word. It was wrong. She knew it was wrong, but given the opportunity, she would do exactly the same thing again.

Glenn stared at her with such shocked dismay that Maggie wanted to throw herself at his feet and beg his forgiveness. She yearned to explain that she hadn't purposely searched through his drawers or snooped into his matters. But she could see that expounding on what had happened wouldn't do any good. Reasoning with Glenn when he was consumed with such righteous indignation would be impossible. She felt wretched and sick to her stomach. The ache in her throat was complicated by the bitter tears stinging her eyes. With everything in her, she struggled not to cry.

"What else did you try to find?" he asked. "How many drawers did you have to search through before you found the letter? Did you take delight in reading another woman's words to me? Is there anything you don't know?"

"It wasn't like that," she whispered, her gaze frozen in misery.

"I'll bet!" He moved to the other side of the living room. His anger died as quickly as it came, replaced by a resentment so keen he could barely stand to look at Maggie. She couldn't seem to let up on the subject of Angie. For months he had loved Maggie so completely that he was amazed that she could believe that he could possibly care for another woman. Worse, she had hounded the subject of Angie to death. It was a matter of trust, and she'd violated that and wounded his spirit.

"Are you satisfied now? Did you learn everything you wanted?" His voice was heavy with defeat. "You don't trust me or my love, do you Maggie? You couldn't, to have done something this underhanded."

"That's not true," she cried. Glenn wanted to wound her; she understood that. She had hurt him when all she'd ever wanted to do was give him her love, bear his children and build a good life with him. But their marriage had been clouded with the presence of another woman who stood between them as prominently as the Cascade mountain range. Or so it appeared at the time.

With a clarity of thought Glenn didn't realize he possessed, he knew he had to get out of the room...out of the house. He needed to sit down and do some serious thinking. Something was basically wrong in a relationship where one partner didn't trust the other. He loved Maggie and had spent the past few months trying to prove how much. Obviously he had failed. He stormed across the living room and jerked his raincoat off the hanger.

"Where are you going?" Maggie asked in a pathetically weak voice.

He didn't even look at her. "Out."

Trapped in a nightmare, her actions made in slow motion, Maggie came to her feet. The Christmas card and letter were clenched in her hand. Glenn turned to look back at her and his gaze fell to the brightly colored card. His mouth twisted into a dark scowl as he opened the door and left Maggie standing alone and desperate.

Maggie didn't allow the tears to escape until she was inside their bedroom with the door securely closed. Only then did she vent her misery. She wept bitter tears until she didn't think she could stop. Her throat ached and her sobs were dry; her eyes burned and there were no more tears left to shed. She had hoped to build a firm foundation for this marriage and now had ruined any chance. Glenn had every reason to hate her. She had deceived him, hurt him, invaded his privacy. And he was sure to detest her for it.

The room was dark and the night half-spent when Glenn came to bed. His movements sounded heavy and vaguely out of order. The dresser drawer was jerked open, then almost immediately slammed shut. He stumbled over something and cursed impatiently under his breath as he staggered to the far side of the bedroom.

Remaining motionless, Maggie listened to his movements and was shocked to realize that he was drunk. Glenn had always been so sensible about alcohol. He rarely had more than one drink. Swallowing back a sob, she bit into her lower lip as he jerked back the covers and fell onto the mattress. She braced herself, wondering what she'd do if he tried to make love to her. But either he was too drunk or he couldn't tolerate the thought of touching her.

She woke in the morning to the sounds of Glenn moving around the room. Her first thought was that she should pretend to be asleep until he'd left, but she couldn't bear to leave things unsettled any longer.

"Glenn," she spoke softly, rolling onto her back. At the sight of his suitcase she bolted upright. "Glenn," she said again, her voice shaking and urgent. "What are you doing?"

"Packing." His face, devoid of expression, told her nothing.

He didn't look at her. With an economy of movement he emptied one drawer into a suitcase and returned to the dresser for another armload.

Maggie was shocked into speechlessness.

"You're leaving me?" she finally choked out. He wouldn't...couldn't. Hadn't they agreed about the sanctity of marriage? Hadn't Glenn told her that he felt divorce was wrong and people should work things out no matter what their problems?

Glenn didn't answer her; apparently his actions were enough for her to realize exactly what he was doing.

"Glenn," she pleaded, her eyes filling with stinging tears. "Please don't do this."

He paused midstride between the suitcase and the dresser. "Trust is vital in a relationship," he said and laid a fresh layer of clothes on top of the open suitcase.

Maggie threw back the covers and crawled to the end of the mattress. "Will you stop talking in riddles for heaven's sake. Of course trust is vital. This whole thing started because you didn't trust me enough to tell me about Angie."

"You knew everything you needed to know."

"I didn't," she cried. "I asked you to tell me about her and you refused."

"She had nothing to do with you and me."

"Oh, sure," Maggie shouted, her voice gaining volume with every word. "I wake up the morning after our wedding and you call me by her name. It isn't bad enough that you can't keep the two of us straight. Even...even your friends confuse our names. Then...then you leave her picture lying around for me to find. But that was nothing. The icing on the cake comes when I inadvertently find a letter tucked safely away in a drawer to cherish and keep forever. Never mind that you've got a wife. Oh, no. She's a simple-minded fool who's willing to overlook a few improprieties in married life."

Rising to her knees, Maggie waved her arms and continued. "And please note that word 'inadvertently,' because I assure you I did not go searching through your things. I found that stupid letter by mistake."

Glenn was confused. His head was pounding, his mouth felt like sandpaper and Maggie was shouting at him, waving her arms like a madwoman. Nothing made sense.

"I need to think," he announced.

Maggie hopped off the bed and reached for her bathrobe. "Well, think then, but don't do something totally stupid like...like leave me. I love you, Glenn. For two days we've behaved like fools. I'm sick of it. I trusted you enough to marry you and obviously you felt the same way about me. The real question here is if we trust our love enough to see things through. If you want to run at the slightest hint of trouble then you're not the Glenn Lambert I know." She tied the sash to her robe and continued, keeping her voice level. "I'm going to make coffee. You have ten minutes alone to 'think.'"

By the time she entered the kitchen, Maggie's knees were shaking. If she told Glenn about the baby he wouldn't leave, but she refused to resort to that. If he wanted to stay, it would be because he loved her enough to work out their differences.

The kitchen phone rang and Maggie stared at it accusingly. The only person who would call her this time of the morning was Denny. If he asked her for another penny, she'd scream. It used to be that he'd call once or twice a month. Now it was every other day.

On the second ring, Maggie nearly ripped the phone off the hook. "Yes," she barked.

"Maggie, is that you?" Denny asked brightly. "Listen, I'm sorry to call so early, but I wanted to tell you something."

"What?" Her indignation cooled somewhat.

"I'm going to work Monday morning. Now don't argue, I know that you're against this. I'll admit that I was, too, when I first heard it. But I got to thinking about what Glenn said. And Maggie, he's right. My attitude toward life, toward everything, has been rotten lately. The best thing in the world for me right now is to get back into the mainstream of life and do something worthwhile."

"But I thought..." Maggie couldn't believe what she was hearing.

"I know ' thought all the same things you did. But Linda and ⅃ had a long talk a few days ago and she helped me see that Glenn is right. I went to an interview, got the job and I feel terrific. Better than I have in years."

Maggie was dumbfounded. She lowered her lashes and squeezed her eyes at her own stupidity. Glenn had been right all along about Denny. Her brother had been trapped in the same mire as she had been. Maggie should have recognized it before, but she'd been so

defensive, wanting to shield her brother from any un-
pleasantness that she had refused to acknowledge what
was right in front of her eyes. Denny needed the same
purpose that Glenn's love had given her life.

The urge to go back to their bedroom and ask Glenn
to forgive her was strong, but she resisted. Denny was
only one problem they needed to make right.

Glenn arrived in the kitchen dressed for the office.
Silently he poured himself a cup of coffee. Maggie
wondered if she should remind Glenn that it was Saturday and he didn't need to go to work. No, she'd let
him talk first, she decided.

He took a sip of the hot, black coffee and grimaced. His head was killing him. It felt as if someone
was hammering at his temple every time his heart beat.
No wonder he rarely had more than a drink or two.

"Who was on the phone?" he asked. The question
was not one of his most brilliant ones. Obviously it
had been Denny, but he hoped to get some conversation going. Anything.

"Denny."

Glenn cocked a brow, swallowing back the argument that sprang readily to his lips. If she was going
to write WELCOME across her back and lie down for
Denny to walk all over her there wasn't anything he
could do. God knew he'd tried.

"He . . . he called because . . ."

"I know why he phoned," Glenn tossed out sarcastically.

"You do?"

"Of course. Denny only phones for one reason."

"Not this time." Her pride was much easier to
swallow after hearing the excitement and enthusiasm
in her brother's voice. "He's got a job."

Glenn choked on a swallow of coffee. "Denny? What happened?"

"Apparently you and Linda got through that thick skull of his and he decided to give it a try. He feels wonderful."

"It might not last."

"I know," Maggie agreed. "But it's a start and one he should have made a long time ago."

Her announcement was met with silence. "Are you telling me I was right?"

"Yes." It wasn't so difficult to admit, after all. Her hands hugged the milk-laced coffee and lent her the courage to continue. "It was wrong to take matters into my own hands and visit Angie. I can even understand why you loved her. She's a wonderful person."

"But she isn't you. She doesn't have your magnificent eye for color, your artistic talent or your special smile. Angie never made up crazy rules or beat me in a game of tennis. You're two entirely different people."

"I'll never be like her," Maggie murmured, staring into the creamy liquid she was holding.

"It's a damn good thing, because I'm in love with you. I married you, Maggie, I don't want anyone else but you."

Maggie's head jerked upright. "Are you saying...? Do you mean that you forgive me for taking matters into my own hands? I know what I did wasn't right."

"I'm not condoning it, but I understand why you felt you had to do it."

If he didn't take her in his arms soon, Maggie thought, she'd start crying again and then Glenn would know her Christmas secret for sure.

He set the coffee cup aside and Maggie glanced up hopefully. But instead of reaching for her, he walked out of the kitchen and picked up the two suitcases that rested on the other side of the arched doorway.

Panic enveloped her. "Glenn," she whispered. "Are you leaving me?"

"No. I'm putting these back where they belong." He didn't know what he'd been thinking this morning. He could no more leave Maggie than he could stop breathing. After disappearing for a moment, he returned to the kitchen and stood not more than three feet from her.

Maggie's heart returned to normal again. "Are we through fighting now? I want to get to the making up part."

"We're just about there." The familiar lopsided grin slanted his mouth.

"Maybe you need a little incentive."

"You standing there in that see-through outfit of yours is giving me all the incentive I need." He wrapped his arms around her then and held her so close that Maggie could actually feel the sigh that shuddered through him.

She met his warm lips eagerly, twining her arms around his neck and tangling her fingers in the thick softness of his hair. Maggie luxuriated in the secure feel of his arms holding her tight. She smiled up at him dreamily. "There's an early Christmas gift I'd like to give you."

Unable to resist, Glenn brushed his lips over the top of her nose. "Don't you think I should wait?"

"Not for this gift. It's special."

"Are you going to expect to open one of yours in return?"

"No, but then, I already have a good idea of what you're getting me."

"You do?"

Maggie laughed outright at the way his eyes narrowed suspiciously. "It wasn't really fair because your mother let the cat out of the bag."

"My mother!"

"Yes, she told me about your grandmother's ring."

His forehead wrinkled into three lines. "Maggie, I'm not giving you a ring."

He couldn't have shocked her more if he'd dumped a bucket of ice water over her head. He wasn't giving her the ring! "Oh." She disentangled herself from his arms. "I . . . guess it was presumptuous of me to think that you would." Her eyes fell to his shirt buttons as she took a step backward.

"Just so there aren't any more misunderstandings, maybe I should explain myself."

"Maybe you should," she agreed, feeling the cold seep into her bones. It never failed. Just when she was beginning to feel loved and secure with their marriage, someone would throw a curve ball at her.

"After the hassle we went through with the wedding rings—"

"I love my rings," she interrupted indignantly. "I never take them off anymore. You asked me not to and I haven't." She knew she was babbling like an idiot, but she wanted to cover how miserable and hurt she was. All those months she had put so much stock in his grandmother's ring and he wasn't even planning on giving it to her.

"Maggie, I had the ring reset into a necklace for you."

"A necklace?"

"This way you won't need to worry about putting it on or taking it off, or losing it, for that matter."

The idea was marvelous and Maggie was so thrilled that her eyes misted with happiness. "It sounds wonderful," she murmured on a lengthy sniffle and rubbed the tears from her face.

"What is the matter with you lately?" Glenn asked, his head cocked to one side. "I haven't seen you cry this much since you were six years old and Petie Phillips teased you and pulled your braids."

Maggie smiled blindly at him. "You mean you haven't figured it out?"

"Figured what out?"

Glenn's dark brown eyes widened as he searched her expression as if expecting to find the answer hidden on her face. His eyebrows snapped together. "Maggie," he whispered with such reverence one would assume he was in a church, "are you pregnant?"

A smile lit up her face, and blossomed from ear to ear. "Yes. Our baby is due the first part of August."

"Oh, Maggie." Glenn was so excited that he longed to haul her into his arms and twirl her around the room until they were both dizzy and giddy. Instead, he pulled out a chair and sat her down. "Are you ill?"

"Only a little in the mornings," she informed him with a small laugh. "The worst thing is that I seem to cry over the tiniest incident."

"You mean like me packing my bags and leaving you."

"Yes." She giggled. "Just the minor things."

"A baby." Glenn paced the area in front of her, repeatedly brushing the hair off his forehead. "We're going to have a baby."

"Glenn, honestly, it shouldn't be such a shock. I told you in the beginning I wasn't using any birth control."

"I'm not shocked...exactly."

"Happy?"

"Very!" He knelt in front of her and gently leaned forward to kiss her tummy.

Maggie wrapped her arms around his head and held him to her. "Merry Christmas, my love."

Glenn heard the steady beat of Maggie's heart and closed his eyes to the wealth of emotions that flooded his being. She was a warm, vital woman who had made him complete. Wife, friend, lover...the list seemed endless and he had only touched the surface.

"Merry Christmas," he whispered in return and pulled her mouth to his.

The Silhouette Cameo Tote Bag Now available for just $6.99

Handsomely designed in blue and bright pink, its stylish good looks make the Cameo Tote Bag an attractive accessory. The Cameo Tote Bag is big and roomy (13″ square), with reinforced handles and a snap-shut top. You can buy the Cameo Tote Bag for $6.99, plus $1.50 for postage and handling.

Send your name and address with check or money order for $6.99 (plus $1.50 postage and handling), a total of $8.49 to:

**Silhouette Books
120 Brighton Road
P.O. Box 5084
Clifton, NJ 07015-5084
ATTN: Tote Bag**

SIL–T–1R

The Silhouette Cameo Tote Bag can be purchased pre-paid only. No charges will be accepted. Please allow 4 to 6 weeks for delivery.

N.Y. State Residents Please Add Sales Tax

Offer not available in Canada.

Available July 1986

Texas Gold

The first in a great new Desire trilogy by Joan Hohl.

In *Texas Gold* you can meet the Sharp family—twins Thackery and Zackery.

With Thackery, Barbara Holcomb, New York model, embarks on an adventure, as together they search for a cache of stolen gold. For Barbara and Thack, their gold is discovered in the bright, rich vein of their love.

Then get to know Zackery and his half sister Kit in *California Copper* and *Nevada Silver*—coming soon from Silhouette Books.

DT-1RA

COMING NEXT MONTH

SOMETHING ABOUT SUMMER—Linda Shaw
State Prosecutor Summer MacLean didn't know what to do when she found herself handcuffed to a suspect determined to prove he was innocent . . . and who happened to look like her late husband.

EQUAL SHARES—Sondra Stanford
When Shannon Edwards inherited fifty-one percent of a troubled business, she went to check it out. She expected a problem, but not the sexiest man alive . . . her partner.

ALMOST FOREVER—Linda Howard
Max Conroy was buying out the company where Claire worked, and used her to get the vital information. What he didn't figure on was falling in love.

MATCHED PAIR—Carole Halston
The handsome gambler and the glamorous sophisticate met across the blackjack table, and it was passion at first sight. Neither realized they were living a fantasy that could keep them apart.

SILVER THAW—Natalie Bishop
Mallory owned prize Christmas trees, but had no one to market them. The only man willing to help her was the man who had once sworn he loved her.

EMERALD LOVE, SAPPHIRE DREAMS—Monica Barrie
Pres Wyman had been the school nerd. But when Megan Teal hired him to help her salvage a sunken galleon, she found the erstwhile nerd had become a living Adonis.

AVAILABLE THIS MONTH:

MISTY MORNINGS, MAGIC NIGHTS
Ada Steward

SWEET PROMISE
Ginna Gray

SUMMER'S STORM
Patti Beckman

WHITE LACE AND PROMISES
Debbie Macomber

SULLIVAN vs. SULLIVAN
Jillian Blake

RAGGED RAINBOWS
Linda Lael Miller

FOUR UNIQUE SERIES
FOR EVERY WOMAN YOU ARE...

Silhouette Romance

Heartwarming romances that will make you laugh and cry as they bring you all the wonder and magic of falling in love.

6 titles per month

Silhouette Special Edition

Expanded romances written with emotion and heightened romantic tension to ensure powerful stories. A rare blend of passion and dramatic realism.

6 titles per month

Silhouette Desire

Believable, sensuous, compelling—and above all, romantic—these stories deliver the promise of love, the guarantee of satisfaction.

6 titles per month

Silhouette Intimate Moments

Love stories that entice; longer, more sensuous romances filled with adventure, suspense, glamour and melodrama.

4 titles per month

SIL-GEN-1RR

A terrible family secret drives Kristi Johannssen to California, where she finds glamor, romance and...a threat to her life!

BEYOND THE RAINBOW

MARGARET CHITTENDEN

Power and elegance, jealousy and deceit, even murder, stoke fires of passion in this glittering novel set in the fashion world of Hollywood, on the dazzling coast of Southern California.

Available in August at your favorite retail outlet, or reserve your copy for July shipping by sending your name, address and zip or postal code along with a check or money order for $4.70 (includes 75¢ for postage and handling) payable to Worldwide Library Reader Service to:

In the U.S.

Worldwide Library
901 Fuhrmann Blvd.
Box 1325
Buffalo, New York
14269-1325

In Canada

Worldwide Library
P.O. Box 2800, 5170 Yonge St.
Postal Station A
Willowdale, Ontario
M2N 6J3

Please specify book title with your order.

 WORLDWIDE LIBRARY

BOW-H-1

Take 4 Silhouette Intimate Moments novels
FREE

Then preview 4 brand new Silhouette Intimate Moments® novels —delivered to your door every month—for 15 days as soon as they are published. When you decide to keep them, you pay just $2.25 each ($2.50 each, in Canada), *with no shipping, handling, or other charges of any kind!*

Silhouette Intimate Moments novels are not for everyone. They were created to give you a more detailed, more exciting reading experience, filled with romantic fantasy, intense sensuality, and stirring passion.

The first 4 Silhouette Intimate Moments novels are absolutely FREE and without obligation, yours to keep. You can cancel at any time.

You'll also receive a FREE subscription to the Silhouette Books Newsletter as long as you remain a member. Each issue is filled with news on upcoming titles, interviews with your favorite authors, even their favorite recipes.

To get your 4 FREE books, fill out and mail the coupon today!

◖ *Silhouette Intimate Moments*®

Silhouette Books, 120 Brighton Rd., P.O. Box 5084, Clifton, NJ 07015-5084

**Clip and mail to: Silhouette Books,
120 Brighton Road, P.O. Box 5084, Clifton, NJ 07015-5084***

YES. Please send me 4 FREE Silhouette Intimate Moments novels. Unless you hear from me after I receive them, send me 4 brand new Silhouette Intimate Moments novels to preview each month. I understand you will bill me just $2.25 each, a total of $9.00 (in Canada, $2.50 each, a total of $10.00)—with no shipping, handling, or other charges of any kind. There is no minimum number of books that I must buy, and I can cancel at any time. The first 4 books are mine to keep. *Silhouette Intimate Moments available in Canada through subscription only.*

IM-SUB-1   **BM1826**

Name _____ (please print)

Address _____ Apt. #

City _____ State/Prov. _____ Zip/Postal Code

* In Canada, mail to: Silhouette Canadian Book Club,
320 Steelcase Rd., E., Markham, Ontario, L3R 2M1, Canada
Terms and prices subject to change.
SILHOUETTE INTIMATE MOMENTS is a service mark and registered trademark.